Land of Ice and Intrigue

Seasons of Fae Book 2

Sonya Lawson

SauceBox Press

Contents

Note to Reader (TW)

This book contains scenes that may depict, mention, or discuss: abduction, assault, attempted murder, blood, death, fire, kidnapping, murder, and violence. Please take care of yourself as you read.

To my dad, who taught me a lot, including how to fight and how to love a river.

Prologue

Jarok - The Night Before Prince Ghel and Lady Strella's Betrothal

Prince Jarok Borau rubbed his tired eyes. He'd been squinting at scout reports, letters from men in the field, and security logs for a few hours, doing all he could to organize the information he had at hand. So much was happening in the Winterlands, what with the rising Monti Clan rebellion, traitors invading their home, and his older brother, Prince Ghel, set to become betrothed to a lady neither had met before. At least the last bit would change the next afternoon. Jarok wanted to be prepared, needed to be prepared, to help his family and his land as best he could.

It was all tiring, and more than anything, he wished for a hard drink and a soft body in his bed to relieve some of the stress. Prince Jarok lived up to his reputation as the more genial, fun-loving Borau brother, even if most of his time was spent like tonight: taking his duties to his family and homeland seriously. The bulk of which centered on where he stood: making sure the Winterlands Palace remained safe and secure. He'd taken over the daily charge of palace security from his mother decades ago. One reason for the switch was his other benefit to his family: he was good with a mask. He could laugh and play and wheedle his way into the good graces of the lords and ladies with a flippant smile the court seemed to indulge. All fake, for the most part, but necessary, especially when he wanted to keep track of information and attitudes regarding his royal family. It was a skill he wished he could employ on his broody, gruff brother before his meeting with his betrothed the next day.

A pain shot like a lance through the prince's skull at the thought of what might happen with his brother the next day, how the betrothal would go. Much was at stake. Ghel needed to secure the union to help solidify alliances, but more importantly, to keep an eye on the traitorous father of his soon-to-be bride. And what if the lady herself was a traitor helping her father? It remained to be seen, so Jarok had a great deal to look out for in the next days.

To elevate his now-aching head, he stood from his seat, his civil and warrior training making his posture ramrod straight as he stretched his long, golden-brown neck left to right, back then forward, trying to ease the tension there. He hung his head, the floppy cut of his short black hair causing the effortless yet artful looking tangle at the top of his head to skim across his eyes, feathery and soft. As he pushed his hair out of his face once again, his mind homed in on a small half-moon scar at the base of his thumb—something he received gods knew when or how. All he knew was it had happened before he was saved from the frozen waste of the Ice Plains during a particularly vicious and sudden blizzard.

He didn't often think back to that time he could barely remember. He knew he was a Windin by birth, his distinctive looks having spurred him to do a little digging later in life, but now he was all Borau, dead set on keeping the royals who had taken him in, made him a prince, and more importantly, made him a real part of their family, safe and in power. Hence the late night, the headaches, and the worry he felt along with the pressure. If he had to stay all night in his study off the royal wing, he would.

A faint yet distinct sound drew him back from his stray thoughts. The skid of feet on gravel. An animal perhaps. Or a misstep by someone trying to circle the palace for a different reason. Jarok slinked toward his window facing the south side of the Winterland Palace so as not to draw attention with his movement in the firelight. When he was close enough to the edges, he peeked around, searching the small gravel path four stories down for any sign of an intruder. Nothing came at first, until he saw a single leather-clad foot kick up from rounding the nearest corner. Godsdamnnit, there was someone skulking about the grounds in the dead of night, and there was no good reason for anyone to do so.

Long ago, his mother, Queen Alene, derisively referred to by some as the Warrior Queen, had taught him several secrets of the palace she'd learned from her husband, King Frit. Some she had also discovered on her own. One of which was there, in his study. An extra perk of being a royal prince: having a secret set of stairs behind one of the overstuffed bookcases. He pulled an old, worn-leather volume by the spine, triggering the spring to release a hidden door, which opened wide into a dusty, cobwebbed corridor. Jarok grabbed a candlestick before running down the winding staircase, unconcerned with the grime or the spiders hovering. He made it to the door to the outside of the palace in a flash, then eased it open as he secured the lit candle in a holder by the interior, being slow and methodical for the first time since he had spied the boot on the path below him.

With stealth and grim determination, he picked his way across the frozen ground, avoiding the gravel path so he wouldn't make noise. He was surprisingly silent for a tall warrior made of lithe muscle. Whoever was ahead had also learned a lesson and made nearly no sound. When Jarok concentrated, he could hear the occasional slip of gravel once again, as if whoever ran ahead was unused to the area and the loose, rocky path.

He neared a bend in the palace, a spot along the western edge where a large turret stood towering ten stories high. Spanning several yards, the outcropping caused a tricky blind spot for someone trying to track an unknown intruder. He paused and leaned his back to the wall, inching across the stone so as not to present an open target to anyone waiting beyond the arch of the structure. As he came to the apex, his foot skidded across gravel, and a second later, a large brown-leather-clad foot shot into the air, barely skimming his face. If he'd been running straight ahead, the blow would have blindsided him. He was momentarily dazed, but because of his forethought, he was more angry than anything else.

He leaped into the path, lunging blindly in the direction of the kick that'd landed across his right cheek, and managed to catch whoever it was in a bruising grip, bringing them down hard to the ground. He scrambled for purchase as the unknown fighter twisted and kicked to free themselves. Prince Jarok was wiry and wily, and had been trained by his brother and mother and cousins, some of the best warriors in the land. He wasn't about to let go of his prey and managed to position himself on top of the struggling brown-leather-clad figure on their back.

When the large moon freed itself from the clouds and shone silver light on them both, he froze. On her back, he corrected himself. She was tall for a Fae woman, strong, as most Fae were, and obviously trained as a fighter. But those weren't the reasons Jarok froze in the moment. He knew plenty of Fae female fighters, a number of whom were members of his family and could beat him if they tried, so the idea of a female threat to the palace wasn't outside the realm of possibility for the prince.

What stopped him dead was the body and face pinned below him. Her compact muscle, thick and strong thighs, and ample breasts strained against the traditional Winterland fighting leathers the woman wore. His hands clenched at her wrists and his thighs clamped around hers, holding her firmly in place, but not without a great deal of effort on his part. She had a powerful body Jarok could imagine doing many dirty things with in different circumstances. Her face was broad, wide for a female. Not what a noble Fae would call beautiful, but then again the nobility were often stupid. She was handsome and striking, her cheeks a shock of pale skin and her nose regal though slightly large and pointed. Her big eyes squinted in anger just as her wide, full-lipped mouth curled back in an animalistic snarl. Her hair, pinned tight to her head, glimmered darkly in the moonlight, a slight reddish tone to it which somehow snagged Jarok's attention.

Enough of his attention, in fact, to cause his arms to loosen a bit, and she was able to whip one wrist free. She brought it up in a sweeping arc, nearly connecting the side of her balled fist to his temple. It would have been a punishing blow if he hadn't managed to block it with his forearm. He leaned down, pinning her entire arm under his own.

"Now, now, now. None of that," Jarok gritted out. "That's not how our introduction will go."

"Get off me, you brute," she said, bucking under him in a way Jarok had to push out of his mind.

"No, intruder."

"I'm no intruder."

"Funny, as I've never seen you before."

"You know every single Fae in this palace?" she asked, her thick, reddish arch of eyebrow rising high in obvious disbelief.

"Yes," he said, with all seriousness. He made it part of his duties to know all that went on in this palace, all those who came to be around his family. His brother, Ghel, protected the family and the Winterlands with their army, and Jarok helped as his second. He also helped as the man of information, the one who could be counted on to know, to track or schmooze, or do whatever was necessary to keep those he loved safe, as they'd kept him safe since he was a babe of four.

Something in his tone brooked no argument, so the leather-bound Fae woman made no reply, simply giving a humming sound as if thinking over things. She was silent long enough he thought to prod her more, but her bucking suddenly picked back up, surprising him enough she got him to his side. She wrapped a powerful leg around his and twisted, flipping them completely around so he landed on his back, looking up at the woman straddling him.

As he often did, he went for innuendo to disarm his opponent. "If you liked it on top, lovely, all you had to do was ask."

She sneered, the perfect mask of noble entitlement flashing long enough for him to be intrigued by it. He didn't know who this was, but she was a tangled mess of contradictions Jarok wanted to unravel.

He didn't have time to do so, and he needed to contain her, get her secured in the dungeons of the palace before he went at this puzzle. He shook her hand off and shot his right arm to her right side, leveraging it so he took her off him and to her side once again. They wrestled for dominance for several seconds, enough to both be panting. Jarok discovered an odd thrill in the push and pull before he narrowed his gaze and decided they'd had enough tussling on the ground.

The prince shoved her back hard to the cold earth and held her shoulders down. "Fun and games are over, now, lovely. Sorry to say."

His eyes darted toward the sky when he heard wings close by and tried to catch if it were one of his mother's birds of prey somehow on guard, come to assist. A red hawk cry sounded too close, and he scanned the sky and grounds for the bird or his mother, knowing one or both had to be nearby.

A stupid thing to do given the fight he'd just had with the woman below him, but he was certain, somehow, help was near. However, nothing was there to help when she popped her knee up, forcing his hips to go up as well. A split second later, her loose knee reared back down and up, connecting to his balls. Pain blinded him, and he lost his hold. She scrambled to her feet and was running away at top speed before he caught his breath again. Like a good warrior, she didn't stop, look back, or second-guess herself. When Jarok was finally up again, using his wind magic to help himself breathe easier, she'd disappeared somewhere on the grounds.

He didn't sound an alarm for all to hear. No need to worry everyone with this just yet. Instead, after recovering from the blow to his body and ego, he found the guards on duty, questioned them about any possible encounters, and searched with them until dawn kissed the western sky above the Winterland Mountains.

Jarok found nothing then, but only hours later, he saw that arresting face and shock of auburn hair seated at the side of his brother's soon-to-be-bride, the fighter masquerading as her lady-in-waiting. In the following months, he hounded her every step, waiting for her to reveal the secret he was certain she possessed. The secret he just knew hovered above his family, waiting to drop and possibly harm them all. When she finally did reveal it, all to help save his brother and his kingdom, he was shocked—by both her power and her willingness to use it for such ends. Then, and only then, he begrudgingly admitted she might be more than a beautiful but potentially deadly problem to solve. She might actually be a solution.

Chapter One
Piris

Lady Piris Volesion strode into the royal meeting rooms on long legs covered by a simple navy travel dress, which just happened to conceal her sharpest blade, strapped to her thigh. Head held high and back straight and sure, she gave a wide smile to her best friend, Princess Strella, who was seated at the impressive oak table. Princess Strella had been princess of the Winterlands for about a month, but she'd been Piris's friend, her sister, for most of their lives. When she saw her friend's worried expression, her suspicions about this meeting soared, although her sure steps didn't falter.

As expected, King Frit and Queen Alene were at the head of the table. The frail king was seated, his warrior wife standing at his side, gripping his shoulder as one of her snowy owls gripped her own and surveyed the room with a fighter's attention. Prince Ghel sat close at their right, his eyes as hard as one of his mother's birds of prey, always at the ready to protect if necessary. He looked forever cold and hard, like the landscape of his kingdom, the Fae Winterlands, but Piris knew different. She'd witnessed firsthand how his gruff exterior vanished at the touch and concern of her friend, the princess seated close to his right. Strella's icy exterior appeared as impeccable as always—white-blonde hair artfully wavy and impossibly light-blue eyes fixed on Piris. Her shimmering gray dress, the color of the Winterland skies most middays, echoed the skies around the Ice Plains just outside the Winterlands Palace gates.

Lady Piris took all of this in, running scenarios in her mind, as Prince Jarok, who'd fetched her for this meeting, brushed past her to take his seat at the left hand of his parents. Her teeth ground, the sound grating in her own head and loud enough to get a smirk from the arrogant prince as he moved away from her.

The Fae male was a fighter, like most in his family, except he was all lean-   muscled strength and stealth compared to the bulk of his brother. Made sense to her, as they weren't blood related. No one brought it up, of course, or implied he was less a part of the family. She'd heard stories of years ago, when nobles occasionally whispered about the differences and what they implied, but Ghel and Queen Alene shut such talk down with force, and King Frit, before his illness, was equally as impressive in his anger and wrath. All who knew the royals had learned early on they'd have a serious fight on their hands if they so much as hinted at Prince Jarok not being a true part of the family.

Piris wondered if this had instilled his arrogance and entitlement, but squashed the idea quickly. It was love, true and simple, that made his family defend him. He, for his part, acted the same for them, something she had to at least begrudgingly respect when she found little else to respect about the man. He cared for his family, at any cost, something she'd experienced firsthand when he'd focused his attentions on her, his mind certain she was a threat because of their disastrous first meeting. He'd eased some over the weeks they'd known each other, which was surprising, given he now knew the secret of her magic: that she was no null as everyone had believed but a mimic, wielding the affinity most feared in the minds of many Fae. He said little of her magic, but his wicked tongue still lashed out at her every chance he got, and his condescending sneers and looks lingered long on her.

Lady Piris Volesion was curt, prickly, and sarcastic at times. She was able to hold her own in a verbal or physical altercation, so she wasn't worried about Jarok getting in too many hits. She was worried about spending more time with him, although the idea of going home put a pit in her stomach. She'd miss Strella, and didn't want to have to confess to her parents the royals now knew the secret they'd kept for so long. Her father would likely erupt and, even worse, her mother might cry, but she would be happy to have distance from the infuriating prince who always seemed to get a rise out of her, no matter how hard she tried to ignore him.

"Lady Piris Volesion, please. Come closer." The king called her forward, waving a hand for her to the edge of the table. She'd stopped several feet away before giving a deep curtsy of respect. Too far away for his liking, apparently. She spared a quick glance at Strella, who'd started twirling a strand of hair on her forefinger, then braced. The outward sign of Strella's worry made her even more wary than Prince Jarok's words to her when he showed in her room earlier: *"We are required in the royal meeting room."*

"Thank you for agreeing to meet with us, lady," the king said, a small but tight smile on his face. His words brought her back to the issue at hand.

"Of course, Your Graces," she said, doing another dip and small bow of the head to the king and queen.

"As you are well aware, Lady Piris, we have... issues we need to overcome, for the good of all the Winterlands," the king said. Piris managed to keep herself from snorting at the understatement. They'd defended their land from an internal warrior rebellion, thanks to Ghel and Strella.

Ghel and the Winterlands forces had met the amassed army outside the palace, in the cold, frozen wastes of the Ice Plains, and struck down many who came against him, including the rebel leader himself. He had only had the chance because her brave friend had ridden out in the heat of battle, alone, to warn the prince of the treachery of her father. Despite winning the battle, Prince Ghel's mercy allowed the leader of the rebellion, Engad Monti, to slip from their grasp, killing a slew of Winterland soldiers who guarded him and disappearing.

Now, word in the land said he was hiding with the Monti Benders, a contingent of elite archers he'd groomed to fight at his side. They were formidable and, now hidden, enemies the Borau royals couldn't afford to leave free in their lands. More importantly, the group seemed bent on destruction, killing any who opposed them as they gathered what forces they could. To what end, she could only guess. Likely some devastating attack on the royals again, which made her blood boil. Her best friend, her sister, was now one of those royals who very well could be under attack. Soon, if Monti was given enough time.

Queen Alene nodded in support of her husband, her dark eyes assessing Piris so thoroughly she itched to squirm under her gaze. She knew—they all now knew—what she was. A piece of her also knew what they would be asking of her, at least in the abstract. The details would be different, sure, but her fighter trainer had told her what was coming before the words were spoken.

Prince Ghel waded into the conversation, taking ownership, as a good man would. "Piris, I've come up with a plan which could help us uncover the Monti's whereabouts in a more covert manner."

"A plan you may or may not take up," Strella interjected, conviction in her words. Strella would always fight for her, and if Piris didn't agree to the ask coming her way, the princess would ensure there would be no consequences, even going toe-to-toe with her new family to do so.

Because Strella and Piris were old family, not by blood but by bond, and the loyalty for each ran deep. Which meant Piris would agree to whatever plan they had concocted if it meant keeping her best friend safe from future Engad Monti attacks. Gods be damned, she was stuck either way, despite the fact she would be asked rather than commanded to do something.

"Given your special gifts..." Ghel continued, slightly uncomfortable.

"My magic?" she asked, her brows arched. She'd revealed her secret, her magic, of the power of mimicry, to help Strella save Ghel in battle. Now the entire royal family, and the Autumnlands Lord Cylian Padalist more than likely, knew she could manipulate sound, mimic anything she heard, and mimic the powers of others, reproducing any form of magic she'd witnessed. It was a formidable magic, historically manipulated and used by Fae leaders for their own advantage. Or hunted down and erased so it couldn't be passed, thought by some fanatics to be an abomination for whatever ridiculous reason they concocted in their heads. Hence the reason why no one beside her mother, father, and Strella knew of her abilities until recently. Everyone'd thought her a null and had shunned her because of her lack of power, never realizing she held one of the rarest and most coveted or condemned gifts in all of Fae, depending on who one asked. Now, the royals of the Winterlands knew, because she'd chosen to reveal it in service of her friend. In service of Prince Ghel. She trusted Strella to be at her back and ensure they didn't use it to take advantage of her, but it didn't mean they wouldn't ask things of her, things they might not ask other ladies to do who weren't mimics.

"Your magic is impressive, yes," the Queen said, "and might well come in handy on such a mission. However, we are more concerned with your fighting ability."

Ah. They knew she was a fighter from Prince Jarok, or simply because one Fae trained in combat could always spot another. The movements of the body, the look in the eye, always seemed to give it away to anyone paying attention to such things. Her father, Lord Brettly Volesion, had trained her in secret after they had spread the rumor she was a null, helping her control her magic while also teaching her offensive and defensive skills. It was written on her body, as it was written on all the Boraus, so it was a toss-up how they knew about her training. She, however, liked to blame Prince Jarok, so she cut him a scathing look before continuing the conversation. "What do you wish of me?"

Ghel said, "We wish, Piris, to escort you to your home. You planned to leave soon, correct? We suggest you leave with Lord Padalist, my cousin Gem Aurora, and Prince Jarok as escort."

"I don't require an escort."

"Of course not," the Queen said, "but it gives my son and Lord Cylian an excuse to ride through the land, picking up information along the way, while not attracting too much attention."

"Excuse me, Your Grace, but why? Could they not simply journey alone, themselves, to gather information?"

"True," Prince Ghel answered for his mother. "However, having a justifiable reason helps with such missions. A prince can go anywhere they wish, but after an open rebellion? With a lord of another realm? It might create too many questions, which in turn draws too much attention. Possibly the attention of Monti and his Benders. While we wish to find and confront them, we would like to do so with additional information and on our own terms."

Piris swallowed hard at the thought of Lord Cylian, whom she liked, being attacked by the Benders without additional aid. She told herself she didn't care if the same happened to Prince Jarok.

"I'm a fighter, as you say, and far less suspicious given your logic. Why not have me journey home, as planned, gathering any information along the way, which I can then relay back to you once I reach Volesion Peak?"

King Frit, quiet for so long, spoke. "Dear Lady Piris, we are assured by the fact you can take care of yourself in any possible scrimmages along the way. Your strength, however, is not all the help you can provide your crown. We might also need the help of Volesion Peak and your father, Lord Brettly Volesion."

"Others would expect you to have an escort, Piris," Strella said, soft and true. She'd want someone to go with her regardless.

The king nodded in agreement, then continued. "Thanks to some scouting, we have reason to believe the missing Monti and his Benders are in hiding close to the Great River. Your family home, Volesion Peak, would be a good starting point to investigate such claims."

The picture cleared for Piris. They'd assembled a group of fighters, along with a few savvy Fae used to gathering information, and given them a plausible reason to travel so far from the Winterlands Palace after a direct attack, and one in the group also happened to have a connection to an ally they needed in the moment. It made sense, but it didn't mean she had to like the plan. Or all of the people she'd be required to spend time with to execute it.

She looked over at the younger prince, and Jarok smirked at her, making her blood pound and her fists clench. Damn, she would say yes, but...

"Are all three escorts necessary?" she asked.

Queen Alene snorted a laugh, then said, "Yes," pinning Piris with a hard-eyed warning. She'd never openly disparage Prince Jarok in front of his family. She wasn't that rude. She also valued her life and health too much to take such a stupid risk.

"Very well." She sighed, resigned. "I'll need more details, and to speak with Lord Padalist and Gem Aurora before we leave, but yes. I will help you in this."

"Piris, you know—"

She waved a hand at her friend's interruption and gave her her most reassuring smile. "I know, Star," she said. "I know. I also know I can help, and I should. Just as you knew you could and should help in the battle."

Strella took the hint and didn't argue, understanding Piris's need to do this. Her best friend had risked her life to help her love, even after Piris had tried to stop her. In the end, she'd let her friend do what she had to. Now she was asking for the same. Piris felt a need, a spark. A small fire inside. The mission, if all went to plan, did not involve much, but it was opportunity to be more than a quiet, secretive lady around everyone but the smallest circle. A chance for her to use her training, and possibly her magic, to do something good in the world, to help her friend and her kingdom. If it meant spending time with a Fae man that made her blood boil, so be it.

Jarok, timing as impeccable as ever, broke into her thoughts with a half laugh her way. "It'll be a pleasure, lady, to escort you through the kingdom." The words themselves were innocuous but they dripped with sarcasm, making Piris bristle at his implication. Gods help her, she wanted to punch the smug look off the prince's harvest-gold face. From Ghel's glower at his brother, he might even let her. The king and queen, however, likely wouldn't enjoy the fight.

She held herself tight, gave her best sneer, and said, "I look forward to time spent with Lord Cylian and the Aurora warrior," before she gave her formal good-byes and swept out of the room. There were now different travel preparations to make. It also might be best that she practiced calming herself before the prince raked her nerves and made her want to punch him. Repeatedly.

Her magic prickled in her ear, a sure sign it needed release. Her father had trained her to fight, her mother had trained her to be a lady, and both had helped her hone her magic as best they could, in secret. It worked because her father's magic was based in vocalizing sound and her mother's magic was based in hearing. Some might say it was a perfect combination to teach a mimic, or possibly even form a mimic. Either way, each helped her hone her skills, recognize when her magic swelled inside and needed release, and how to let it out in small doses. All in secret. All only when necessary, even as they helped her use and grow her power, harness it. As her mother always said, to know something was to have power over it, and she needed ultimate power over her magic to keep it hidden.

Thinking on her past and knowing she'd see her family soon made her pick her mother for this release. She missed the woman, even if she dreaded what she'd have to tell her parents when she showed up at Volesion Peak. Focusing, she sang a line of a lullaby her mother always sang to her, her mother's voice from her lips giving her heart a slight ache. She then focused on her increased hearing, her mother's magic, honing it so she heard the Fae person breathing in the next room. Her room. She wasn't too concerned, because she knew the sound of the steady in and out well.

Piris took a moment to stuff her magic back down in the deep well she'd constructed in her mind. The little she siphoned off was enough to keep her magic calm for at least a week. Enough to keep it and her hidden. Though if she were honest with herself, she'd done a poor job of hiding of late. The guilt of it nagged at her as she thought of her family.

After a few beats and breaths of her own, and a few more notes in her mother's soft voice, Piris walked out of her small closet to find her friend, Princess Strella, peering into her travel trunk.

"Find anything interesting?" she asked.

Strella gave her a dazzling white smile and sat very proper and princess-like on the bed beside the trunk. "No, but I imagine it's because you like to bury your weapons at the bottom of your trunks."

"You know me so well." Piris laughed, moving to toss the thick wool scarf she'd retrieved from the closet into the trunk before closing and latching the lid. She slapped her hands together and declared, "All done," as she plopped a little less gracefully on the other side of the trunk.

Not that her body wasn't graceful in its own way, but Piris often thought her larger frame, with her fighter training, overrode the lady-like poise her mother had and tried to help her build, the same poise her friend wielded with ease. The fact was she took far better to her father's fighting lessons than her mother's lectures on deportment and expectations of civility. She could play the lady, knew all the rules and etiquette, but it felt like play. Fighting, however, felt like an electric charge to the gut, a game of life and death and injury she knew in her heart. She was far more comfortable in her leathers than her traveling gown, which she frowned down at then, picking at the dark-gray flannel traveling dress. She was at least thankful she didn't have to wear a corset when in the carriage. It would've been even more torturous.

"Peep?" Hesitant, Strella reached across the broad, flat cedar top of her trunk. "Are you certain you want to do this? It's not too late to change your mind."

Gods, she loved Strella. Her shining blue eyes darkened with worry, and Piris sent up thanks, not for the first time, that Strella's treacherous father had thought to do business with her own father all those years ago. Her life would've been so lost and lonely without her, a sister despite them sharing no blood—as was clear by the worry, and the general idea she could somehow know best.

"No, Star. I'm sure." Piris's brow dipped down and she put on a fake frown to make her laugh. "I could do without the prince's company, but the mission is no issue."

She half joked in the moment, and Strella knew. Catching her hand, her friend squeezed tight and replied, "Jarok is an honorable man, a good prince. I can't say I enjoy your constant bickering, but I can say I'd trust him with your life. I actually am in this. The goal is to gather information, but anything can happen on the Winterlands roads, and who knows where Engad Monti will next strike."

A nod was all Piris could give her. She knew both the danger and the honor of the prince to be true. Her issues with Jarok ran deeper but hinged almost entirely on personal dislike and distrust. She'd never say he was a dishonorable or disloyal Fae man. He was simply annoying, cocky, and forever frustrating.

"I made Ghel tell me everything about your planned journey," Strella said quickly, likely knowing Piris wished the subject to be changed. "Prince Jarok and Lord Cylian will follow behind the carriage on horseback, and Gem Aurora will ride inside the carriage with you. There are two inns where you will stop, but you will mostly stay in traveling houses. You'll also pick up an ally along the way."

"What ally?" Piris asked about the only new piece of information Strella had revealed.

"I don't know. Ghel didn't give me specifics. He said it was someone from another land who knew Lord Padalist and had some stake in fighting rebel leaders."

"Another fighter then," she said, almost to herself, thinking through the implications. It could be someone from the Autumnlands who was traveling to the Winterlands, which might explain why they didn't meet here to leave with the rest of the group. An odd choice for the Boraus, seeing as most nobles in Fae, in and out of the Autumnlands, had little to do with any emissaries from that corner of the land outside of Lord Cylian. Or, knowing of Lord Cylian's reach, it really could be anyone from any land.

Piris disliked surprises, especially when they interfered with a mission she had in mind, but she would trust Lord Cylian in this. He'd helped Strella during the battle on the Ice Plains, helped bring her back, despite the accuracy of the prophecy of her death her friend had carried all her life. She'd always trust him with her life. He'd saved it once before by saving her friend.

"Have you spent much time with Gem Aurora?" Strella asked, absently twisting a stray strand of blonde hair in a fluttering hand.

"No. Should I have?"

"No. No. I wondered is all."

"Have you?"

"Some. Here and at the Aurora Outpost, but not a great deal of time."

She felt a weird thread of jealousy, which was absurd, as her friend deserved to have legions of people to love and be loved by. She thought hard for a second, wondering if someone else new could come in, take a piece of her friend for themselves in a way Piris had her, not in the way Ghel had his wife. Friendship was a tricky thing at times, a relationship like any other, with its ups and downs and moments of doubt, but

Piris knew she shouldn't doubt Strella's love for a second. She brushed the stray worry aside, and the pain eased in her chest. She'd just had so few people love her—her mother and father and Strella. Less than a handful of other Fae who cared for her in any real way. In a way where they knew her and still her loved despite what they knew.

Shaking her head free of the odd thoughts, Piris asked, "What do you know of Gem then?"

"I suspect you'll either be fast friends or quick enemies. You're too much alike for it to go any other way."

Piris laughed at the assessment. "Fair enough. I suppose we'll find out soon."

Strella hitched a knee up to the bed, turning to face her friend full on. Piris mirrored her movement, giving her the attention she obviously needed. "Be careful, will you?"

"Aren't I always?"

"No," she said, meeting Piris's joking tone with her serious one. "You are sometimes reckless, and your training has often gotten you out of those moments unscathed. But this, what you're doing... there're so many ways for this to go wrong."

"You think I can't handle a simple scout mission?"

"No. No, Piris. You can handle anything thrown your way," she said, a fierce, forceful air to her words. "There are people out there hiding, waiting for an opportunity to hurt the royal family and the Winterlands. You could well be a target. It's no secret you are part of my heart."

"You're most of my heart, Star. I promise, I'll be on guard. Keep myself safe."

She dipped her head, breathed deep, then asked one more favor of her friend. "Will you also help keep the prince safe?"

Piris knew where this was coming from. Strella loved Ghel, her own prince, and he loved his brother fiercely as he loved his whole family, royal or no. He'd be devastated if something happened to Prince Jarok, which in turn would make Strella devastated for him.

"For you, Star. Only for you."

Strella smiled bright and squeezed her hand hard. "If you say so," she whispered, then gathered herself up, rising from the bed. "Come. Let's have a walk together before you leave. Find something interesting and far less sad to discuss for the next hour."

As they walked and chatted, heads close together, they came upon the queen readying for her own walk. "Come," she called to the two friends, "walk with me." Not a question, and not a harsh order, but decidedly a directive they did not want to dismiss. Piris and Strella trailed behind their queen as she took long, quick strides out the door, eating up the distance between the palace and one of the side gardens.

No one spoke for a time, but Queen Alene slowed enough to stay in pace with the princess and lady so they could walk together in silence. The harsh, cold air filled Piris's lungs and ran through her blood.

Eventually, because her friend could not help herself, Strella turned to the queen and asked, "Do you often walk here in the afternoons?"

"I train still and do other activities, but there is nothing like the Winterlands air to make me feel more alive. Plus, it gives my birds some room to roam with me still near." The queen nodded upward, where a massive eagle stretched its wings in a smooth glide high above them.

"How—" Piris pulled back before she completed the question. She thought there was no need to prod the Warrior Queen of the Winterlands about what she may consider personal matters.

"Out with it, Lady Piris. Do not hold back with me. You surely do not with my son." A ghost of a smile flitted over her stony face. If not for that, Piris would have paled at the bite in the words and what they implied about the queen's opinion of her. Opinions never mattered much to Piris, for good reason, as her reputation had been initially smashed to help hide her magic. Yet, for this woman, she cared. And not only because she was queen of her land.

"How does your connection with the birds work, Your Grace?"

The queen cocked her head like one of her birds, studying Piris while still walking, then asked her own question. "Do you not know, lady?"

A fair enough question, given Piris's own magic. "No, not in a true sense." She paused here, not having discussed the intricacies of her magic to anyone outside her parents and Strella all her life. "It's more like the magic knows but I do not. I let the magic do what it needs to do. I control it, yes, and understand how my magic moves in me, but I cannot understand the specifics of each feat my magic accomplishes. It simply does it."

"Fascinating," the queen said, still holding her gaze as they all walked. Strella gripped Piris's arm tight, a silent sign she was there to intervene if her friend felt the need, and she appreciated it. However, she did not need it then. Didn't think she'd need it with this queen, ever.

"With my birds, I—" She turned her face toward the sky when her eagle screeched, high and loud, into the open expanse of gray. "Down," the queen growled, whipping a blade out from under her coat as her eagle dove down from the sky.

Piris did not question the order, grabbing Strella and twisting her so she landed with a hard thump on her back to the left of where Piris had just stood. She covered her friend, searching for signs of danger. An arrow thudded hard into the gravel mere inches away from them.

Piris looked about her for cover of some kind, something to protect her sister, when she heard more birds, hard beats of wings and long cries filling the skies. Queen Alene crouched low but stood strong, her hard face set in concentration, her eyes narrowed on something Piris could not see. Something she guessed the queen only saw or understood through the eyes of her eagle.

Piris, however, did see another arrow, flying fast from a different direction, right at her queen. She yelled, "Move!" as she scrambled low to the ground, to try to stay between her friend and queen, to do something to protect both. The directive wasn't specific, but the queen seemed to understand enough to dive to her right, avoiding the second arrow, and embed itself in the palace grounds.

The queen let out a colorful curse, and Piris appreciated the sentiment. When Strella tried to raise her head, she pushed her friend back down. "Stay low," she warned her as she searched the sky for more arrows.

She saw none, but watched as birds of prey started falling from the sky. On her right, she noticed the queen flinch, and her heart dropped at what Queen Alene must feel in the moment. Everything other thought was cut off by a scream of rage.

"Strella!"

She heard the pounding of feet.... looked behind them and found both princes running at full Fae speed toward them, blades drawn. Jarok kept his eyes toward the sky in defense, but Ghel only had eyes for his princess, tucked tight under Piris.

Another, distant scream rent the air, along with a mass of bird screeches. If Piris had to guess, the archer was now felled. She wouldn't risk the life of her best friend on such a guess though. She stayed planted on her, a shield, until Ghel reached them and dragged his wife into a fierce hug.

"They are done," Queen Alene said, her voice low and harsh. Piris trusted her and began to rise. The imprint of gravel on her hands, and the few cuts and bruises along her body, twinged as she moved. A hand appeared in her vision—a large, long-fingered, and slightly calloused golden-brown hand. The hand of Prince Jarok. She didn't take it. She stared, long enough for him to give a sigh of annoyance and grab her arm on his own. She shook it off as soon as she stood, glaring his way, but he'd turned from her to ask a group of guards coming their way about what had happened.

Piris didn't know specifics, of course, but she could see the outline well enough. Benders, at least two, had breached the palace defenses and tried to kill the princess and queen. Obviously Engad Monti was not done with his attacks on the royal family.

Chapter Two
Jarok

The attack on the palace rattled him, above all others perhaps, because palace security was his domain. He'd also been the one to find the murdered guards along the western wall, their throats slit before they could raise a single alarm. His mother's warrior instincts had saved them from complete disaster. He also had to admit Piris's quick thinking and reflexes in the moment helped a great deal. Still. Still. His defenses were breached, his mother and sister-in-law and whatever Lady Piris might be to him had been attacked on his grounds.

There'd been hours of study and discussion over the matter—more concern over security, but in the end, their best course of action was the one they already treaded; they needed to complete this mission. Find Monti and his Benders and cut the attacks off at their root. Until then, they were certain attacks would continue to come. Some of which might even come on their travels.

Jarok managed to stuff down the guilt and rage at the second attack on his family and their home and steeled himself as he entered his brother's study. For the journey ahead and the danger it may entail.

"Are you prepared, brother?" Ghel asked as soon as Jarok stepped into the room. Slipping into his nonchalant courtly mask to cover his worry and guilt, he gave a hard snort at the question. He exaggerated looking down at himself. His fighting leathers, a grayish black which highlighted the glossy black of his hair, molded to his body while his trusty falchion, with its wickedly sharp curved edge, sat secure at his side. The leather riding gloves hung loosely around his travel belt next to his small purse. His saddlebags weren't hanging around his neck, as they had been sent ahead to his horse, but he thought he looked damn ready himself.

He quirked an eyebrow at his brother, who looked him up and down with his own huff of annoyance, then bent back over his desk to study a map. None in his family blamed him for the most recent attack. No one questioned his security measures or methods, asking only how exactly the Bender had gotten onto the palace grounds, then mourning the loss of his men as he did. He blamed himself, however, and the prodding games he played with his older brother helped him push the blame aside. For a time at least.

When Jarok pulled closer, he noticed the map ran the course of the Great River, or at least the portion of the Great River running through the Winterlands. Smack in the middle, nestled among a visual representation of some type of evergreen forest, sat Volesion Peak, their supposed destination. Ghel managed a glance his way and a huff at his sarcastic look, but he dropped the questioning, going back to whatever he and Cylian were discussing.

"See here," Ghel said, tracing a thick finger along the edges of the river on the map. "This is what I was telling you about. So many outcroppings, cave systems, coves and such. Unless we have more information, we're going in blind. We could search for a year and never find Engad Monti and his Benders unless they wanted to be found."

"How do we gather more information, beyond the normal means?" Jarok's question was valid. He knew how to talk, to laugh... to get others to talk and laugh with him, which he could do while on the road whenever they stopped with others. More than that, and they needed a plan.

"No one knows the river and what happens on or around it better than Brettly Volesion," Ghel said without looking back at Jarok.

"Definitely seems getting into Lord Volesion's good graces is a necessity then," Cylian muttered.

"Yes," Ghel grunted. "I fear we might not be able to do so." Jarok may have imagined the pointed tone in his voice, the accusation there, so he ignored it and feigned ignorance.

"Why, brother?" he asked, leaning a slim hip against the side of the desk. "Do you doubt my and Cylian's ability to charm?"

Hard, dark eyes bore into Jarok with the exasperation only an older sibling can rightfully display. "I doubt he'll be too happy to discover the secret he kept about his daughter, to ensure her safety from any in power, especially those in leadership positions in two different Fae lands, has been revealed to us."

"That was Lady Piris's choice," Jarok replied. He'd known something was off about the woman. Knew in his bones she had a lurking secret, and not only because he caught her snooping on the grounds the night of their arrival, before he even knew she was his sister-in-law's lady-in-waiting and best friend. He had seen it there, a shadow in those bronze eyes of hers, and had set himself to the task of discovering what she hid from everyone. Despite all his needling, his watchful guards, and his own watchful eyes always narrowed on her when she was in his vicinity, he'd never come close to guessing her secret. It rankled a bit. He prided himself on being a man of information, being able to gather and reveal and know whatever needed to be known, especially in and around the palace, which was his particular protective domain. Having a mimic there for weeks, without any clue, was a blow to his ego.

If he were honest, having a mimic in the Winterlands at all was a shock. Their magic was exceedingly rare, hidden away from the old hunts and persecution and forced servitude. Mimicry was a formidable power. The ability to mimic sound as Piris could might be handy, but the real force came with the ability to mimic any magic they felt or observed, ever. In their entire life. It meant Piris could conjure any magic she needed as long as she'd encountered it once. No wonder she was iron and wood, rigid and cold and unbendable. To have such power, and hide it away. Take the whispers of people who thought her powerless and do nothing to prove them wrong. It displayed a level of skill and will he might call awe inspiring if it didn't reside in Lady Volesion.

"Yes. She made her choice," Cylian said, breaking into Jarok's musings about the maddening woman. "Doesn't mean her father will be happy with her for making the choice, or with us for knowing despite her choice."

"Which means we'll have a harder time getting him on our side, or trusting he'll share useful information." Jarok said it out loud, but he knew they were all thinking it.

A big sigh came from Ghel. "Exactly. We need his help. We might even need his ships."

"Darin has access to at least one ship, moored here, if all else fails. The Springlands king has a vested interest in squashing a rebellion so close to his own shores." Cylian spoke as he pointed out a port on the other side of the Great River, along the border of the Springlands.

"Darin Marco? He's our ally in this," Jarok sneered. Now he knew why Ghel hadn't told him before this. He had a grave dislike for Marco, even though he'd only met the man in passing when he had been a teenager. Darin Marco was a known spy and assassin for the domineering royals of the Springlands.

Jarok supposed such a king, bent on retaining absolute power and control, would be more than a little concerned about any whisper of rebellion close to his kingdom. The Boraus were not happy with rebellion, but Jarok, like his family, felt it was a false rebellion, born on a need for power rather than a need for political of social change. Maybe he was biased, but he felt himself proof of the care and concern of the royals of the Winterlands—an orphan nearly dead on the Ice Plains scooped up by the family and made one of their own. It was emblematic of how they led the land, and a reason why Jarok had an ingrained drive to protect his family and help his kingdom. Not because he was born to it, expected it, but because he could help others with the political and social power he possessed.

He suspected Engad Monti did not feel the same. He knew the king of the Springlands did not, and that was part of his problem with allowing a weapon of this monarch into his land. It didn't sit well with Jarok to have such a person come into the Winterlands, at their request no less. He'd serve his king without question, which meant they couldn't trust what he'd do when he fought beside them, if it ever came to that.

"You need to put *all* your issues aside during this mission," his brother grumbled at him as he looked at the map, setting the images to memory.

"All? Whatever do you mean, Prince?" The sarcasm wasn't exactly warranted, but Ghel needled him, digging into old annoyances and wounds, even if he didn't realize he did it.

Ghel straightened and squared around to face Jarok. Ghel had four inches on him, but Jarok stood tall against his brother, despite his shorter, leaner build. He'd fought him many times, in practice and in annoyance, and had never backed down from his brother. Most Fae men, faced with the anger of Prince Ghel Borau, would step away if given the chance. Not Jarok. He'd never step away, never show he wasn't up to the task, despite often feeling like it.

"Jarok. Please. For your own good and for the good of us all, do try to curb the sarcasm and bite. With Marco and, more importantly, Lady Piris."

"Lady Piris doesn't require your protection, Ghel." It was the truth. She hung heavy, a weight around his neck while in his palace. She was no damsel in distress. "A fighter with a sharp mind, tongue, and probably several blades, yes, but not a Fae woman needing protecting."

"She is my wife's sister by bond, so she is now my sister."

"But not your sister," Cylian said with a smirk to Jarok. He wasn't at all interested in the implication there, so he left the comment alone.

"All I'm saying, brother, is she can handle herself."

"Yes, but you don't need to make it harder for her," Ghel countered. With a sad whisper, he said, "Strella worries."

Ah, of course. Ghel worried because Strella worried. He should respect his brother's wishes, wear the congenial, pleasing mask he usually had no problem slipping on when he needed to do so. For his brother, whom he loved with all his soul, and his new sister, whom he also loved, not in small part because she'd saved the brother he loved in a number of ways. Something about Lady Piris Volesion made it damned hard for him to do this. When she was near, the mere look of her riled him, calling for words or actions he'd never consider throwing at another lady.

"I hear you, brother," he finally said, "and I understand the concern you and Princess Strella have, the love she has for this lady. I... I will try."

"Trying is all we can ask, right, Ghel?" Cylian looked between his friends to make sure it would be enough, always the thoughtful diplomat.

Prince Ghel's hair, a wild, massive knot at the back of his head, bobbed as he nodded hard. Then, his bulky, muscled arms shot out toward his brother. Jarok flinched back slightly, always ready for the playful but sometimes painful hits his brother might give him, but a blow didn't come. Instead, those arms wrapped tight around him, pulling him into a deep bear hug. The warmth of him was familiar, a comfort he'd known almost all his life, and he melted into it a touch.

"I worry for you too, you know." Ghel's gruff confession in his ear made Jarok's hard smacks on his brother's back too jerky.

He pulled back, slipping the cocky mask in place, and said, "No need to worry about me, Ghel. I'm far too handsome to die."

Ghel wasn't amused by the joke, not in the least, and clapped Jarok on the shoulder, gripping him tight. "Ensure Lady Piris remains safe from any undue pain, and ensure you return to this palace."

The brothers rarely went off without one another. Only a handful of times had Jarok gone out on a campaign away from the palace, much less without Ghel at his back. He'd thought little of it until the realization hit. He was off, without his brother close, to a mission which might well mean battles. Gem would accompany there, and he loved his cousin fiercely. Cylian was as close as a brother in some ways. Still, neither were Ghel, the gruff, silent Fae he remembered chasing away his nightmares when he had been a boy of four and new to the palace. The one who had taught him tricks in the practice ring. Who teased in his own, dry way. Neither were his older brother. He joked with Ghel, riled him, teased and fought and everything in between, but he knew beyond doubt Ghel would lay his life down for him. Just as Jarok would lay his life down for Ghel.

If the hidden Monti wasn't stopped, he'd come after Ghel again, as he'd done in the Ice Plains battle. The idea steeled Jarok, made him shove the initial fear down so it remained quieted by more important things like duty and respect and love.

"I will, Ghel," he said, no trace of his sarcastic charm or jokes. He stood firm, all seriousness in the face of what could possibly come.

"Good. Good," Ghel said, and Jarok was struck by how much he sounded like their father, the king, when he said that often-used phrase. "Now come. We need to discuss possibilities." Gesturing toward the map, he stepped back to the desk, Jarok following, with Cylian close behind. The three heads bent, searching for answers there, or with each other.

Jarok triple-checked the hooves of his horse. It wasn't that he didn't trust the grooms of the palace. They had exceptional magic and cared a great deal for their charges. One would serve as coachman along the way to keep the magic in place. However, he'd heard, in detail, what had happened with Princess Strella when she had gone off to battle to save his brother, and the idea of the magic wearing off was fresh in his mind.

"All right, cousin?" he heard from behind him, the familiar timbre of the voice telling him it was Gem even more than the words she said. He eased the lifted hind leg of the horse to the ground and spun to sail her way, a genuine smile extended to her twin at her side, her brother Stone. He figured he was seeing her off, as most of the royals were doing with everyone in the party.

Gem stood, her right hip hitched as her left hand sat on the pommel of her short sword. She was in light travel leathers, or light compared to the pile of furs and leather and wool Aurora Clan warriors usually wore. Better for her to mix in with the usual Fae traveling the main roads in the Winterlands. She still stood out clearly as a warrior, what with her stance and her sword and her hard eyes squinting in the abnormal afternoon sun, taking in the scene before her.

"All is fine, cousin," he said, walking up to smack both on the back in greeting. Stone and Gem stood strong against it, and Jarok braced as both hit him, each delivering a punishing blow on the backside of both his shoulders in quick succession. His knees eased, his core flexed, and he prided himself on taking the blows without stumbling a step. Gem and Stone smiled broadly at him, their royal cousins passing their usual little test.

"Aye, all looks fine," Stone said with a touch of admiration in his voice, his warrior's gaze landing on something in the distance. Gem elbowed him in the side and shook her head at his antics, all of which made Jarok turn back around to see Lady Piris in her gray traveling dress saying good-bye to Princess Strella.

"Your brother is a lucky man," Stone said, making Jarok both rankle and breathe easy at the same time for some reason. A long pause stretched before Stone said, "And some other lucky Fae will take on the tall warrior one day."

Jarok ground his back teeth, his jaw flexing while he shifted his shoulders, finally deciding on a noncommittal grunt in response.

"Enough, Stone." Gem shoved him away. "Good-bye." She grunted without fanfare, moving toward the carriage. Her brother didn't let her go far, reaching his long, massive arm out to snag her and give her a big sideways hug. Gem hit him yet again, which he should've seen coming, but the man chuckled and let her loose to go stand with the woman she was supposed to guard as she also played companion and chaperone.

Apparently following Jarok's own thoughts, Stone said, "Seems a little silly, giving that woman a guard."

Jarok said, "Yes," the S a hiss across his lips. He could say a great deal about Lady Piris, most of which would not be flattering, but he'd never be able to say she was a woman who needed a guard along a standard Winterlands road.

Stone hit him again, absently checking the saddlebag at the horse's side before saying, "Be safe, cousin," and striding away without another look.

He was used to the odd mix of jokes and quiet from his cousin, so he took no offense. Instead, he looked around, quirking a dark eyebrow at Cylian, who stood checking his own horse a few yards away. Nodding at the prince, both mounted and reined toward the carriage where he saw Gem, then Lady Piris stoop into the confines. Both women were tall, Lady Piris a little taller even than his cousin, so he wondered how comfortable they'd be stuck in the carriage for long hours.

Princess Strella stood back as Prince Ghel closed the door tight and moved them to their parents. The king and queen stood back a few steps from the ground, waving good-bye to the two in the carriage. Prince Jarok rode up, pausing his horse in front of his family. He'd said his good-byes earlier, but he wouldn't leave without saying something again. Just as they worried about him on the road, he'd worry about what might happen here in the palace with him gone for weeks. He trusted his brother to keep the palace safe, but it was still his responsibility, one he left behind for this mission. He couldn't imagine ever trusting anyone else to take over security. Before he could say anything, his brother's gruff boom sounded. "Take care of yourself, Jarok."

"I will. I always do," he said, getting a small smile from his father and his mother, though his brother shook his head. Not wanting to extend the scene further, he smiled big at the family he was leaving behind and spurred his horse. Pulling into the lead position, he left his home behind, worry over himself and others a ball of heat in his gut.

They'd made it four slow miles past the palace along the winding forest road leading to the main traveling thoroughfare of the Winterlands. It bypassed the Ice Plains and the emptiness there, but the cold, evergreen woods and snow-packed lane felt tedious to Jarok, and he blamed it on the carriage. He knew why they needed it. Part of the plan was for them to appear as protection for Lady Piris as she traveled home, which was completely understandable to most Fae they'd encounter along their route, as everyone knew Lady Piris was a null noblewoman. If only people knew the truth: she was a mimic in their midst. No, he snatched the thought back almost as soon as he had it. She didn't need anyone else knowing about it. Gem, he trusted. She'd obviously been told so she wouldn't be surprised if it came up while they were traveling. Suddenly, a different, exceedingly distasteful idea wormed its way through his head.

"Cylian," he called to his right side. "What exactly have you told Marco?"

Lord Padalist didn't turn his flame-red head to his friend as he scanned the road ahead. "Only what was necessary."

"What was deemed necessary?"

"The outline of the rebellion so far, information regarding Engad Monti past and present, what the Winterlands royals wished as well as what they were willing to do in order to achieve those wishes."

He knew those things too. He'd hashed it out with his family in private before they relayed it all to Cylian, who'd presented them with the opportunity of an ally. The Winterlands royal court was willing to give a great deal to ensure the ex-Monti leader stopped being a threat to their lands and their family. He agreed with it in theory, the high price, but knowing it was Darin Marco, or the Springlands royals, who'd reap the reward made him uneasy.

None of it answered his real question in the moment. "Anything about our party?"

Cylian looked at his friend then, eyeing him up and down from a few feet away as their horses clomped along. His silver eye with its slashing scar flared as the smile spreading across his lips reached his other gold-tinged eye. "I told him who was in our party."

"Come on, Cylian." Jarok was done with the back-and-forth, especially when he saw the tease on his friend's face. He took a second to look back at the carriage, not able to see the woman he wanted information about in the moment. "You know what I'm asking."

"Then why not come out and ask it, friend?"

"Cylian," Jarok growled, sounding oddly like his far gruffer brother in his annoyance. He was a man who rarely became annoyed with others, or at the very least, a man who was able to easily hide his annoyance with a smirk, clever comment, or joke. The mask he wore so often.

The lord beside him barked out a laugh. "If I didn't know better... Ignore my musings, friend. I told him enough, which was there was a Fae noblewoman with us, a formidable fighter who for her own reasons hid her nature from others in this land."

He needed more assurance. "He doesn't know she's a mimic?"

Cylian stopped his teasing with his next words. "He does not, but he very well could, quite soon. Darin Marco is a friend, a sometimes ally, and one of the shrewdest Fae I've ever known. If something happens, if Lady Volesion must use her powers around him, he won't miss the implications."

Jarok jerked his head in agreement. All true, and all worrying. They did not need yet another powerful Fae with knowledge of Lady Piris's powers, if only because her father would be even more displeased with it. At least, that was what Jarok told himself as he worried over the possibilities of her exposure to the Springlands assassin.

Chapter Three
Piris

Gem sighed loudly and asked Piris, "Dull, isn't it?" as the warrior woman let the carriage curtain fall down again. Piris eyed her travel companion—one of four, then five, then who knew how many once they hit a specific point in their journey. Gem Aurora was her immediate companion, the one forced to ride in the carriage with her. To keep up appearances.

They'd left the palace hours ago, exchanged a few pleasantries, but neither woman seemed inclined to talk for the sake of talking, so each had retreated to their separate corners. Gem napped. Piris had closed her eyes but didn't sleep, instead thinking about her good-byes with Strella, which made a lump stick in her throat, and what she'd have to say to her parents in a few short days' time, which made sweat break out across her forehead. It was a jumbled mess of emotions, so sleep was not easy for her. Especially not in the rocking interior of the lush carriage.

It was comfortable, she'd give it that. More comfortable than being on horseback as the lord and prince were, or outside the carriage as their coachman was. Also warmer. The insides stayed toasty thanks to heat spells from the Fae who'd built the contraptions. Still, like a corset, it confined. Hemmed in. Sometimes, she preferred the fresh air of horseback. It might be far more entertaining, which brought Piris back to what Gem had grumbled to her, a familiar thing she'd said herself when crossing the slog of the Ice Plains in a different carriage, on a different sort of mission to protect her friend.

"It is indeed," Piris finally replied, leaning up slightly out of her previously slouched position. She'd relaxed somewhat, partially because she saw Gem relax, and if an Aurora warrior could take a break, so could she.

Gem looked at her from tip to toe, evaluating her. Not in a harsh, overly critical way, like she'd already made up her mind about the woman. That was the way of the other Fae noblewomen she'd encountered who knew she was supposedly a null. Not exactly in the way Queen Alene or Prince Ghel first looked her over either, with a fighter's calculation. Definitely not the way Prince Jarok raked her with his eyes, scraping her skin in his wake. No. More like a curious and jovial stranger, wondering what they might do or whether they could find mischief together.

Piris openly studied the woman as well, since her companion was going to be rude about it. Gem Aurora was a sturdy woman, but not unattractive as people often implied when a woman was called sturdy. It was what she knew others meant when they talked of her own height and muscle and broad features. Gem's limbs were strong, thick. Her shiny dark-brown hair was pulled back in a tight bun at the nape of her neck. Dark-brown eyes, the echo of her hair, sparked on her face, full of something Piris couldn't quiet place, but she thought might be amusement or mischief. Either way they bounced with light, deep rings in stark white. Her face, pale from lack of sun but with an olive undertone, was full and rounded, with a small, fluffy white scar at the corner of her left cheek.

"This?" Gem said, apparently noticing Piris's fixed gaze on her cheek. "White bear."

"You were attacked by a white bear?" Piris asked, leaning forward, excitement and amazement coloring her voice.

"Aye. A few times. Well, chased by a white bear a few times in my life. This, however, wasn't exactly an attack. More like a dying gasp after my brother felled the thing."

"Your brother Stone?"

"Aye. Stone Aurora, my twin. My bane."

Piris heard love there, but a twinge of something else, something she knew. An envy of sorts for someone allowed to be all they could be. She didn't answer, but nodded.

"What about you?" Gem said, gesturing toward Piris and the white, papery slash of a scar along the back of her right hand. She sometimes covered it with longer sleeves, but not often. It was small, barely noticeable, so she forgot about it more often than not.

A smile stretched across her wide mouth. "My father accidentally knocked me with his sword."

Gem snorted. "You sound happy about it. In my experience, sword wounds aren't happy things."

"No, they wouldn't be, I'm sure. But my father... He taught me a lot when he didn't have to, especially about swords."

Gem's eyes shifted slightly, a new look of understanding creeping over her face until her own smile matched Piris's.

"Do I have to call you lady?" she asked.

Piris laughed. "Gods, no."

"Good. Would've forgotten eventually anyway, but don't want to be rude and all that."

Piris waved a hand in dismissal and, after a beat, said, "Strella told me she thought we'd be good friends or hate each other by the end of this."

"A toss-up," Gem quipped.

"I guess."

"I think friends might work," Gem said, her smile going small but not any duller. "You know the bite of the sword and also find traveling in a carriage boring. Common ground."

Piris chuckled, leaning back in her seat as Gem rearranged herself. From a satchel at her side, Gem pulled a small wool blanket over her chest. It was a thing of beauty, a picture of the night sky with streaks of vivid color nestled among mountains in an intricate, tight weave. A picture much like Strella had described to her when she had told her of the fasting ceremony.

"Beautiful blanket," she said.

"Home" was Gem's reply before she closed her eyes again, leaning her head against the lush, upholstered side of her bench. Piris could respect Gem's abrupt end to their conversation. She needed her rest too, though rest wouldn't come easily. Hadn't come easily in so long she forgot what it felt like. She closed her eyes again, willing herself to sleep, except her will, a formidable thing, couldn't help her out in this one task.

Their first overnight stop was not at a tavern or inn but rather at a small traveling house. In the less populated regions of Winterlands, such houses stood close to the roads at certain mile markers. Sometimes they were a cluster of one-room cabins, sometimes multi-room dwellings. The structures were maintained and stocked by a caretaker during daylight hours, and kept open for travelers to use at night. It was an honor system, with travelers agreeing to not trample the place and leave compensation for use when they could. In the harsh weather of the Winterlands, it took a great deal to survive, and people tended to help one another.

Piris had never actually stayed at a traveling house before then. She and her father had camped in the vast forest around their estate often when she'd been training. If the whole Volesion family traveled, they stayed at inns along the way, her father meticulously mapping a route where her mother would be most comfortable. Not that her mother herself had ever said she preferred inns or wouldn't stay at a traveling house, but his concern for his wife's comfort was always paramount.

Piris was struck then by how odd it was he didn't show the same concern for her, a lady by birth as well. She was a fighter by training, but part of her fight came from her mother, who could cut a noble Fae down with a few choice words or a slice of her eye as cleanly as her father could cut with a blade. As she mused about why her father felt the need to treat her so differently, which inevitably came back to the fact of her magical difference and the importance of secrecy for him when it came to her abilities, three of her companions chatted with the coachman about something.

She caught snippets before hearing Prince Jarok exclaim, "You're mad, man!"

"No, Your Highness. I cannot. Will not."

The carriage had pulled into a semicircle of gravel and compacted snow where a single, small cabin stood. Piris had wandered behind the carriage, as Prince Jarok was tying up his horse at a post toward the front of the vehicle and she wanted to avoid him as much as she could. She'd not had much time to look, but she had seen a massive pile of firewood stacked high along the edge of the cabin, the small outhouse beside it, and a cramped structure a few yards down which looked like a shed with a tiny iron chimney snaking up the side.

With the raised voices, she turned from her inspection of their surroundings and decided to walk into the fray.

"What's the issue here?" she asked, looking right at Jarok because she knew, somehow, he would be the center of it.

Gem snorted and threw a hand out at the man beside the carriage, "The daft coachman refuses to stay in the cabin with us."

Lady Piris turned toward him, a groom sent from the palace to care for their horses and steer the carriage.

"Aye, miss. Lady. I cannot. My mother would hang me for such disrespect to the prince. And a lord and lady."

"It's no disrespect, Nore. You are welcome, as I keep saying." Jarok sounded exasperated, but his dark eyes held not shrewd disregard, but a different, softer thing she didn't want to name. Not from him, who she'd already pegged as too cocky and uppity.

"Will you not budge in this, sir?" Piris asked, trying to give him space to make his case or think through the issue. Gem, Jarok, and Cylian urged him to reconsider, as they should. It'd be a cold night in the carriage, as the heating spells took hours to recharge on their own.

He shook his head, barely looking at her, and she huffed out her own sigh.

"Very well. Go check the structure beyond the cabin, just past the outhouse. I think it might be an additional sleeping area, though far smaller. Good enough for one Fae, if it's what I think it is."

Nore, the coachman, perked up at the idea and excused himself to check out the situation.

"You could have given this information earlier," Jarok groused.

"Oh, really? When, exactly? When I was not within earshot of your ridiculous argument or when you, a prince of the Winterlands, was browbeating the poor man?"

Said prince had enough sense to look shamed by her retort and didn't respond. The coachman returned, assured the quartet the structure behind them was a smaller traveling house and said he was more than happy to stay there.

"Good. Good. Take plenty of firewood with you. It will be covered for the night," Jarok said, command in his voice. Enough command to scrape across Piris's nerves.

"Please, coachman, do make sure you keep yourself warm and well supplied," she said a touch gentler, her mother and her kindness again on her mind, before craning her head to the prince to give him a withering stare.

He snorted and walked away to finish tying his horse, Cylian smiling and shaking his head as he trailed behind to take care of his own mount.

"Stubborn men, the lot of them," Gem muttered as she shook her head.

"Couldn't agree more," Piris said. "Let's get inside. They can freeze out here if they want." She'd put on furs when she'd exited the carriage, and her wool traveling dress helped cut the evening chill down, but she knew her leathers would be more comfortable for her. At least, in her mind they were warmer, more comfortable. More secure.

Gem stopped her with a touch on the shoulder before she took two steps from her companion. She'd started to head right into the cabin, but the warrior moved in front, taking point position. Of course she would; she was supposed to be companion and guard. It was her purpose on this trip. Still, it rankled Piris a little, as if her new friend didn't trust her abilities.

"None of that now," Gem muttered, as if she noted the momentary flash of annoyance on Piris's face. "I have to do what I have to do. Might as well get used to it."

Schooling her face, Piris let her lead, staying a few steps behind as Gem opened the cabin door and peered inside. She moved to check corners, look through the small closet that stood behind the only door in the space, and even looked up into the small stone chimney to ensure nothing was there. It wasn't a huge undertaking, checking the security of the cabin. The space sat empty, a near perfect fifteen-by-fifteen-foot square except for the small rectangular cutout of the closet by the door and the hearth, which jutted out a few feet along the far back wall. Not much to take in or inspect, but more than enough to keep the four of them warm for the long Winterlands night.

"Looks fine," Gem finally said to Piris, who stood at the threshold. She opened her mouth to reply but froze when she felt a sear against her left side, landing right at the waist of her dress. Looking down, she saw a hand, with powerful, long fingers and pronounced veins popping in relief against the prince's tawny hand.

"Excuse us, *lady*," a familiar, infuriating voice huffed at her right ear. Close enough for her to feel the puff of his breath, just as she felt the hand at her waist, both equally hot as they skated across her nerves. She didn't reply, but spun away quickly, stepping deep in the room as she did, putting as much distance between her and Prince Jarok as she could in a matter of seconds.

"Finished fighting with the groom, I see," she finally said, jabbing him with words to cover her own shaky reaction.

He stepped toward her, a hard, almost menacing step as if in chase, before he pulled himself short, visibly reining in whatever pushed him toward her. "You may not care if your people freeze, but I do," he said, heat rising in his voice as color smeared across his impossibly high and sharp cheeks.

Cylian and Gem ignored the two standing off in the middle of the room, instead deciding to light a fire in the hearth, which was the smart thing to do.

Piris ached to say more, to jab and hurt, but she stopped herself. She knew it was a ridiculous impulse, not worth her time or effort, but the prince always did this to her, made her feel shaky and off her game, so she tended to strike back without thinking. Just as Strella had accused her of, just as she'd promised her friend she'd stop doing.

"I—" She held her tongue a moment, thinking better, before she sighed. Her hand skimmed over her forehead and paused a second to rub her temple. "I'm tired. I-I'll rest," she said, directing it to the room at large.

Jarok stared, then turned his head to the side, and she saw he bit the inside of his cheek. He stopped his own words as well. Maybe, just maybe, they could begin to be more civil to one another.

"I'll get my roll," she called and moved to the door.

Jarok stopped her with a raised hand. Without a word, he turned sharply and strode into the darkness, presumably to fetch the rolls for everyone, not just her. It was a very un-princely thing to do for his companions, but Piris stuffed the thought down as soon as she had it.

J arok took a while fetching the bedrolls, which Piris learned was because he had gone behind their cabin to make sure the coachman was comfortable and secure for the night, an action she decided to ignore.

They'd talked little to one another as Cylian prepped a simple stew pack over the fire, mixing water with dried ingredients to provide them a hearty, warm meal. Piris offered to empty the pot afterward and scrape the dishes, but Gem stopped her, taking the outdoor duties so she wasn't exposed.

Instead of taking offense or being annoyed, she tried to do what Gem had suggested and get used to the idea. She took the time to set up her and Gem's bedrolls close to the right side of the hearth, placing Gem's a little in front of her own so she'd get more heat. The Aurora warrior snorted at the position when she saw it, but said nothing, apparently also getting used to the idea the lady wasn't going to be treated like a lady at all times.

It was full dark as all four Fae bedded down for the night, saying little to one another above what was necessary. Jarok and Cylian discussed when they should leave in the morning, what might need to be prepped again for the continued journey. Gem stayed quiet, so Piris didn't add to the conversation either and was thankful the talk lasted only minutes. Seemed everyone was tired enough to sleep early and hard, which was what Piris wanted to do.

She squirmed a moment in her roll, twisting so she could cradle her head in her left arm and face the two Fae men who were thankfully turned toward the opposite wall. Piris thought she needed to get used to sleeping on her back or right side, but let the thought drift away as she went down, down, down into sleep.

She was a gangly thirteen-year-old, two years past the revelation of her powers, sitting on a rock beside a roaring fire. She looked through it, around it, trying to see anything other than the flames, but little showed itself. From across the bright expanse, she heard her father's words. Words he'd drilled into her over and over again when she had been in training: "Secrets keep you safe."

Piris had been terrified when her magic manifested as a preteen Fae. Most Fae found their affinities between ten and twelve, around the same time their bodies started to slowly change. She knew of mimics, of course. They were the hushed boogeymen of children's stories, a history so dark the truth of it wasn't learned until Fae were much older, if at all. Except she knew a little more, as mimics ran in the Volesion family long ago, and she'd drilled her father about their abilities and history. When she'd started imitating her mother and father, along with their magic, the ability slipping out of her without thought or direction, she'd told her father first. She remembered the tears and fights between her mother and father, days of worry and stress, until they came to her with the plan: they'd pretend she'd never manifested an affinity, marking her a null instead of confessing to anyone she was a mimic. She'd be a different type of target as a null, open to gossip and derision within the nobility they slowly started to distance themselves from, but she'd be safe from the worst that could happen to mimics.

At the same time, her education as a lady would continue, along with new combat and magical training from her father. In secret, of course. All in secret. All in hiding. He'd been tough with her, which she now appreciated, but in the face of her roaring dream fire, her adult mind slammed back in the too-stretched teenage body she felt she had no control over, and just as she felt she had no control over her life then, the anger once again rose. Anger at the unfairness, the burden, the whittling away of who she was and could be, all in service of a secret she'd been told must always be hidden away.

Strella was the only one let into the secret, a mistake she'd thankfully made at a young age. Her parents had been so angry with her, but after discussing it with both her and Strella, they were confident in her friend, as they should have been. Strella never gave away her powers, never would have. Piris had done that all on her own, and she'd do it again, to help her friend save her love.

Adult Piris's eyes looked down at her tinier self and flexed her cracked knuckles, hands hurting from hours of practice with daggers and combat training every week. She spoke with older Piris's voice into the fire, a choked confession. "I told, Father."

"You are not safe," her father said, his voice melting into the roar of the rising flames, the heat searing itself across her face.

"I can make myself safe."

"Can you?" It was not her father now, but another voice, one more grating, one with enough heat to sear through the fire in front of her.

"Yes," she hissed at the sound of Prince Jarok, rising, her body transformed into what it was in reality, an adult Fae woman. She stood clad not in the traveling dress she wore to sleep but in her brown fighting leathers, the leathers she'd worn the first night she was at the palace, the first time she had encountered the prince.

A shadow of a body flitted across the flames, and the wind picked up, warm and caressing in a way Piris wanted to lean into but wouldn't allow herself to, as an unnerving and infuriating chuckle sounded. "Maybe. Maybe not, *lady*. Some flames you can't extinguish when they start to burn."

"Nothing burns yet," she bit back, her eyes trying to follow the direction of the prince's disembodied words. Another chuckle... then all was darkness, sound and feeling and sight snuffed out in a second like a small death.

Piris started awake a moment later, her breath quickening as her eyes sprang open. She didn't often dream like that. Not that she didn't dream. Sometimes she even had delicious dreams. This one had been heartbreaking and infuriating in equal measure.

After blinking a few times, her eyes adjusted to the soft glow of the banked fire in the hearth. She looked ahead and saw the prince facing her, his golden face and dark eyes blurred in the darkness but still sharp enough for her to see they were trained on her. Slamming her eyes shut, she rolled over on her back before looking at the ceiling, determined to sleep like this. She'd try anything to avoid the eyes she couldn't quite see but still felt on her, just as she'd felt the heat of her dream.

Chapter Four
Jarok

Jarok slept little the night before. He'd been woken by a sharp intake of breath and turned from the wall to find Piris looking tired but alert, her eyes scanning the space before boring into his. She looked away quickly, and he did the same, not needing to think on her more when he should be sleeping. However, sleep eluded him as he obsessed over what had woken her, why she had been so alert, and the pang of now knowing what she looked like rumpled from sleep.

Eventually, he fell back to sleep, getting a few precious hours before Gem woke at dawn and stomped around to make sure everyone else got up and got ready to continue their journey. They had another full day and another night at a traveling house, then a second full day, before they stopped at the first inn as planned.

The traveling houses were preferred because they were isolated, more secure, more within the prince's control in many ways. At an inn, anyone could come and go as they pleased, and the thought of it made the security-minded prince's teeth grind. Luckily, he and Cylian had mapped out a six-day route where they stayed at inns only twice. The idea still made him even more on edge than the loss of sleep did. He was not happy when Gem asked, "When do we meet with the other Fae?"

He couldn't be mad at his cousin for the question. She needed to know to properly plan, even if it was merely planning in her mind for future possibilities. But did she have to say it as Piris bent down on her knees beside his cousin, packing her bedroll as the rest of them did?

"At the first inn," Cylian said, cutting his eyes to Jarok as if he sensed the tension pulsing from the man.

"Who is it?" Piris asked, setting herself back on her heels, facing the two Fae men who'd just finished putting their own rolls away.

"No need for you to concern yourself with it," Jarok muttered, hoping she'd drop the topic. Knowing her, her dogged tenacity, and her uncanny tendency to clamp onto anything that annoyed him, she wouldn't.

"Lord Padalist?" she asked, quirking a thick, perfectly arched auburn eyebrow at the diplomat.

"Cylian. Please," he replied.

"Piris to you, then," she said with a sweet smile Jarok had never seen directed at him, a stray realization that oddly hurt his head and chest for a fleeting moment. "Again, who is this mysterious ally?"

Cylian looked at his friend and cocked his head. Jarok knew she also deserved all the information, needed it just as Gem and he and Cylian needed it. Didn't mean he had to like it.

"Darin Marco," Jarok growled, shoving to his feet and slinging his pack over his shoulder.

Gem cracked out a laugh. "Oh, now I know why you're so surly, cousin. Or at least, one of the reasons."

"Enough, Gem." Jarok stood and planted his feet, staring down his cousin, daring her to continue. She smiled at him completely uncon-cerned, rising herself, never one to back down from a fight in any form. Gem opened her mouth, likely to give him some snarky comeback, but Piris's voice cut through first.

"Who is Darin Marco?"

Cylian gave her the bare-bone facts. "An ally from the Springlands."

"Your ally from the Springlands," Jarok said.

"Our ally now, friend. You must keep that in mind."

Piris's head whipped back and forth between the two men, soaking in all they said and what they didn't say, her shrewd mind whirling behind those assessing bronze eyes.

With a sickly-sweet smile, she said, "Someone the prince dislikes so much must be rather interesting."

"You be careful with Marco," Jarok snapped before he could hold his tongue.

"I'm all carefulness, Your Highness."

Jarok gave a dismissive snort before giving her another command. "You will steer clear of the Fae."

"What makes you think you can tell me who I shouldn't spend time with, Prince?"

"For your own good—"

She surged to her feet, stalking the distance between them as her feet remained light and silent, her training etched in every movement of her body. She stopped inches from his face. They were nearly the same height, Prince Jarok having only an inch or two on the woman, so her squinting, heated eyes stared easily into his from the short distance.

"You get no say in my good."

A cocky smile tripped across Jarok's lips, and his words tumbled out before he could stop himself. "Someone should, as you appear to lack the ability yourself."

Piris cursed loudly before striking him with more honed words. "I apologize, Your Oh-So-Elevated Highness. Please, do command me as you do everyone else around you."

Jarok ground his teeth, hating the words, hating she thought he was like that, and hating how sometimes he was, as he had spent the bulk of his life commanding in one way or another. He didn't get a chance to lash out with his own barbed words before Cylian's heavy hand landed on his shoulder. "Come, Jarok. Let's ready the horses."

Jarok's head was jerky, stiff, as he nodded in the lady's face. He swiveled on his heels and stomped away from her, far less graceful than her, despite his own years of training. He made his way out the door and to his horse, his jaw locked tight and his movements precise as he did what he had to do to get them on the road—get Lady Piris back in the carriage and away from him with her too-smart gaze and too-quick tongue.

The morning stretched long and cold. The coachman had prepped the carriage quickly and seen to the horses' spells to keep the snow and ice from packing their hooves and making travel dangerous for rider and horse both. No one spoke on it, but everyone there had either seen or heard of the accident with Strella's horse during the Battle of the Ice plains, how it had thrown her and Ghel had only just managed to avert utter disaster for his princess. The five travelers tore into a quick breakfast of crisp travel bread with a tub of cheese Cylian had smartly brought along. Easy enough to keep it cool in this weather, which was the usual gray bleakness of the Winterlands. Not that anyone minded a great deal. It was their home, their land, and the frozen scenery around seeped into them, energizing them in some ways.

All except Cylian. He was a son of autumn, used to a certain chill, but the slight coolness of autumn was no match for winter, even when a Fae piled on the furs over their leathers.

After the fifth time Jarok heard Cylian blow into his gloved hands and rub them together for a little friction, he chuckled, the puffs of hot air creating white clouds of laughter around his head. "Cold, are you? Here I thought your magic could warm you."

"Some, yes, but not enough for riding hours across this freezing land."

Jarok used his own power to break the headwind so Cylian wasn't directly bombarded. "Let me know if my mind slips, and I'll pick it back up." His wind power required some intent, but not a great deal of concentration. He'd honed his skills with a tutor. His father, having something similar in the ice and cold he could direct, had helped him practice his magic to become nearly automatic to him, something he could bring up and down, command and shut away with little thought. If he wished, he could command a gale from a small breeze and whip wind around an enemy, which he'd done enough in his past. This barrier, winds of protection, was a piece of his magic he enjoyed. It gave him the ability to defend, not simply attack.

The Autumnlands lord called to him, "No need, friend. You should reserve your energy for more important things."

"The comfort of my friends isn't important?"

Cylian, who'd been a few horse lengths ahead, slowed enough to get side by side with Jarok. The prince saw the dark look on his face and worried his teasing had gone too far somehow. A problem he sometimes had, and usually only regretted when it bit into family or friends.

"We've had a quiet day and night. Does not mean it will remain so, even in this desolate stretch—maybe most especially here. It was in a similarly isolated place where your brother and the princess were attacked by the Benders."

Jarok looked away, partially shamed by the fact he'd spent a good bulk of the morning sulking rather than keeping himself alert and trained on the area. Gods damn it all, he wouldn't—couldn't—allow agents of Engad Monti to get at their group. He, and his family, figured he might be a direct target. He knew the Benders' leader wanted to lash out at the royal family for his own twisted reasons he called noble.

Engad Monti wanted power. Oh, sure, he wrapped it in talk of bettering the lives of warrior Fae like his clan, but his domination of other clans, his aggression and acts of war, told otherwise. He was a Fae out for himself, cloaking his actions in words like honor and freedom. Because it was about power, about what he could gain. His actions hadn't ended with Ghel winning the battle over him and his clan. No. They'd end when he was imprisoned or dead, which was why Jarok was out here to begin with. To gain knowledge or, hopefully, stop the Monti outright before he could bring more chaos to his land and his family.

He concentrated more, sending the barrier he'd placed at the head of Cylian in an arc, then a circle, creating a wind tunnel of sorts where their horses and the carriage were engulfed in a small stream of air. Enough to confuse and misdirect any arrows that might surprise them. Jarok had done the same the day before, all day, but he hadn't put it back into place that morning because of his absurd bickering with Piris.

His friend heard the click of his teeth and saw the tightness spread over his shoulders and said, "All is well, has been well, Jarok."

Cylian was attempting to reassure him, let him off the hook for failing in his duties. Something Jarok himself couldn't quite do, not yet. Not with himself.

Early afternoon, they stopped to rest and reset the magic of the horses, eating more bread and cheese with little talk between them. Jarok found himself staring at Lady Piris as she stretched. She wore the same gray traveling dress as the day before. The color was dull and drab, but touches here and there showed its expense: the double stitching in the seams held strong; the fabric, while dull in color, was thick full wool guaranteed to keep out the cold; and the cut was modern and in keeping with the latest Fae fashions in their land. His mother wore dresses as often as she wore leathers, something she said was a different form of armor she needed as queen. Jarok thought Lady Piris likely felt the same, which was why her traveling dress was as nicely made as the leathers he knew she had in her trunk.

"Problem, Prince?" he heard her sneer a second before he realized his eyes had snagged on the gathered ruffle at her chest as he thought about dresses and ladies in his odd, haphazard way. Jarok shook his mind out of thoughts of fashion and necessity and muttered something incoherent.

"Excuse me?" Lady Piris asked, her hand hovering over her pocket, her eyes squinting at the prince.

Jarok cleared his thoughts, gave her his eyes so she could see he was serious, and answered, "I said, 'Apologies, Lady Piris.'"

Her eyes widened a flash before she went back to a tight stance in front of him. Neither said anything for long beats. They stared at one another, dark-brown eyes locked to bronze, assessing.

"Yes, *Lady Piris*," Gem snickered as she returned from her rest stop behind a nearby mound of dirt and snow pushed off the road. "Oh, do forgive the utter rudeness of His Royal Highness, daring to lay eyes on such a delicate lady."

Jarok watched Piris flinch, fascinated by the play of thoughts on her face at his cousin's words. He'd made her flinch before, of course, as she had him, but dark, hot wind stirred in him when someone else, even his own cousin, did the same. He popped his mouth open and frowned at Gem, but before he could get a rebuke out, he heard Piris mutter something herself.

"Huh?" he asked, turning in time to see her head down as she moved closer to him. She stopped a few good feet away, close enough he scented her, the smell of clean ice and steel he associated with the bite of her tongue.

Keeping her eyes on the ground, he just managed to hear her say, "Call me Piris. Please."

He could give her snark, offer a snide comment her way, but he stopped himself. For the peace of their journey and because of the emotions he'd seen on her face when Gem called her "lady" in her joking tone. So he nodded at her, a nonverbal acknowledgment before he croaked out, "Jarok," his voice oddly broken even to his own ear. Why not? Everyone else on the trip called each other by their given names. He and Piris could as well.

She blinked his way, rapid movements taking him in, before she turned at a quick clip and stalked back to the carriage, her long, leanly muscled legs eating the distance, or so he imagined. He couldn't see them under her dress.

"Easy now, cousin. Some might see such a look and think dirty things," Gem said, hitting him on his shoulder as she passed. He muttered and hmphed and sputtered in reply, but the one thing he didn't do was correct her.

The second night at a traveling house went differently than the first. They stopped at a clearing with five small cabins, each unoccupied for the night. Piris declared she and Gem would stay alone, and the coachman again refused to stay with the prince, which left Cylian and Jarok in a single cabin together. It wasn't bad, but Jarok found himself looking out the one small, dirty window in their cabin over and over again, checking no one else showed and nothing amiss happened in the cabin where his cousin and Piris were staying. His wind absently whipped around the structures, a moving shield.

"Sit," Cylian ordered after the tenth time he'd paced to the window, and Jarok listened. Not because he had to do so—he was a prince, after all—but because Cylian was a friend, an intelligent Fae diplomat and strategist, a solid fighter, and in this, right. Jarok needed to calm down. He was hovering, even from a cabin away, and he really shouldn't be. Not with her. He'd witnessed both Piris and Gem in fighting form, had taken hard blows from each. Knew they could hold their own against anyone who might attack. Still, the idea of not being there, with them, in person, made his skin stretch tight and itch. It was best for everyone, especially himself, if he sat and tried to think of something else.

Even sitting, Jarok moved, his leg bouncing as he tapped the toes of one foot on the floor. Cylian looked from his dancing foot to his face and back again before his face softened. "They are secure in that cabin, friend." Understanding shone through Cylian's eyes.

Jarok stopped him before he could say more, flipping his hand in the air. "It's fine. I'm fine. Obviously they are fine. Everyone is fine. No need to discuss further."

"If you say so," Cylian called, moving to unroll his pallet, though Jarok saw the ghost of a smile crack his lips before he fully turned away. Jarok decided to follow Cylian's lead and prepare for bed.

As he tried to make himself comfortable in his roll, Cylian said, "We will meet with Darin tomorrow."

Immediately, any comfort Jarok could've grasped flew away like a snow owl. He stiffened and simply replied, "Yes."

Cylian sighed deep, hard, and said, "Maybe, Jarok, you should give Darin a chance."

"Don't worry, Cylian. I can play the part as well as you. I'll be civil."

"Being civil and being open to knowing someone are two different things."

"Is it necessary we become friends for this to work?"

"No, Jarok, but it might make things easier in the long run, especially if certain concerns you have come to light." He didn't need to name Piris and her powers for Jarok to know exactly what he meant.

Jarok stayed quiet, not talking about why he distrusted Darin so much. He did eventually say, "He's a killer."

"As are we all, in one way or another," Cylian replied. Jarok couldn't argue the fact.

"He kills for a fickle and cruel ruler."

Cylian ended the conversation by embedding a verbal dagger right in Jarok's skull. "Unlike you, who became part of a kind and just royal family, Darin Marco and I come from corrupt houses. With only a worthless, long-forgotten title to his name, he had few options outside his arrows and his wits. The various Fae lands are not always kind to those born within certain power structures, friend. I've seen it, time and again. Felt it myself, my whole life. You know this but chose to ignore it for a man from the Springlands who had little he could do with his life because of where he was born."

Jarok remembered little of his time before being folded into the royal family—flashes of cold and hardness with dashes of hunger thrown in. He was thankful, both for being taken in by his family and for not really remembering what he had before them. Cylian, on the other hand, had been born into privilege, as he freely admitted, though his privilege came with its own harsh reality, one example of which shone like a fork of lightening on his face in the scar running through his one silver eye. His words buried themselves deep into Jarok's brain. Before he closed his eyes to sleep, he thought maybe he'd give the Fae a chance after all.

J arok's wind died down as he slept. He didn't need a great deal of thought to keep up his protective winds, but he did need consciousness. When his ears caught something, a shift in frozen ground outside the cabins, he bolted up in his roll.

He saw nothing from the window, but he knew someone was there, close by. He felt them like a burn on his skin. Jarok couldn't pinpoint them yet, so he snuck out of the cabin as quietly as possible, thinking he'd spare Cylian in case it was a winter fox moving around instead of some nefarious Fae.

With his falchion unsheathed and gripped tight in his hand, he crouched low and moved swiftly around his cabin, the one at the end of the row. A sound, soft but ringing in the silence of night, alerted him whoever lingered there was just around the corner. Quick as a flash, he shot out his hand without looking, grabbing the Fae by the throat and slamming them against the far side of the log wall of the cabin.

He smelled icy steel a second before he realized Piris was staring at him. Her eyes were trained on his, unblinking and unafraid, despite the fact he had his blade to her neck. She remained cool, calculated, and utterly unconcerned, at least on the outside. Jarok's keen eyes saw the pulse in her neck jump slightly.

"Can you let go of my neck?" she asked, calm and blasé as if he weren't holding her throat in his palm or pointing a blade to her skin. Gods, she felt hot under his hand, searing, her throat working with the words in a delicious way he tried to shove down, way down, as he let her go.

In a split second he was steps away, hand flexing as if burned by her flesh, sword now at his side. "Piris, I—"

"Thought I might be some agent or intruder? Understandable. However, I was just visiting the outhouse." She waved behind them vaguely. He cursed himself mentally for not thinking of that, for automatically jumping to fight.

"Yes, well." He didn't have words. What could he even say? *Sorry I nearly choked you without permission and put a sword to your throat?* Instead, he straightened, looked toward the cabin where his cousin obviously still slept, and wondered aloud, "Why is Gem still asleep?"

"I made sure not to wake her."

"Impressive," he muttered, then gave her more, an olive branch of sorts he could offer in the cold, dead night when it was only the two of them. "Not many could say they snuck past Gem Aurora without waking her."

Piris nodded, not verbally acknowledging what he said, but he saw her eyes glint in the moonlight.

He chuckled, thinking of the night they met. "We should stop fighting in the dark."

Piris didn't laugh; she simply walked away, heading for her cabin. Before she got there, she did turn back, a tentative look in her eyes.

Jarok understood it, as he was also trying to find footing on this new ground they were attempting to cultivate between them.

"I like you in the dark."

He cracked out a laugh. Such an odd thing to say. "So you don't have to look at my smug face, I assume," he said, though not with the bite and snark he'd have used with her before.

She shrugged and turned away, neither confirming nor denying. Piris left Jarok to stand in the cold for long minutes, wondering what she meant by those words.

Chapter Five
Piris

After the incident in the middle of the night outside the traveling house, Piris and Jarok operated under a calm truce the next morning. Piris missed it slightly, the back-and-forth she'd had with Jarok since they met, the push and pull that caused her heat to rise and the sensation to zip across her body. She knew it was for the best. She and the prince would be in each other's lives for a long time, what with her best friend happily married to his brother. Better they remain cordial instead of causing scene after scene sniping back and forth, or even worse, one day coming to blows.

Never mind the disaster that might arise if she was honest about her words the night before, or how his hand on her naked throat had caused her pulse to race in lust instead of fear.

She could admit, at least to herself, Prince Jarok Borau was handsome. Devastatingly so, despite the smug look often plastered across his face. She'd learned it was often a type of mask. He was a prince, surely used to a certain amount of deference whether he realized it or not, but she could honestly say he didn't always try to put himself above others. The way he treated everyone on this trip—from her to the coachman who he made sure stayed safe and warm wherever they were—proved as much.

The mask was the perfect visage of noble snobbery and jest, something she'd heard other ladies of the Winterlands whisper about when she was allowed to be close to them. They deemed her insignificant enough to ignore as they freely gossiped among themselves. Ghel was the blood Borau, but that didn't matter to the king and queen, which meant it no longer mattered to most Winterlands nobles, at least that they admitted aloud. Which meant, because of Ghel's gruff nature and warrior demeanor, the women in her world gravitated toward the joking, flirting, and chivalrous Prince Jarok.

Piris had thought them crazy when she'd first met the man. He was rude, infuriating, and snide. She saw nothing to admire even if his outward package was devastatingly beautiful, with his full lips, glowing flaxen skin stretched tight over high cheek bones, a wide-set nose, a strong and broad forehead, and a slightly pointed chin. His hair, short on the back and sides but left artfully floppy at the top, glistened like thick-threaded onyx. And those earth-brown eyes with a small upturn on the outside edges, surrounded by wisps of black lashes and haughtily arched black brows, were deep and dark and sometimes sparkling when they sparred. He could drag someone under like the currents of the Great River with the depths of those eyes. Nevertheless, his attitude, how much it reminded her of other lords she'd known, combined with his instant dislike of her, made her skin prickle in his presence. Yes, she could admit he was lovely to look at, but it paled against who he was.

Then she'd seen him in action, not fighting but in the royal ballroom. He'd moved from group to group effortlessly, without a care in the world, flirting and laughing and dancing as he did. She knew then why the women in the room leaned deep into him, breathed him in, fluttered their lashes and gripped his shoulder tight when they danced across the floor. Because when he focused on someone, he could make them feel as if they were the only person in the room.

Unfortunately for Piris, he'd often used that skill to needle her, make her feel watched and studied like something other, a feeling she already fought in her mind without him helping the matter along. He had the night of the ball and had continued to do so, up until he'd stepped into her with his blade pushed into her throat ever so slightly, his warm fingers loosening around her when he realized who she was. Something had shifted between them and her blood pumped harder, fiercer, not in fight but in another, more enjoyable response. She'd be an idiot to pursue it, but sitting in the carriage in the light of day, hours after she'd felt him against her, she could also admit to herself she wanted him. Her body wanted his body.

Her personal revelations were halted when she heard the coachman call a warning "whoa" seconds before the carriage thumped over some large bump in the road. She thought nothing of it, as Winterlands roads were icy and rather bumpy at the best of times, until she heard a soft sound of feet landing on top of the roof.

Gem heard it too and pulled herself up straight, threw off the blanket she'd been burrowed under, and unsheathed her short sword in seconds. She put a finger to her lips, signing for Piris to remain quiet as she moved toward the carriage door close to her side. Piris had already pulled a sharp dagger from her thigh holster, ripping the pocket of her traveling dress as she did, but she freed it easily, flipping it in the air so she held the hilt firmly in her fist in case she needed to quickly stab someone with force.

The dark curtain of the carriage had barely lifted before the ghost of a hand appeared and, in a flash, the door was unlatched and opened. A Fae man in a gray cloak and leathers came in the door feet first while the carriage swayed, the coachman having finally noticed something amiss and calling out to Jarok and Cylian ahead.

The carriage slowed and the hooded figure crouched low to the floor. She and Gem were at a disadvantage, pinned against the opposite door as they were, but Gem used one had to push Piris back as she sliced out with her sword. The man easily maneuvered around her wicked blade, quite a feat in the confined space. He even managed to grasp her sword hand at the wrist. With a vicious pull, Gem stumbled forward, and the man used her own momentum to send her tumbling out the open door of the nearly stopped carriage.

Piris was enraged at the treatment of her new friend and stood as tall as she could, her forearm a band across her body, ready to lash out and stab if the man came any closer. He didn't, and instead moved to sit on the back-facing bench, pulling this hood back as he did.

If she'd thought Jarok pretty, she could say the same of this man. His white-blond hair was short-cropped, a thick, glowing mass around the sharp angles of his pale face. His nose was strong, pronounced in a masculine way, and showed the slightest sign of crookedness, like it'd been broken a time or two. His eyes, a green like ice freezing the boughs of an evergreen, took her in quickly as she studied him. His lips were a stark ruby red adorning his pale face, full with a perfect bow crowning the top.

He had another type of bow slung across his back, along with a large quiver of arrows. Piris shook off these quick observations and went on the offensive, kicking out with a leg instead of her dagger hand to try to catch him off guard.

No such luck. His strong, sure hands gripped her ankle and twisted, not enough to hurt but enough to show her he could in an instant if he wished. Given the circumstances, a reevaluation was necessary on her part.

She stared at him, waiting, as he blinked her way. Finally, a forced smile spread across his lips, showing a slight skew to his teeth. "Lady Piris Volesion," he stated with a dip of his head. "A pleasure."

A second later, the door beside her flung open and wind tore through the carriage, forcing the stranger back against the bench and causing him to drop her foot. She didn't wait to look outside. Piris bolted out of the space to have more maneuvering room, the wind somehow keeping the man frozen as it also helped her alight.

"You have to be kidding me," Jarok growled when he glimpsed the man in the carriage for the first time.

Their Fae attacker, now freed for some reason, stepped from the carriage, causing Piris to back up and crouch into a fighting posture.

"Greetings, Prince Borau," the man said, straightening his cape as if he weren't facing down a ring of armed fighters.

With a sigh, Cylian said, "I thought you were meeting us at the inn."

The man shrugged and turned to look Piris up and down before stepping forward. Jarok growled like an animal, which made the stranger pause.

"Apologies, Lady Volesion. Allow me to introduce myself. I am Darin Marco, emissary of the Springlands Court. At your service and pleasure, m'lady." She didn't believe the pleasure part for a second. Because those beautifully green eyes were cold as ice, unfeeling. Unconcerned with anyone around them. A chill snaked up her spine. The man screamed danger with every look and movement. She hoped the service part of his introduction was true. As dangerous as he seemed, she'd admit it would be nice to have such a Fae on their side.

P iris grinned to herself, trying hard to remember the tentative truce she'd been thinking about earlier in the carriage. Gem, dirtied by the road, had taken her confrontation with Marco with a good-natured smile and a swift, hearty pat on his back. Impressively, the man remained tall and straight when even Piris herself flinched at the sound the slap made against his leathers. Gem had quite an aggressive way of greeting and testing.

Her half smile, hidden as she took more time than necessary to slip her dagger back into its thigh sheath, centered around the curses Jarok was flinging at the newly met ally. Darin Marco ignored the prince in favor of greeting Cylian.

"How are you, Lord Padalist?" the man asked, a firm, clipped nod in Cylian's direction punctuating his words.

"Fine, friend. And please, call me Cylian."

"As you say," he said, turning to take in the surroundings. "I take it you are Gem Aurora?"

Gem simply looked back at him, obvious in her perusal of his figure. It was quite a figure; Piris would give her that. He was lean, tight muscle over a tall frame. His shoulders, broad and honed, tapered down into a small waist. Long arms, muscled in all the right places, crossed a chest that looked like it might have been poured into his leathers. With his blond hair, angelic face, and that body, he'd have women everywhere drooling. Piris would be too, if it weren't for the edge of danger hanging around him.

Maybe it was the fighter in her, but she saw it shimmering around him like a dark aura. Partly communicated with the hard planes of his face and partly shown in the stiff lean of his muscles, he practically screamed, *"Do not touch."* At least to her. Maybe Gem appreciated a dangerous tumble, but Piris thought his type of danger was too real, too dark for her liking. She preferred the adrenaline of controlled danger in her lovers, not this clear, uncontrolled menace leaking from this man for anyone with trained eyes to see.

Jarok stalked up and placed himself in front of her slightly, as if protecting her. Piris rankled at the move, although a small part of her felt a shiver from the heat of his back lightly touching the front of her right shoulder.

"You are reckless, Marco," Jarok spat.

"Now, Prince—"

Jarok cut the prince off with a withering look. The diplomat knew to pick his battles, so he simply shook his head and raised his hands in front of him in surrender.

"Why attack us?" Jarok asked, leaving her front chillier as he moved closer to the man staring at him with cold green eyes.

Darin Marco looked unconcerned with the wind whirling around the prince or the anger oozing toward him with every word. Instead, he stayed calm and aloof, as if nothing could move him if he did not wish it to do so. "A test, Your Highness."

"A test which could have hurt my cousin or Piris, for no reason," Jarok hissed back, stopping an inch from the other Fae's face.

Marco didn't flinch, didn't falter. Simply replied, "They are perfectly well."

Again, a growl like soft howls of wind bubbled up from Jarok's chest, and he turned to his left, ripping a hand through his thick black hair. Together like that, one in front of the other, the differences between the two Fae were drastic, light and dark in appearance, the opposite in feeling and comfort for Piris. Rather interesting, in her assessment.

She finally stopped pretending to do something else and joined in the fray. "Jarok, all is well, as Marco said. Right, Gem?"

"Aye," she huffed out before Piris kept going.

"We need to get back on the road if we want to reach the inn by sunset."

Jarok visibly stilled himself, forcing his tight muscles to relax before he agreed. Eyeing the Springlands ally, he finally asked, "Where is your horse?"

"I don't have one with me now," the man said, no hint of care in his voice, his words basic fact and nothing more.

Jarok again cursed. Loudly. Looked between Marco and Piris for a few beats, before straightening his stance and giving a command. "You'll take my horse. I'll ride in the carriage with Piris and Gem."

The other Fae didn't argue. As he walked forward, Cylian gestured toward his and Jarok's lead horses as he slung an arm across the man's shoulders, which tensed at the contact as if disliking the touch. Or maybe unfamiliar with touches of friendship or affection. It tempered Piris's assessment of the man; anyone not used to care would be a dangerous person, but also a lonely person.

The coachman, reassured by Jarok after he noticed the man's nervous energy, went back to his perch as the two other Fae men mounted the horses a few feet ahead. Gem swept into the interior, Piris followed, and Jarok took up the rear, then snapped the latch of the door closed a little too aggressively as he muttered under his breath about thoughtless assassins.

Piris started at the title. They'd never mentioned his job title, what he might be in the Springlands Court, to her. Thinking about the man, his demeanor and overall impression, she had no problem imagining him as a killer for his king. He practically exuded assassin energy.

"I see why you dislike him," Piris mumbled to Jarok as he moved to the bench across from her to sit beside his cousin.

"Exactly," he bit out, shaking his head as if trying to get the man from his thoughts. "He could've... What he did was stupid and irresponsible."

"Smart, actually," Gem admitted, "even if it bruised my backside."

"Smart? You've got to be kidding, Gem. It was impulsive and uncontrolled."

"You can call that man many things, but stupid and uncontrolled are not two of them, Jarok. It'd be in your best interest to remember that."

"You're being ridiculous," Jarok bit back. "He had no reasoning behind his actions."

"Sure, he did," Gem said, snuggling into the corner with her ubiquitous Aurora sky blanket and closing her eyes as if she weren't having an argument with an angry Jarok. "He tested our security. If he's to be our ally, an ally in service of his royal patrons in his own court, he needs to know how we'd react to an attack. He seems to know Cylian fairly well. I know you don't know him well because you avoid him whenever possible. I've never met the man, and neither has Piris. He needed to know our reaction times and fighting styles in order to evaluate."

It made perfect sense to Piris when she heard it put that way, and from the grinding of Jarok's teeth and the clenching of his jaw as he looked away from his cousin, he thought the same. Gem huffed a mirthless laugh and flipped the blanket over her head, something she'd not done up to that point in the trip. As if giving Piris and Jarok some privacy for whatever reason.

Jarok closed his dark eyes, heaved in a deep breath, and thunked his head back against the wall of the carriage. Piris left him to his thoughts, but she heard his voice, so soft it was like another breath, ask, "Are you okay?"

Piris looked around, making sure he was speaking to her, before she replied. "Yes. He startled me, but Gem took the brunt of his attack. Well, except for a misplaced kick I tried to land, which meant he trapped my leg for a time."

"Trapped how?"

Piris shrugged. "He held my ankle, not in a way that harmed but firmly, so I couldn't get loose. Not until your wind whipped through the space."

More teeth grinding came from Jarok, and Piris couldn't help herself. "You keep that up, you won't have any teeth left."

Jarok relaxed his face and jaw and muttered an apology.

"No need to apologize. You did nothing wrong."

The prince smiled. "Something my mother says. Often. She hates people apologizing for no reason."

"Good on her," Piris said with a little sniff. "People do it far too much. It's annoying."

Jarok barked out a deep laugh, which startled Piris, not only because she'd rarely heard him make the sound but because it made a sharp zing trail down her back, a bolt of something heated but comforting she'd not felt before.

They dropped the conversation and sat in a peaceful silence for long miles, winding their way down the wintery road ahead.

Chapter Six
Jarok

Despite knowing full well the carriage temperature was enchanted to be comfortable for all travelers, Jarok leaped from the thing like it burned him, his skin hot and itchy after being confined in the space. He stretched, bending his back and neck for long seconds to hide the other sources of his discomfort—the Fae lady who descended from the carriage behind him, all tall fighter's grace and luscious form.

They'd finally reached the first inn on their journey, which meant a hot, full dinner, maybe a glass of ale, and a warm-ish and somewhat cushioned bed for him. Jarok smiled at the idea, despite the security nightmare such a space presented. He was no stranger to rough rides, cold nights, or hard bedrolls, but he much preferred the creature comforts of Fae over their previous arrangements. A Fae'd be a fool not to in this cold corner of the world.

"I'm glad for a warm, rowdy room," he heard Gem call as she stepped up from behind him.

"Reminding you of home?" Jarok asked with a smile. The Aurora Outpost, Gem's usual residence, was lively most nights. The warriors there appreciated warmth and merriment in all its forms.

"Not quite, but it'll do," she said, knocking his shoulder with hers as she passed him to enter the inn first.

He turned to see Piris chatting with the coachman about something and noticed her own secret stretches, her height rising and falling in slow, controlled bursts as she stretched up on her toes, then lowered herself back down on her heels. He smiled to himself before his eyes scanned the rest of the scene. A scowl marred his face at seeing Darin patting his horse down.

Jarok managed to hold back his stomp as he moved in that direction. "I'll take him," he said, reaching a hand out to grab his horse's reins from the assassin.

Darin didn't acknowledge the prince's arrival until he tightened his grip on the reins and held them in place. Jarok wasn't about to have a tugging match with the man over the horse, so he stared, the arrogant princely mask slipping into place. Darin's hard gaze evaluated him a beat before stepping back. "Apologies, Prince Jarok. Where I am from, royals do not tend their own animals, and anyone who rides has the responsibility for caring for their steed."

Cylian had walked up during their odd non-confrontation, nonchalant but to Jarok seeming to insert himself purposefully. He'd positioned himself so he could step in if need be, and Jarok pulled back once again, reminding himself they needed Darin. For his resources and his skills. His words, also, caused a little pang in the prince, who'd used his royalty against the man before he'd known full well that being a royal meant something different when it came to behavior in the Springlands.

"No need to apologize, Marco. I simply prefer to care for my own horse. He's been with me many years and is my responsibility. Well, as much my responsibility as I can claim. Here, grooms must do more than I can with their magics."

Darin stepped back several feet in the blink of an eye, so fast Jarok would guess his own magic was speed if he didn't know better. Darin was a Shadow Fae, which was one reason he was such a good spy and assassin. It was a weighty magic to have, one not as dangerous as a mimic's but fairly close. The affinity was often used by those in power for their own ends whenever a Fae with the ability to manipulate shadows was found. Unlike mimics, they weren't exactly demonized by the general population. They were feared more openly, which gave Shadow Fae a certain level of safety mimics didn't enjoy.

The prince didn't say more, leaving his thoughts as they were, and instead went to pet and soothe his horse before calling Nore over after he'd tended the carriage pair.

"Are we to have yet another row over where you will sleep tonight, Nore?" Jarok asked, half-frustrated with the man and half-amused by his continued insistence over what his mother would deem appropriate behavior around nobility.

"Aye, if you continue to demand I stay with you. The stable here houses many coachmen and grooms, with plenty of space for each. I'd feel more comfortable there, Your Highness."

Jarok shook his head at the man but waved him on, not arguing again. He'd given up on it, but he'd continue to ask, hoping one day Nore'd take him up on his offers.

"You talk to the man with great familiarity," Darin said from behind him.

Jarok glanced back, seeing the stiff lean of the assassin, and shrugged. "I've known him for most of his life. He cares for all the family horses."

The groom took his and Cylian's horses and led them into the stables and out of sight. To Cylian at his side, Jarok muttered, "I'll go talk with the stable master, make sure Nore has a warm meal and a bed. Corral Piris and Gem, then grab us a table inside, would you?" His friend dipped his head, both heading in opposite directions. Jarok felt the itch of Darin's gaze between his shoulder blades for several beats before he assumed he went off with Cylian to secure food at the inn.

The inn was a rowdy place, as Gem had observed earlier. Packed too. He moved between patrons, sometimes having to squeeze through the crowd, to get to his party. The Boraus didn't hide from their people, which meant every few feet, a cry of "Your Highness" or "Prince Jarok" went up to cheers and he would stop for a few words and handshakes and grins.

When he finally made his way to the table in the back of the open dining room, he found Piris and Gem bent together laughing over ale as Cylian casually observed all around them. Darin sat back, nearly lost in the corner, his hood up to cover most of his face. He moved to Cylian's side along the wall, across from the women, and sat on the end, plopping down a touch too hard and wincing at the harsh sound it made, which brought more eyes to him.

"Oh, you grace us with your presence, Your Highness?" Gem asked, teasing, and in his peripheral vision, Jarok noticed Darin actually tense for the first time ever. He ignored the assassin and reached over to his cousin to ruffle her tightly bound hair, loosening it in a way he knew would annoy her, just as she knew her words would annoy him.

"Jealous of my fame and renown, cousin?"

"Would be, if I didn't know I could drag you out to the yard and beat you in hand to hand any time I wanted."

Jarok snorted before answering. "Big words from a woman who hasn't sparred with me in ages."

Cylian, not missing a beat, said, "My money's on Aurora."

Piris let out a laugh, forceful and loud and slightly husky in tone. Jarok sat staring, mesmerized for a second as she raised her glass to Cylian in recognition of his joke.

"Enough with maligning my fighting prowess," Jarok said. "What do we have to eat?"

Before anyone in his party could answer, the innkeeper and several servants came over carrying huge platters of roasted chickens and vegetables, all piled high and trailing an intoxicating steam as if fresh from the oven. He thanked Jarok for stopping at his inn, fussed over him to Gem's endless amusement, and left them to eat. Everyone was hungry, so they dug in and made occasional rumblings about how good everything tasted.

After decimating a whole chicken and what felt like pounds of carrots and potatoes, Jarok sat back and patted his stomach, content and sleepy after so much food. "Excellent choice on my part," he said, referencing the inn.

"Good food, good drinks, and lively people," Gem said in agreement, finished her meal, and scanned the crowd behind her. A small band had started playing in the opposite corner and a makeshift dance floor had formed. Gem's body swayed to the beat of the single drum, wanting to move.

"Come. Let's dance," she finally said, leaning into Piris.

"I don't know—" Jarok began to protest, but he couldn't finish before Piris gave Gem the widest, brightest grin he'd seen from her. He wasn't about to wipe such a look from her face. In the name of keeping the peace, he told himself.

Without a word, both women tore off to the dance floor, forming a private little clutch and moving to the beat. It wasn't the dancing of formal balls and such, the type of dancing Jarok suspected Piris was more used to doing, having learned from a young age as a Lady of the Winterlands. This dancing was freeform, relying on beat and intuition rather than prescribed sets. He watched, fascinated, as the lady's posture eased. Her stiffness turned into something fluid and joyful, until during a particular refrain she threw her hands up above her head with abandon, her eyes closed at the feel of the beat driving her body.

"Lovely," Darin mumbled from his corner, and before Jarok knew why, he let out a growl.

Cylian chuckled beside him. "Why not go dance with them, Jarok?"

"No," he said, shaking his focus from Piris. "We need to secure rooms if you haven't already."

"I thought you had?" Cylian said, an eyebrow raised.

"The innkeeper had disappeared when I entered, likely prepping the mountain of food he brought us not long after, so I didn't have a chance."

"Shall I?"

"Let's both," he said, moving to rise. Before he did, and against a large part of his judgment, he called to Darin, "Watch them, would you. Please?"

The assassin's head tilted up so Jarok could see his face for the first time inside the inn. His green eyes, hard as jade, blinked at him before he nodded and turned his full focus on Piris and his cousin still dancing together. For his part, Jarok made himself move forward, not turn his head, and not move himself toward the duo as they enjoyed themselves on the dance floor.

Continuing to internally curse himself and his misstep, he stalked from the quaking innkeeper. He hated the man was afraid. It wasn't his fault. Jarok should have secured their rooms prior, or thought about what the gathering clouds on their afternoon travels might mean for the occupancy of the inn. Snow was coming—not an unusual thing in the Winterlands, but it meant any traveler along this road who paid attention to the signs had stopped for a room when given the opportunity.

The innkeeper had offered his family space behind the kitchen, but Jarok wasn't about to displace him, his wife, and his children because he'd been foolish. No. They'd simply have to deal with the consequences of his actions.

His mood didn't improve when he noticed the two Fae men now grouped with Gem and Piris on the dance floor. The women seemed fine with it, not uncomfortable or unhappy with the two men leering at them as they danced. When one loomed too close to Piris, going so far as to land a hand on her hip and pull her in close to whisper in her ear, Jarok changed direction and stalked across the makeshift dance floor.

"Come, we have things to discuss," he bit out. He stood there, staring down at the offending hand on her hip, seething in rage he couldn't name as his breath came out in harsh pants.

His cousin laughed hard to his right. "We're enjoying—"

"Now, Gem!" he yelled, finally looking up into the frozen and confused face of Lady Piris.

Gem, smartly, didn't push him as she might on a different occasion. He noticed her lean over and say something to the Fae man she was with before giving him an up-and-down look as she passed him.

Jarok flicked his head to the side at Piris, not saying anything and not moving until she swallowed hard and moved past him, brushing against his front because he refused to make room. The Fae who'd dare touch her watched her walk away, eyes again on her hips, and Jarok stepped up with his fists and jaws clenched, not even thinking about what he'd do, reacting in some primal way. He felt an unfamiliar hand on his shoulder and saw a gray leather fingerless glove—Darin's glove—gripping him tight. Stopping his steps. Looking over his shoulder, he saw the assassin give him a grim, closed-mouth shake of his head.

He turned back toward the Fae man stepping away, hands up in supplication, saying, "Apologies, Your Highness," fear plain on his face. It was the fear that brought him back to himself. The man didn't deserve his surprising rage for dancing with a pretty woman. He had no way of knowing what he did would cause Prince Jarok's temper to burn white hot. Hell, Jarok hadn't even known until he saw the man's hand.

Hanging his head low, Jarok felt shame at what he'd nearly done. The hand at his shoulder, from a man he might have before called a foe, squeezed him for a beat. In a low but clear voice, Darin said, "Come, Prince. As you said, we have things to discuss."

"Thank you," he muttered to the man behind him, glad he had time to mask the churning confusion of anger and shame in his chest before he reached their table.

Cylian stood whispering with Gem, who had a too-familiar mischievous grin on her face caused by whatever the Fae lord was saying to her in the moment. Jarok knew whatever she was turning over in her mind wouldn't be good for him.

Piris sat against the wall, her face flushed from dancing and her eyes bouncing around the room, landing everywhere but on Jarok.

When he made his way to the table, he leaned down to whisper harshly at Piris, "Did you know the man you danced with?" Honestly, he didn't know which answer would be worse: no, she danced close to a stranger or yes, she danced with someone she knew before him.

She shook her head no and he watched, hesitant for a moment before she gathered herself. Piris pulled on her own mask, tucked it tight as she sent him a hard smirk and stare, the perfect dismissive combination he'd come to expect from her when they fought. "Why does it matter?" she asked, ending with a scoff his way before turning from him.

Jarok's hand whipped out before he could stop it, grabbing her face, gentle yet firm, tilting her chin slowly back in his direction. "Not a smart move, lady."

"So *you* say, Prince. It was only a dance."

"With a man you do not know," he bit out, grit and anger hardening his words like stone. "He could have done anything."

"Like what, step on my toes?" she shot back, meeting his look, her bronze eyes blazing. Still, she made no attempt to move her chin from his grip.

A polite cough behind him brought Jarok back to focus, to the conversation they needed to have about arrangements for the evening.

He straightened, looking in turn toward the three in his party who hadn't been with him when he had reserved their rooms with the innkeeper. "The inn is full. We have only two rooms for the night."

"Not a problem. Gem and I can take one while you, Cylian, and Darin take the other," Piris said.

Simple enough, and what Jarok figured, until Gem said, "Sorry, lovely lady. I have other plans for the night," and quickly turned on her heels to make her way back to the Fae man she'd been dancing with earlier.

Jarok intercepted his cousin in four quick giant strides, grabbing her by the bicep when she was halfway to her target. "You can't, Gem."

"Oh, really? And are you going to stop me?"

Exasperated by both women at this point, he said, "Look, cousin. You can sleep with whoever you want. I have no issues. But on another day. Someone must stay with Piris."

"Why? She's a warrior, capable of handling herself."

"First of all, she's supposed to look like a lady, not a warrior, and you are supposed to act as her chaperone. Though you've done a poor job of it today."

At that, Gem whirled around, ripping her arm from her cousin, and snarled. Unless she was in battle or sparring, Gem rarely looked so serious. "Watch yourself, cousin. I take my duty seriously. I also have come to know the lady in question. She's more than capable, whether you think so or not."

Jarok pushed a hand through his floppy black hair, his voice strained but still low in the crowded space, not wanting anyone else to hear. "Gem, please. For me."

Gem's face softened and she leaned in close, giving him an affectionate squeeze on his hand before dropping it. "After what I just saw, I *am* doing this for you, you fool."

With that cryptic line, he watched her walk away from him. He could follow, demand she come back, do her duty, but he knew it would mean a real fight. He didn't want to fight his cousin. He also didn't wish to deal with the fallout of her leaving. Because someone would have to stay in the room with Piris, and of the options left, he knew, without doubt, the only acceptable solution was him.

Chapter Seven
Piris

It was odd. Moments ago she'd been dancing with Gem, giddy excitement a sweet taste on her tongue. Now she was sitting, fuming, at their table, watching Jarok and his cousin argue. Just like he'd argued with her. The man was insufferable, even if every time he touched her she felt it coursing through her blood like a fever.

She'd not danced at an inn before. Hadn't danced outside the strict confines of ballrooms or dance lessons, and even then, rarely, because most who would partner with her after she had come of age dismissed her out of hand because of her supposed lack of magic. Fine by her. She could barely stand the lot of them, save Strella. Especially Prince Jarok... until this trip. Now she could admit to herself her attraction to him, despite his frustrating traits and her tendency to dismiss men as little more than partners who could scratch the occasional itch.

Said itch intensified as she watched the hard lines of Jarok's body, jerky with anger and his attempts to control it after whatever Gem had said to him before she left. He stalked back to the table, his dark eyes black and boring into her so she felt them like a touch—a touch making her shiver all the way to her core. Anything between them would be a bad, bad idea, but the longer she was around him, the more convincing she needed to believe it.

Piris turned away from his stare before he arrived at the table, pulling her earlier anger at his interruption over her like a shield. He was beautiful and mesmerizing to look at and interact with, but so damn frustrating, especially when he acted as if she couldn't take care of herself. So much of her life was training, or being constantly mindful of where she was, what was around her, how she presented herself. For him to dismiss her abilities hurt more than she'd admit. Why should this prince have the power to hurt her feelings?

"Gem is... occupied for the evening," Jarok said to no one in particular.

Piris shrugged. "Fine, I can stay alone."

"Out of the question."

She sucked her top lip between her teeth, attempting to calm herself a moment, and Cylian stepped into the fray. "Jarok is right, Piris. There are too many questions, too much at stake, for anyone to be alone."

Jarok's tense muscles stood in stark relief, and she felt herself staring at their cut against his leathers before she dragged her eyes away. "Piris, please. I... It's not about you being unable or unprepared. I made a promise to protect you. And as Cylian says, we all need to watch one another. No one of us should be alone while on our journey."

Piris huffed, clinging to her anger out of stubbornness at that point, because what they said made sense. It stung her pride, but it was true. She'd made a promise herself, to Strella, to ensure Jarok stayed safe. If he claimed he'd go off alone for the evening, she'd protest too. Not because he wasn't a great warrior. He'd gotten the jump on her the other night when she'd felt the bite of his blade. She'd also felt the power of his body, on top of and under her, months before, when they'd first met. The memory of that encounter caused her to flush, but she shoved the thoughts away as soon as she had them, trying desperately to focus on the matter at hand.

"What of Gem?" She was pressing both out of worry and to be contrary.

Jarok snorted. "Gem won't stay gone. She definitely also won't be alone."

"She'll be alone and in a likely vulnerable position for a while. Or, at least I hope for a while, for her sake."

Cylian snorted at the innuendo but covered it with a fake cough, because they were having a serious conversation after all.

Jarok rubbed his forehead, hanging his head. "I can't reason with her. If you want to go try, by all means, help yourself. She is set on this course. She'll return before the night is over, I'm sure of it. Gem also knows better than to be alone for long here."

Piris wanted to argue more. The fact they'd traveled for days and the closest they'd come to an attack was from their own ally jumping in their carriage was high on her list of points to make. She dropped it, as she dropped her anger. All for the sake of the group and the promise she'd made. Her voice was a sigh of resignation when she said, "Very well. What are your ideas for the arrangements?"

Cylian chimed in, saying, "Darin and I will stay in the smaller room. You and Jarok will take the larger room. Gem will likely show up there later, so you need the extra space."

Piris stared open mouthed at the suggestion. It made the most sense, of course. She didn't know Darin at all, and his coldness put her off. Jarok and Darin had some form of truce going now, she'd noticed, but it was fragile enough they shouldn't room together. Just in case. Which of course left her and Jarok together.

Jarok looked like he wanted to argue, opening his mouth to speak, then snapping it shut before he could get anything out. Piris rose to end the ridiculous conversation. "Fine. Me and Jarok will stay together. Just someone, please, show me where the rooms are so we can be done here."

Jarok stood straight, tall, his golden skin tight and showing the barest hint of a flush as he swept an arm out, inviting her to move from the table as Cylian took the lead, making his way to a back set of stairs tucked on the other side of the inn, as far from the open dining room as they could be to give the overnight guests some semblance of quiet and privacy. Piris wished she could have that too, but she suspected such a thing wouldn't come tonight, not with Jarok in her room. Something hot and dark slithered through her chest, a different desire she wanted to keep locked away tight, but that also might not happen with Jarok sharing her room.

For a supposedly large room, the space was small. So small, in fact, there was only one bed. Piris blinked at the single mattress atop a basic wooden frame, no headboard or footboard, a simple blue wool cover draped over it and two pillows nestled at the top. Nothing extravagant, but serviceable. For one person, as it was one bed. In their current situation, not helpful.

"Stay here," Jarok called behind her, closing the door with a snap before she could reply. She stayed, mainly because her mind was whirling too fast for her to do much else. Jarok's incoherent yell from the distance drew her out of the odd stupor she'd found herself in. She shook it off, muttering to herself about her father being disappointed in her. She needed to be on her toes, even if there'd been no attacks up to this point. There was no need to let trouble have an easier time of it when it found her and her party because she'd been shocked there was only one bed in the room. With her luck, she should have seen it coming. A niggling in the back of her mind tried to whisper it was actually a good thing, but she ignored the urging.

Jarok's voice was harsh, raised, but unintelligible through the hallway and two doors separating them, so she chose to ignore it and do something more productive. Piris moved to the bed, checked to see if there was a second mattress to be lain on the floor. None was there. She studied the thickness of the cover, which was barely enough to keep someone warm on the bed, much less as a pallet or cover on the floor. Bending down on her hands and knees, she checked under the bed, thinking she really should have checked before even approaching the bed. Whatever had gotten into her today was making her incredibly sloppy, and she didn't like it.

She didn't hear any more shouts from the room across the hall, so it appeared Jarok had calmed some, for now. There was a small chest of drawers along the wall opposite the bed, not far from the small dent from the door handle marring the walls, which had once been white but were slightly cream with age and continual use. Not dirty, simply old. Much like the drawers, which squeaked as she opened each, the smell of cedar drifting up and soon overpowering the space. Nothing was there to help the situation, so she snapped each drawer closed.

A water basin stood in the corner by the bed, but it was the only other thing in the room—no closet, no trunks, nothing where another mattress or blanket would hide. No solution to the one-bed problem, but the longer she sat alone, the more it seemed not like a problem at all.

She rose from sitting when Jarok banged back in the room, pacing even before the door completely shut behind him. If she didn't know better, she'd say he looked nervous about something. It was not the usual vigilant nervousness or worry he wore like a cape around him most days when he thought no one was looking. She was more than familiar with that part of Jarok, the part she'd witnessed bear down on her since their meeting. This was a different nervous energy, something making light sweat gleam on his golden brow and the corners of his dark eyes pinch tighter than normal.

"The other room is even smaller, if you can imagine, with only a twin bed and barely enough room for a man to stretch across the floor."

When he didn't say more, she answered with an "okay," thinking maybe he wanted her to fill the silence. He stopped pacing in front of the dresser and leaned against it so it took his weight as he crossed his tightly toned arms across his leather-clad chest. She took him in, letting herself really wonder, for the first time, what his body might feel like in a position other than fighting. Usually, if she felt her thoughts wandering in such a direction, she shut them down quickly. As she spent more time with him, she found him both more and less infuriating, and she couldn't stop herself from thinking on what they might feel together.

Her head jerked when a quick series of knocks sounded at the door, and Cylian's voice, half-muffled, called out before he entered the room. He carried two bedrolls with him, his and Jarok's. She'd seen them enough in the past few days to recognize each.

"Here," Cylian said, handing off his package, then turning to look at her before staring back at his friend. "We'll be across the hall if you need anything."

Jarok stared down at his bedroll, a heavy sigh on his lips. "I was so looking forward to..." His voice drifted and he never finished, moving to kneel on the floor and roll out his makeshift bed.

"Looking forward to what?" Piris couldn't help the question. It slipped out, as if compelled by some magic.

He turned his head, and from his position, it looked for a moment as if he were kneeling at Piris's feet, a supplicant of some sort. The image made her heart beat faster and her mouth water, but she locked the outward signs down as best she could, waiting for his answer.

He rose, facing her, only inches away, and said, "No need for you to worry, Piris. I just—Gods, I feel like the pampered prince you and others think me to be for even admitting it, but I just really wanted to sleep in a bed, not spend another night on my bedroll." His smile twisted as he laughed and shamed himself at the same time.

"Nothing to be ashamed of, Jarok. In fact, you take the bed. I'll spend the night on the bedroll. I don't mind. I did it often enough as a teenager."

He squinted at her as he shook his head. "Not happening, Piris. You're in the bed. I'm on the floor."

She threw her hands up. "I'm not some delicate flower, unlike the cover we're using. Though, given our current position, seems the cover might well be blown anyway. I can sleep a night on the floor."

"No," he said, his firm words echoed in his cross-armed, feet-planted stance in her face.

"Fine. Fine. Then we share the bed."

He blanched, clearly taken aback by her suggestion, and Piris felt a clench in her gut at his perceived rejection. "No," he said again, this time less firm.

"Why not? The bed's big enough. Are you too good to share a bed with me?"

"No, not too good. Never too good. Too much."

"What does that even mean?" she yelled, her arms flinging out at the absurdity of this fight when they'd had so many others in the past. There they were, once enemies with a current truce of sorts, maybe even an understanding, arguing not to hurt but to make sure the other would be comfortable.

"I desire you too much to leave you alone if we slept close," he growled before closing the half step of distance between them and grabbing her face in his hands. He squeezed slightly, bringing her closer and closer, until their lips met, and the world exploded in sensation.

Gods, he tasted good, like the clove smell he exuded mixed with fine man and the tang of the wind. His tongue burrowed into her mouth, seeking shelter, and she gave it entrance, sucking it deep and wrestling for dominance. Even in this, their first kiss, they seemed to be in a type of battle. She yielded easily, letting him bend her body back as he deepened their kiss, taking all he needed and giving her back so much in turn.

Suddenly, he was gone, back a few paces before she even realized the kiss had ended. "I should never have done that." He spoke as if chastising himself, not admitting something to her.

She panted, catching her breath, but no way would she let that fly. "Am I not good enough for kissing?"

He cut his molten brown eyes at her, his voice low and guttural as he said, "I'd do much more than kiss you, Piris, if there weren't other issues at play."

She jutted her chin out, goading him with a sneer, the best way she knew to make him break his cool. "Prove it, *Your Highness*."

Jarok stalked forward, crowding her until she gave up one, two, three steps, her knees hitting the back of the bed with a soft thud. "Don't test me, Piris. Not in this. Not unless you're prepared to take every bit of what I'd give you."

"Empty threats unless you back them up."

She watched, fascinated, as he searched her face for something. Her hardness cracked some then, her outward ice melting, so she could give him a piece of herself, the honest truth that she wanted him as well, even for a split second.

"Positive?" he said, reaching between them to grab both her wrists in one hand.

He gave a sure squeeze, enough to hint at what he might wish to do, and Piris turned to goo inside, wanting to scream yes at the top of her lungs. The lust riding her hard meant all she could do was nod.

"I need the words, lady," he said, taking his other hand to sweep a finger down her face, from ear to chin, gripping her there once again so she was forced to look deep into his earthy eyes.

She licked her lips in anticipation. "Do your worst, Jarok."

He wasted no time, pushing her down so she sat on the bed, then shoving her restrained hands into her own chest, forcing her back until she lay across the fairly comfortable blue sea of the bed. He climbed on top, straddling her thighs as he'd done the first night they met, and a different driving need coursed deep in her core at the sight of him hovering above her, at the firm grip of his hands, at the illusion she was not in control in the moment. By the gods, her mind reeled at the idea she might be able to give up control of something, anything, for once in her life.

Jarok said nothing as he leaned down, devastating the square neckline of her traveling dress with kisses. She had a moment to think about how she'd only managed one change and a few quick rag baths in the days she'd been on the road, but the idea fled when he used his free hand to plump her breast as he continued his kisses. The prince obviously didn't mind.

His mouth moved up, not the direction she wished it to truly go but still nice as he nibbled, giving quick nips at her neck, causing her body to buck under him. A dark chuckle escaped his lips, puffing against her ear as he leaned up and said, "Hands above your head."

He'd let go of her wrists and she hadn't even noticed, but she did as she was told, without question. This time, she turned her head to the side as his tongue oh so slowly edged the outside shell of her ear.

"The number of times I wanted to shut your mouth with mine," he muttered before he turned her face to him and ravished her lips again, plunging deep so all she could taste, feel, sense was this luscious man on top of her.

Piris felt his knees pop hers open and ease in between, and she met his hips when they sank down into hers. He was hard, and very large, digging into her through his own leathers and her traveling dress. She moaned into his mouth at the contact, which made his lower body jerk as he leaned harder into the kiss. Jarok pushed her further into the mattress as he swallowed the sounds she made against him.

Gods, the friction felt delicious and maddening, enough to give her a thrill but not nearly enough to get her where she needed to go. Not like this. She wanted Jarok skin on skin. She wanted to feel his hard cock inside her, invading her like his tongue, taking what he needed and giving her pleasure in return. She'd ripped her head away to the side, partially to breathe and partially to demand he do what she wished, when they heard it. Heavy, loud boots on stairs. Yells from below. The echo of a word yelled in the distance.

"Fire."

Jarok growled out a string of curses seconds before the door to the room burst open and Gem entered. She didn't even blink at her cousin splayed on top of Piris but repeated what they'd both apparently vaguely heard.

"Fire!" she yelled, her arms waving them on, urging them to get up and out of there.

Jarok rolled off Piris and took a second to adjust himself in his leathers. She sat up quickly, unconcerned about her appearance, and she was facing Gem the moment she saw an arrow sail from the smoky hallway and embed itself right into her back.

Chapter Eight
Jarok

Jarok vaguely wondered how one second he could be blissfully grinding on top of Piris, aching to be inside her, and the next second find his cousin bloodied on the ground at his feet. Lust pounded in him still even as rage welled up to meet it, and he had no idea how the two could stay contained in his body.

He dropped to his knees, pulling Gem forward to shield her with the bed as best he could. She hissed at the movement, the arrow with the distinct Monti fletching embedded in her back, though luckily, not very deep. Sadly for her, it wasn't a clean through and through, so someone would have to dig out the tip.

"Go, you fool," Gem said, her eyes half-closed as she sucked in short, hard breaths.

"I can't—"

"You can and you will," she clipped out. He spared a moment for Piris, watching her square up in a defensive posture at the foot of the bed, her wickedly sharp dagger at the ready, her body crouched low to present less of a target. She positioned herself as defender of his cousin, and a different sort of warmth pulsed in his blood at the sight.

"You and her, you need to go. Now."

"But—" Jarok said.

"It's a scratch. Practically nothing," she gritted out. "They're here for you, Jarok. I heard one of them yell something about taking the prince. Don't let them get what they want."

Jarok nodded, knowing full well she was right. The only reason the Benders would risk an open attack would be to kill or kidnap, and the only useful victim in such a scenario was him, as Engad Monti seemed forever focused on gaining the power of the Borau royals. However, only a short ride from Volesion Peak, and the resources Lord Brettly Volesion could muster, Piris might also be a solid bargaining tool for any Bender smart enough to see her potential. Both needed to flee and regroup at a safer location.

He couldn't just leave Gem there, alone and unattended, however. "Cylian!" A beat later, the red-haired Fae parted the growing smoke of the hallway to enter their room.

The lord immediately started to give a report of the situation. "They're downstairs, at least the ones left. I've tried to contain the flames as best I can. Darin dispatched the Benders above—"

He stopped when he saw Gem bloodied on the floor. A curt nod was all he needed to replace Jarok beside her. "Go," he said, echoing Gem's assessment.

Piris, squinting toward the hallway beyond, said, "We can't go that way. The window." She'd understood the situation so fast—had seen and executed a plan in her mind. He would have stopped in appreciation at the way she thought if there was any time to do so.

Jarok moved toward her after lashing his sword back on his hip, grabbing her waist as he did, causing her to tense before he said to her side, "Good call."

She turned without a word when Jarok grabbed her hand and led them to the old, framed casing. At least they were only one floor up. Not a bad jump for any Fae, much less two trained fighters. He took the time to survey the ground, for anyone waiting below or any obvious hazards. He couldn't see deep into the shadows, or tell if anyone lingered close by, so it wasn't a complete sweep of the area, which made him more than a little nervous.

"Okay. Seems clear, but anyone could be waiting below, so we jump and immediately run toward the stables, yes?"

Piris nodded, looking out the window herself and apparently coming to the same conclusion.

"Follow after as soon as I clear the landing," Jarok said as he climbed onto the windowsill. He had no time to hesitate or think too hard. The other way was fire and enemies with ready bows. This way likely also held Benders, but it at least gave them better odds and an open space in which to fight. He hesitated a split second before leaping down, bending his knees and loosening his muscles so they'd take the impact with as little damage as possible. The hit was hard, rattling him up to his teeth, but he sustained no injuries.

After he sidestepped, Piris followed. Her own thud to the ground sounded painful, but there was no sign of it on her body except a slight tightening around her eyes and a tick in her jaw.

With no time to spare, he grabbed her hand and they ran together, slowing only when they came to a blind corner at a line of three outhouses situated between the inn and the stables. It was a perfect place for an ambush, so he wasn't surprised when a group of four Benders stepped in their path.

"Your presence is requested, Prince," one said, a sneer on his face and a promise of violence in his words.

He didn't get a chance to reply before Piris lashed out at the Fae with a swift, high kick to his chin, causing him to reel back, his hands windmilling to try to keep him upright before he landed hard on his ass in the middle of his group.

The Benders were fierce fighters, highly trained and with a clear purpose, so they lost no time attacking. At least one was momentarily down when the other three advanced, two coming at Jarok while one made to grab Piris. With his own fighters to contend with, he didn't have the ability to help her. He ached to, his attention divided in a way that wasn't good for either of them, but in a flash, he understood, as he had somewhere in his mind before, he really didn't need to protect her. Piris held her own against the hardened warrior trying to contain her. She'd landed at least three harsh blows with her fists, weighted by her clenched dagger, in as many seconds. The last landed hard in the man's gut, causing him to double over and let out his breath in a rough whoosh of air.

Jarok had no more time to consider her as the two men bore down on him with daggers of their own. He flicked his falchion out of his scabbard and gripped it tight with both hands as he brought it up to block, then repel their blows. The leverage the larger weapon gave him pushed the men back, but they weren't amateurs. Without a word, one went back in for a high hit while the other crouched, moving in to take out Jarok's legs. He called his wind to him, using it to topple the crouched man with a short, focused gust as he met the other's dagger once again, pushing him farther back and hopping over the man sprawled at his feet.

He switched positions, trying to keep both in his sights, which meant he lost his peripheral view of Piris. It burned through him, turning his back on her, but he did it to help them both. He could still hear the unmistakable sounds of a fight in progress: grunts, curses, and the smack of hard fists or feet on cloth and flesh. As long as he heard those noises, Piris was still fighting, which meant he could concentrate where he needed to at the moment.

Both his opponents were up, trying to circle him. The one he'd pushed to the ground with his magic came at him from behind. They pounced at once, managing to take the prince down to the ground despite the swipe of his sword at one of their stomachs. Blood oozed, but the man didn't let up his attack. Both Benders worked their way on top of him, the one with the stomach wound wresting the sword from his grip as he pushed all his weight on Jarok's arm with bony knees, while the other pinned his other arm, moving to plant his dagger in the prince's gut. His wind howled in defense, but they were prepared for his magic and huddled low against it.

The blade swung down, but before it could connect, a blur in a traveling dress knocked the Bender down from the side and rolled with him on the dirt and snow and ice. Jarok didn't hesitate to reach across and use his left hand to punch the other Bender in his wounded stomach, causing a wheeze of breath from the man and making his knees ease up on his prone arm. A second blow brought the man down, and Jarok flipped their positions, took the man to the ground, and moved to straddle him. His falchion wasn't in reach, but he managed to block the upward swing of the dagger, pushed his weight down on the arm, twisted the Bender's hand, and slowly but surely forced the blade down, down, down until with a final push he embedded the thing in the man's chest, right into his heart.

Jarok didn't look back down at the man he'd just killed, and instead pushed himself up to help Piris. She'd grabbed his sword at some point and was volleying back and forth with the Bender who'd been on him moments before. The one she'd originally fought was on the ground several feet away and looked to still be bleeding. The one she'd felled first had fully recovered and was coming at her from behind. Jarok flew toward the man, the impact aided by an icy wind at his back, and he took the man down, shoving the dagger he still clutched through the back of the Fae's neck, killing him in an instant.

Piris spared a glance his way but was only distracted a moment, not enough time for the Fae she was fighting to take true advantage, though he seemed to think it was. He jumped toward her, trying to knock her over with his muscle and height, but she swung back the falchion and stabbed forward in a flash, burying the wicked sharp, curved blade all the way through the Fae's chest.

The two of them froze like that, blood dripping down her hand. The look in her eyes told Jarok it was the first time she'd killed. He didn't have time to comfort her in the moment. They needed to be gone before more Benders streamed from the inn and tried once again to stop them. He rushed to her and she started, eyes wide and wild, when he laid a gentle hand at the small of her back.

"Piris. Come." He took the sword from her and shoved it into his hip-belt, not bothering to wipe the blood from it. He'd have to clean it later. He grabbed her now-free, bloody hand and moved her with him, toward the stable and the horses he knew Nore had bedded down there.

Nore, the blessed man, already had his and Cylian's horses saddled and ready when Jarok pulled Piris into the stable. "They're prepped, Your Highness!" he shouted, moving to fling open the large double doors at the end of the row so the two could flee.

"Piris. Piris!" Jarok yelled in her face, trying to snap her out of the fog she'd been in since killing the Fae. He gripped her shoulders and shook her slightly, which seemed to do the trick. Her head straightened and her eyes narrowed on him, focusing once again. Good enough for Jarok.

"Get on Cylian's horse. We need to ride. Now!"

She didn't hesitate then, and he didn't either, both mounting and moving toward the doors at top speed in a blink. Jarok shouted, "Run, Nore," not wanting the groom to be punished for helping them when the Benders in the inn, or the ones they'd left breathing by the out-houses, saw they'd escaped on horseback.

They pounded down the snow-filled lane, kicking up bits of snow and ice as they fled, only slowing momentarily as they rounded the corner to pass the inn and get back to the main Winterlands road.

As they passed the inn, fire lighting the sky with a menacing or-ange-yellow glow, an arrow whizzed past Jarok's ear.

"Down," Piris called beside him, flinging her body to hug tight to Cylian's horse, making herself as small a target as possible. Jarok mimicked her until the shouts of the Benders faded in the distance.

Their horses were swift, prepped well, and ready to run. Jarok hoped it'd give them a solid lead. They were headed back in the direc-tion they'd arrived, away from where they needed to be, so a different plan formed in his mind. When he finally saw the opportunity he needed, he yelled over to Piris, "Follow me." She veered off the road behind him and they trampled into a break in the tree line.

It was slower going, clomping through the dark woods on horse-back. Not only did the closed-in trees make maneuvering difficult, but the deep pockets of snow were hard to catch before stepping through them, making each hoof drop potentially treacherous. Jarok, to offset this, stirred the snow several feet ahead and covered up their sounds with a vortex, taking most of his concentration. He also used his wind to sweep over their trail, making it near impossible to track them, though not entirely impossible for the right Fae, like Gem with her tracking affinity. He hoped she was well, and well enough to find them by the morning. They had no supplies and no hope of surviving in a Winterlands forest for very long without help.

It was quiet between the two Fae, Jarok concentrating on the path ahead. Piris was lost in whatever thoughts crowded her head, and the prince tried not to think too hard on it. There was nothing for it at the moment. He could dive deeper, consider a way to help her, but only when they were safely away.

The forest itself wasn't quiet. Owls hooted in the trees, reminding Jarok of his mother, his home, and causing an ache to lodge in his gut for long minutes. Other creatures, small and furry, scurried in the shadows of the night, doing what woodland creatures did in the Winterlands—looking for shelter and food where they could find it. The wind, what Jarok commanded and the gusts moving on their own, whistled through the evergreen needles at odd intervals, keeping both Fae on edge. What Jarok didn't hear was the clomping of hooves behind them, which, after several miles of picking through the forest, made him ease a touch.

After hitting a rise in the trees, Jarok looked down on a small open hollow, evergreens ringed in a circle blanketed with pristine, pearlescent snow. He guided his horse down, cooing to him all the while, encouraging each step. When the slope ended and Jarok dismounted, he bent to the horse's ears, whispering more words as he patted the steed. He gripped the reins tight a beat, gave a quick clicking sound with his tongue, and released the horse to move on its own.

The horse listened, whinnying at Cylian's stallion once Piris dismounted and urging it along in front of him. Jarok coiled a rope on his arm, his hands deft and familiar with the fibers he'd snagged from his saddle.

"Where are they going?" Piris asked.

"Back to the inn, though not via the road. My horse can find Nore anywhere, so they will be fine. We don't need to have them out longer than necessary." The prince worried about trackers but also the health of the horses, who needed the groom's help to not get hardened hooves in all the ice and snow in the forest. He did not have the magic to help them, so best to send them on to Fae who could.

Piris didn't acknowledge the answer but moved to rub her hands up and down her arms, warming herself. They had no furs and no leather outerwear, nothing to keep them from the cold besides the basic traveling gear they'd been wearing when they'd jumped from the second floor of the inn. Jarok didn't say anything, as nothing could be done about their clothes, but he redirected the wind to act as a shield, keeping the windchill at bay for Piris.

"We should keep moving," he said, jerking his head toward deeper into the forest on the opposite side of the clearing.

"Are we on our own now?" Piris walked as she talked, refusing to look at Jarok as she did.

"The others will find us."

She glanced back at the lack of tracks they left, Jarok's magic making it easy to cover their steps.

"As long as Gem is well... No, Gem will be well. She will find us."

Piris didn't question him further, pulling her arms tight around herself as a shield against the cold and possibly the events of the evening. Jarok worried about her and what everything, the delicious and the horrendous, made her feel, but safety was the first concern. Soon, he'd consider them far enough into the depths of the forest to rest for the night. Then he'd talk to her... get her to talk to him.

"Come on," he called, staring at her with his feet planted as he encouraged her to move. "The woods are lovely but deep, and we have miles to go."

Chapter Nine
Piris

"This should do," Jarok said, breaking the silence they'd walked in for what felt like miles. He'd looked back at her on occasion, pointed out snow drifts or other hazards, but he hadn't spoken a word since he let the horses go. Not that Piris minded. A lot had happened, and having the time and space to run through it in her mind helped.

She'd killed a man. Sure, she'd fought before, but it had only been sparring. She'd not been in a real fight against an opponent bent on hurting her, unless she counted her first encounter with Jarok. She didn't. Even when they'd fought before knowing one another, there had been a difference, a way the prince moved against her. The threat of hurt had been there, but never the threat of death or other, more vile things.

The fact was she was a trained fighter, but never a tried fighter. She'd had no opportunity. Piris had been hidden away—at the understandable request of her parents, given her magic—spending any fighting time sparring with her father and his guards or training on her own. Her fight with Jarok had been her first real-world experience, but there was a mountain of difference between what had happened between her and Jarok and their encounter with the Benders earlier.

She didn't regret what she did, killing the Fae. Didn't mean she experienced some sick joy in taking another's life. In the moment, she'd known it was her or him, and her training had kicked in, seeing her through. Her father would be happy about that at least, when or if she told him.

Still, blood had soaked her hands until she'd stooped outside the clearing, picked up a fistful of snow, and rubbed her hands together to clean them. After wiping the remnants on her traveling dress, they were better. Colder, but not near as bloody. Except it lingered in spots, under and around her fingernails, and in other places snow couldn't quite reach.

Pushing herself to focus on the here and now instead of earlier in the evening, she looked up and noticed the intense frown on Jarok's face. She'd say he worried for her if she didn't know better. The prince would never worry over her, even if they'd shared a few lust-filled moments before a life-and-death fight. Too much picking and bickering existed between them for him to worry over her.

She arched a brow at him, hitching a hip as she did so in her best attempt at cool and collected.

Jarok took her in, head to toe, blinked at her blankly several beats, and gestured up with his hand. "We'll stay here for the night."

"Here" was a giant fir tree, its base branches spread out in dips and folds, stemming from a surprisingly narrow trunk given the number of heavy branches it supported. The thing was beautiful and massive, stretching out at least twenty feet around and towering high above them, reaching so far into the inky night sky she couldn't see the top.

"How, exactly, are we staying here?" Dubious, Piris stretched her neck around dramatically, looking this way and that in an exaggerated manner to make her point.

"Don't worry," Jarok said, his cocky smile set.

Her dismissive snort sounded even more harsh in the cold, quiet air of the wintery night, so she intentionally turned her tone warmer. "All I do is worry."

"Same, Piris. Same," he muttered back, a flash of something she didn't recognize in his eyes. "For now, however, follow me."

He jumped on top of a low-hanging branch, all nimble limbs and solid footing himself, much like the tree. When he reached back to help her up, Piris was already climbing without any aid. She followed his lead, as he'd asked, step for step and jump for jump, until they reached a rather large branch about thirty feet above the ground. The needles, crowded in thick, stung her face, and the smell of pine and sap seeped from every corner of the tree, lingering heavy in the air.

Jarok pulled himself up to the larger branch with a soft grunt, swinging his leg around it so he straddled the thing, and a flash of memory shot through her mind of how it'd felt to have him straddle her in the inn. With no time for such thoughts, she made to follow. He was firmly planted, so she had to take his hand, the familiar zing of contact with him something else she ignored so she could get a good grip on the trunk.

Piris moved to swing her leg over as well, to face the prince several feet down the limb, but he stopped her, taking her firmly in hand and planting her between his legs. She stiffened, asking, "Is this necessary?" with a touch of breathiness she wished would stay locked down tight.

A hand shot out from behind her, gripping a rope. "If we're spending the night in the tree, we need to secure ourselves. Just in case." He moved again, his head brushing her hair as his breath whispered across her ear. "So, yes. We need to be close."

A shiver rushed through her, but she managed to tamp it down before she embarrassed herself with how much his touch affected her.

She shrugged, all uncaring and indifference, as he chuckled to himself. She opted to ignore it.

What she couldn't ignore was the way he worked the rope around them. He wove it like an intricate tapestry, cinching her tightly to both him and the tree branch. Layering it so there was pressure and assurance but no signs of pinching. Piris wiggled, trying to gain room even if she didn't necessarily need it, and a gruff command came at her from behind. "No. Stop moving."

She stopped, though she was uncertain why. She also didn't argue. Maybe because the feel of Jarok's warmth at her back and the security of the tight rope around her thighs and torso caused her muscles to lose some of their usual tension, melt and relax. Piris leaned into it, leaned into Jarok, and decided as they were stuck in a tree for the night, she might as well find comfort where and how she could.

"Good girl," he whispered from behind her as he made one final knot in their bindings. Her mind wanted to snap at him for it, but something deeper inside made her pause, so instead she pretended she didn't hear him. Opting for feigned ignorance over acknowledgment or confrontation worked better then.

A few minutes passed, enough for Piris to drift closer to sleep, when Jarok spoke. "How are you?"

"The rope is fine," she said.

"No. I know the rope is fine," he said, so sure in his use of it. "How are you feeling? After everything."

His voice drifted off, asking her to fill the stretch of silence. She didn't at first, not wanting to expose herself to him. Yet he knew a bit of what she felt. Had to. Maybe it wasn't such a bad idea to give him this, a piece of shared experience neither could deny.

Her voice sounded clear to her ears, though a slight vibrato creeped in where she was usually so steady, enough of a tremor she noted it and was certain Jarok would too. She hoped he wouldn't comment, though, and would just let her get it out.

"I killed a man. He was going to kill me, or you, but instead I killed him. I'm not sorry I did it because the alternative... I am sad I was forced to do it."

"All warriors go through this at some point. The first person I killed was in a battle between two Winterlands clans. We'd been called to mediate, but the battle raged before we got there. I was twenty, so young and new, and within the first five minutes of being on the battlefield, a Fae man came barreling at me, blade high and eyes narrowed. Targeting me. My hand shot out on instinct, with the same sword you used today, and cut him clear across the belly. A hard death, and not pretty. Not that any death in battle is pretty."

"He was someone's son. Maybe a husband or father or brother," Piris said. She didn't clarify she meant the man she'd cut down, but Jarok understood.

"He also made a clear choice to follow a rebel and attack two fighters," he countered. All true, but it didn't ease the guilt over what consequences might stumble down to others because she'd killed the man.

"It was very different. Not the action itself. That was all instinct. The feelings after. They were very different than I imagined."

"They always are," Jarok whispered, and he moved to wrap his arms around her from behind, bringing some of his warmth around her at the same time. She allowed it, leaned into it even.

"Next time..." She stopped herself. Gods, she wished there were no next time, but with the Benders clearly following them, it could not be guaranteed. Plus, she wouldn't be completely honest with herself if she didn't admit the fighting thrilled her... caused adrenaline to course through her veins. During the fight, her world focused, narrowed, and despite the consequences, she'd never felt more alive. Never felt so useful, which was something rarely offered to Fae ladies in any realm.

"Next time I'll be ready," she said, though she was uncertain of that as well.

Jarok didn't correct or counter her assertion. He squeezed her middle and leaned his head down to hers, as if resting there, cheek to crown. Piris closed her eyes, not to fall asleep but to quiet her mind as best she could with the prince all around her.

Piris floated in warmth, the scent of pine and sap, wind and clove, surrounding her. She breathed deep and shifted her back against the cushion behind her, snuggling deeper into whatever was making her toasty and happy. Then a shout sounded, startling her awake and straight into mortification.

"You two finished up there?" Gem yelled from the ground.

Piris blinked, sleepiness and comfort fleeing in an instant. Jarok, the warmth at her back, chuckled in his annoyingly knowing and cocky way. "Sleep well, m'lady?"

She didn't answer. Shoving away as best she could while still roped to the prince, she growled out, "Could you untie us?" with a great deal of snark.

More annoying chuckles. "Someone is not a morning person," Jarok muttered, but he unwound the ropes, unweaving the work he'd done last night to secure them to the giant fir tree.

As soon as she was able, she leaned over deep, and Jarok shot out a hand to steady her. She didn't think she needed it, so she elbowed him with one arm, looking down, down, down, at a grinning Gem far below. A Gem grinning up at them despite her arm in a sling.

"Coming," she called, a touch too bright and chipper. More chuckles all around, this time from Jarok and Gem, as if it were some weird family trait. She scoffed and swung a leg over, ignoring Jarok's protest for her to wait for him. Her limbs were a little stiff and tingling from being tied to the tree in one position for hours, but she was used to moving through pain and discomfort. Something her father had made sure she understood in all their training. She stomped hard on her feet as she planted them, forcing the sensations out and waking her muscles in quick succession. In moments, she was scrambling down the tree, following the exact path they'd used to climb the night before, her memory sharp even in the light of morning.

When she jumped down from the final branch and landed with a firm thud on the ground, Jarok was a split second behind, dropping in so close, he pushed into her space and grabbed onto her shoulders to steady himself. Piris shook his hands off and stepped to Gem. "Are you well?"

Gem shrugged her one good shoulder. "Will be. Those damn Benders and their bloody arrows. If only I had Ghel's healing, this would be no issue at all."

Jarok, who'd stood so close behind her she could feel the length of his body like a warm wall at her back, stiffened at Gem's words.

"What happened last night?" she asked, wanting more information about the events after they left.

A crack of a twig made Piris shoot her eyes to the left, where Cylian and Darin stood. They definitely hadn't been there a moment before, and as they could be silent when they wished, she knew they were announcing themselves.

Gem nodded at Cylian, whose mismatched eyes were tight at the corners. "Five Benders were killed, the rest managing to escape in the chaos. The fire was contained to the inn, but sadly, the inn was destroyed by the smoke. Thankfully no one else was injured."

"The horses?" Jarok asked.

"Arrived late in the night and were taken care of by Nore," Cylian said.

"What of Nore and the people around the inn? And the innkeeper?"

"All taken care of, Prince. I sent Nore back to the Winterlands Palace with a message so aid could be brought to the inn as they rebuild."

Darin, who'd been standing stiff-straight and silent the entire time, visibly started, something Piris suspected was a rare occurrence for the assassin. He pushed his gray hood back, revealing the sharp planes and angles of his pale face and short crop of white-blond hair, looking from Cylian to Jarok.

"Good. Good," Jarok muttered, mostly to himself, about what Cylian had done.

Darin continued to stare at the prince, intense and steady, and Piris's hackles rose for a moment before he swept his eyes to her and she saw a softness there she'd never imagined possible. A light of something like wonder at what Cylian and Jarok had revealed about themselves shone in his green depths.

Piris of course knew plenty of history about the Springlands Court. Not as much as the Winterlands, which was her homeland, but enough. Her father thought it important for her, especially as their lands bordered the Great River, which itself was the border between the Winterlands and Springlands.

She knew the history of their monarchy on a cursory level and, more importantly, knew the talk of how the monarchs there, past and present, ruled absolutely and at their own whims, sometimes caring for their people and sometimes not. The sometimes was more often than not mandated by whatever advisers were in favor at the time, how cruel or capricious the sitting monarch was. From the astonishment Darin showed, she'd guess the monarchs cared little for helping their people.

She thought of Ghel, of King Frit and Queen Alene, of her best-friend-turned-Princess. Even of Jarok. Piris could never say these royals didn't care for their people. She'd seen throughout her life, in small and large ways, their attempts to make the Winterlands a good place for all who lived there. It wasn't perfect by any means, so few monarchies were, but they tried and succeeded in truly significant ways. She wondered what Darin had endured in his life, close to his monarchs, that made him so very surprised Jarok would be concerned about a coachman and an innkeeper. Sadness planted itself in her chest at the idea, and she felt a sort of thawing toward the assassin. Enough to make her more understanding about his behavior and intensity.

She also looked at Jarok, thinking of him and his family, giving him a smidge more grace than she had before.

Gem interrupted all these thoughts, coming up beside her and knocking her with her good shoulder. "Looks like we're walking."

"Huh?" Piris asked. She'd been so lost in her own thoughts, she'd drifted far from the conversation.

"Walking. To Volesion Peak. According to Cylian's calculations, it will take us about five to six days if we don't dawdle." Gem picked up a pack from the ground and slung it toward Piris, who caught it with a grunt of surprise. It held her bedroll strapped to the bottom and was packed with supplies, including her fighting leathers and a few extra blades. "Hope you don't mind me going through your trunks to get things."

"Thank you," Piris said, happy to see the leathers. She moved deep into the woods to change after letting the others know what she was doing. She wished she could burn the bloody traveling dress, but she opted instead to leave it where it lay. No need for it any longer or the odd reminder it would bring.

Coming back to her party, she adjusted the pack on her shoulders and said, "We head northeast, yes?"

Nods all around, and they moved in their small group, walking through the dense, cold woods, each step bringing her closer and closer to home.

Chapter Ten
Jarok

The first three days of their journey on foot was uneventful, much to Jarok's relief. He remained tense, as did everyone else after the attack at the inn. For Gem, it meant more ribbing on him, which was a way she let off steam when she couldn't spar or do any training because of her shoulder wound. It continued to heal cleanly, but Jarok had to keep on her to rest her shoulder and not take off the sling or do any number of things, which made him the perfect target for her barbs. He didn't mind if it meant she kept herself well and not sniping at others in their party.

Cylian was quiet, intense in the way he had when totally focused on what was around him. Often the Fae diplomat could at least pretend to not be so intense, to joke and tease and cajole. Like Jarok, he was able to slip on the mask of lordly diplomacy as needed, had a particular method of putting others at ease one might call magical if they didn't know fire and heat were his to call. Here, intent on their surroundings, his courtly demeanor slipped and showed the Fae man underneath: a man with a singular focus when those he cared for might be in danger. The care part was crucial. Jarok didn't doubt his defensive calm would be in place if there were Fae present Cylian did not trust. In their small group, he knew everyone well, and everyone knew him as best they could, so he let his mask ease in favor of helping keep all safe.

Darin interacted little with them, going off on his own during the day. Jarok assumed he was scouting ahead and left him to it, hearing faint traces of him every so often. Maybe he was scouting or maybe he didn't want the company. Either way, Jarok didn't ask because it mattered little to him. He'd proven himself to be an actual ally, shoving his reservations about the Fae down because of his trust in Cylian and what he'd seen of Darin himself in the last few days.

Piris oscillated between biting comments toward him or completely ignoring his existence, enough it caused his blood to boil with anger and lust. The first day, he'd pressed her to talk more. She'd experienced a great deal the night of the attack at the inn and he wanted to offer her space to work through her feelings. He'd be lying if he didn't also admit to himself he wanted to remain close to her, her body, and the heat that he still felt like phantom pains against his body. Gods, the few moments at the inn and the night she slept on top of him seeped deep into his mind and body, so much he was dreaming of her every night. He would be embarrassed if he hadn't heard a gentle moan slip from Piris one night as she'd slept. He suspected she suffered from the same issues.

It was maddening because he disliked her. Had disliked or did still, he couldn't quite tell any longer. She'd been his opponent for long months, someone he couldn't trust even after the secret she kept was revealed and he begrudgingly admitted it was worth her keeping for so long. He'd been attracted to her even before. Jarok couldn't imagine a Fae male who favored women not being attracted to her tall, strong frame, her fighter's grace, her wide mouth with strong lips, the sheen of her dark-auburn hair, and the spark of intelligence and fight in her bright-bronze eyes. He'd not acted until after a sort of truce had been called between them and, admittedly, he'd seen another man touch her. He'd raged at the idea of her being with another, and it had driven his actions at the inn. Now, when he should be cool and rational, he yearned to touch her again, feel her fire against him and taste her flesh.

He told himself it was simple attraction. One Fae desiring another. In his mind, if he tasted her, his lust would wane and they could continue. Maybe not as friends, ever, but something better than opponents constantly at each other. As they stood, her sniping mixed with the sneers and eye rolls and attitude she threw his way, he ached to tie her down and tease her until she expressed something other than annoyance and attitude. But, alas, she seemed over whatever lust had driven her to let him taste her nights before, determined to stay as far away from him as she could both night and day.

A sharp snort came his way. "What is it you need, Prince?" Apparently he'd been staring at her as he mused about what he'd like to do to her.

He wasn't too quick to shift his thoughts from the fantasies running through his head, so what came out first was "huh?" as he shook his head clear. Piris gave him a hard, derisive laugh.

"Maybe keep your mind on the wood, cousin," Gem said from behind, her snicker at her own joke grating over his strained nerves. He gritted his teeth but let her have the dig because he'd noticed her wincing in pain earlier.

When he focused on Piris again, she had stopped, arms crossed on her chest and a hip kicked out to the side, her ice and steel smell hovering even in the evergreen-drenched air. She nodded, but not at him, more like at something she'd thought herself before she spun on silent feet and started walking again.

"We're getting nearer to Volesion Peak."

"How can you tell?" Cylian asked. It wasn't dismissive but curious. Jarok also wondered. The area looked the same as what they traveled the last few days.

Piris waved toward a small spot several yards away on their left, where a cluster of fir samplings grew. "Those are great silver firs. They only grow closer to the Great River. The deeper in the forest you get, the less chance there is you encounter them. So, we have to be close to the river, and therefore close to Volesion Peak."

Jarok moved over to the small, barely growing trees. Determined little things, they reached up toward what little sunshine they could find in the gray Winterlands sky. A sky also covered and crowded by the massive firs around them. They tried, and he respected them for it. He reached out to stroke a tiny branch and breathe in the sweet pine of their scent, then stood from his crouch and found Piris staring at him once again. "What is it you need, lady?" he asked with a smirk as he pushed past her and continued.

Cylian, Darin, and Jarok discussed how much longer it might be before they hit Volesion Peak. The small fire they had allowed themselves burned down to tiny embers as they talked.

"We estimated five to six days of travel on foot, but we might be closer if Piris is correct," Cylian said.

Jarok thought about it, running over the Winterlands map locked in his head. He knew the land better than Cylian and Darin, that was certain, but he was no expert on the eastern edges of his homeland. He could kick himself for not knowing more, but there was nothing to do about it now. Each day he learned something new, tucking it away for future use for his family, as he did with most information.

"We have no reason to doubt her," he said aloud, looking up from their small clutch to find the woman they spoke about, the one who should herself be party to the conversation.

"She went into the woods," Darin said, not looking up as he studied some lines he'd traced in the snow at their feet to demonstrate how far they'd likely come from the inn.

Jarok froze at the news. He should have noticed, but he'd been deep in conversation with Cylian and Darin for several minutes by then. "When?"

Darin looked up to give his cold, jade stare to Jarok. "Five minutes ago."

"What?" Jarok jumped up. "Why didn't you say something? Or ask her where she went?"

The assassin shrugged. "I'm not used to questioning the actions of a lady, Prince."

Jarok bit back his curse. It wasn't on Darin, as he'd implied with his matter-of-fact answer. Jarok should've been paying attention.

"We go after her?" Cylian asked, rising.

"No. She hasn't been gone too long and may just need time alone to relieve herself. I'll go alone. You two stay here in case she returns. Point me in the direction she went, and I'll search for her. If I'm not back in thirty minutes, come looking for us."

Cylian nodded but didn't sit again, choosing instead to remain at the ready. Jarok grabbed his falchion belt from atop his pack and lashed it around his waist as he stalked off in the direction Darin pointed. He moved into the dark, deep woods in search of the infuriating woman who caused him so much frustration.

"About time," he heard Piris say from his right. She was seated in the deep V of a large branch and had to jump down two feet to reach the ground, landing with a soft thud when she did.

"Come on. It's not safe for you to be out here alone."

"Only me?"

Jarok sighed. "Of course not only you. Everyone needs to stay with the group to be safe."

"Oh, well then," she said, moving up close to him. So close. Closer than she had been to him in a few days. Close enough his breath hitched at the warmth of her and the lungful of ice and steel he got whenever she was near. "But we're not alone now."

"No..." he drawled out, hesitating, trying to understand what he thought might be going on here. "Why exactly did you come out here, Piris?"

"So you'd follow me," she said without a hint of concern, as if the words didn't land a blow right to Jarok's gut.

His hands flew out on their own, without thought, clasping down on her waist and dragging her even closer to him, until the tips of her leather-clad breasts brushed up against his chest and he heard her suck in a shaking breath.

Implications, ideas, needs, and wants whirled in his mind in a mess he couldn't disentangle for several seconds. Eventually he narrowed his eyes at her, studying her face, which was almost level with his, her eyes shining like molten metal even in the dark of the forest. "Are you certain you want this?"

"If by this you mean a quick release of the tension between us and nothing more, then yes."

"Nothing more?" He pressed her to be certain, not because it had twisted something in his gut when she'd said the words.

"Nothing more," she asserted, her voice husky but firm. Sure.

Nodding, he said, "Very well," before stepping her backward. "We have maybe ten minutes before the rest of the group comes looking for us. Not nearly enough time for what I'd like to do to you, but enough to do something fun."

Her back hit the tree she'd been in moments before, which stopped his progress. He moved one hand down to his sword belt and the bit of thin rope he kept there. "Hands," he demanded.

Piris looked taken aback by the statement. "Why?"

"No questions. You want this, yes? If so, we do it my way."

A shudder moved over Piris's face, a beautiful thing for Jarok to see. She closed her eyes a beat then opened them, her mind as set as her jaw. She lifted her hands up between them, offering them to him palms up.

He took them, rubbing a thumb over the inside of one wrist softly, reverently, before he wove the rope around her, tight but not tight enough to hurt. He then threw the excess up, over the branch he'd spied above them, caught the falling end, and pulled it, hard. Her breath pushed out in a gasp as her arms shot up over her head and the sound went right to his cock. Jarok quickly tied off the end to a root on the ground, trailing kisses along her fighting leathers as he came back to standing.

"I do wish I could take my time, Piris. Maybe another day."

"I said nothing about another day."

Jarok shrugged. "We'll see," he said, distracted as a finger traced lazy circles around the sliver of pale skin now exposed between her leather shirt and her pants from the stretch of her body upward. "Beautiful." He breathed before he went right to the button of her pants and snapped it open, wasting no time getting the leathers down past her hips, exposing her to him and the night air.

Gods, he could smell her, sweet and metallic and mesmerizing, and he dropped again to his knees to breathe her in deep and watch closely as he ran a finger over the damp, dark red curls at the apex of her thighs. She mewled above him, squirming at his touch, and started to shout his name before he popped up and covered her mouth with a hand.

"Oh, no. No words. Definitely no shouting. Don't want the others interrupting what little time we have, right?"

She shook her head, desperation and need warring in her eyes. Jarok felt the same pull, so he didn't make her, or himself, wait. He kept her mouth covered with one hand as he snaked the other down to her dripping pussy, flicking a finger over her clit in a flurry as she squirmed against him. He paused only to dip down, test her opening with one finger. He slipped in with ease, so he added another and pumped in and out in hard, quick thrusts that made a moan leak from around his hand at her mouth.

The angle was not the best, and her hips still being encased in leather meant it'd be a tight fit, but his fingers worked well enough, so he decided to go for it. He eased his hand from her mouth as he continued to play with her, eyes locked on hers, and said, "Be quiet, or we'll have to end this."

She said nothing as he unbuttoned his leathers and pulled his cock out. It was already weeping, begging to be deep inside her.

He licked his lips, looking down as he rubbed himself against her exposed mound. She whimpered, pushing her hips forward, silently demanding more contact. He smiled and angled her hips to pull her away from the tree trunk, steadying her with firm pressure as he adjusted his angle and height to ease himself inside of her. "Gods damn." He breathed out as he watched himself disappear inside her slick, tight heat.

She moaned, thrashing her head, turning the noise into soft, nearly silent pants as he went in inch by delicious inch. When he bottomed out, he moved his hand from her mouth to her other hip, hitching her higher, going in a fraction more. His head fell forward and he stayed frozen for several seconds, savoring the feel of her all around him.

Her hips flexed, causing her inner muscles to grip him even tighter, making his mind blank before it roared back to life, driving him to pull back and thrust deep in a flash. He was lost, the sensation too delicious, too deep, too much for him to process as his body drove him on and on and on. Piris thrashed beneath him, as much as she could while still confined by her leathers and his grip on her hips, but she moved along with him, meeting him thrust for thrust, driving them both higher and higher.

He felt himself barreling toward release at an embarrassing speed, so Jarok left one hip to dip back down where they joined and rub tight, hard circles on her clit. She bit her mouth hard as a cry almost escaped her lips. Without thinking, he bent deep so he could clamp down on her mouth with his, thrusting his tongue into her in time with his cock, both of them clashing together in a melee of teeth and lips and slick flesh. He felt her walls flutter around him, and she stiffened like the trunk behind her before splintering, a scream echoing from her mouth into his. He sucked it down like the best ale. Seconds later, his hips stuttered as he found his own release deep inside her.

Jarok kept his mouth on her, easing them both down with a softer, more languid kiss before he released her hip and pulled himself free of her. He thought about loss, about want, about a myriad of things he couldn't name when the warmth of her fell away, but he stuffed it inside, like he stuffed himself back into his leathers. Because that was what she'd asked him to give her.

Chapter Eleven
Piris

As Jarok pulled out of her, Piris bit the inside of her cheek to stifle the moan crawling up her throat. She wouldn't show that, not to him. Not after she'd set clear boundaries she'd meant. Piris didn't want attachment of any kind. Her secrets were hers to keep, locked up tight. She had all she needed with her parents and Strella.

That wasn't exactly true any longer. Gem had shoved her way into Piris's small circle rather quickly. Cylian had made his way there before the trip, thanks to him helping save Strella's life, but his presence these past few days had made her appreciate him more and more. Even Darin, whom she remained wary around, was becoming something like a friend.

Jarok... Well, Jarok riled her in the most infuriating ways. A simple smirk or side slide of his dark eyes or a flip of his floppy hair could get her hackles up in an instant. Yet, he'd shown such care and concern this whole time, she'd come to think of him as someone who could be her friend at some point in the future. She didn't know if it could ever go that far, not with the way they constantly rattled one another.

The delicious kiss-and-grope session in the inn had heightened things, as did his reveal about his first kill when she'd desperately needed those words. Earlier that day, when he'd stooped to admire the silver fir saplings, something in her chest had twisted at the sight, growing tighter and tighter like a twining rope around her ribcage until she'd made her decision. She needed to have Jarok, get him out of her system somehow. Before she burst with desire.

She wanted him. Sure, she'd wanted a number of Fae in her life—and had had them. She was secretive by nature and need, which meant she often followed desire only with people she could ignore or dismiss after: young lords who'd also want to keep their dalliances with her a secret and the occasional sailor or merchant visiting Volesion Peak from other Fae lands. Like most Fae, she saw no issue with sating desires when they popped up for her. Desire for someone she knew and would have to interact with again wasn't something she'd dealt with before. She'd thought ignoring the pull of the prince would be enough, but each day after their first kiss, after feeling the heat of him on top of her, strained her resolve.

Unused to denying herself her physical desires when she had to stuff down so many other desires and dreams, she'd decided if she set clear boundaries, they could enjoy one another and be fine after. Piris hadn't counted on the way he dominated her, the delicious pull and tug of his rope work, or how every thrust into her drove her pleasure and emotions higher and higher, as if they somehow intertwined when she was connected to this Fae man.

Not good. Not good at all.

She was left biting her cheek, hanging limp from the ropes, unconcerned with the pinch in her shoulders because her mind was whirling too fast.

Jarok bit out a curse after straightening himself. He looped an arm around her waist, pulling her tight into his hold. She kept her mouth locked down because another moan wanted to leak from her lips. Told herself to get a grip when he pushed her up, taking her weight in his strong arm as he worked to untie her wrists with deft fingers.

When she was free, she sagged against the man, and he shifted his hold to make sure her feet were on the ground while still keeping her weight in his arms.

"Can you stand?" he whispered, the words a caress across her flushed cheek.

She gave a nod and stiffened her legs, shifting herself to take her own weight. Jarok hesitated a moment, as if he wanted to keep her where she was, but dropped her back without a struggle, letting her find her bearings.

She absently rubbed one wrist with her opposite hand and muttered, "Thanks."

Jarok's eyes narrowed on her hand, then he touched her again, the zap and heat of him roaring back to life in her blood. He rubbed her wrists in soft, gentle circles with his deft fingers, loosening the small sting there. He brought them up to look as close as he could in the dim light and turned each over several times before satisfied with whatever he saw. "No bruising or chaffing," he said.

He let his hands fall with hers still in his grasp, so they stood inches apart, hand in hand, facing one another. It was too close, too much, after a whole lot of too much had just happened. "They're fine. No problem," Strella said as she shook his hands off. An odd blush hit her, someone rarely embarrassed, when she realized her leathers were still down, leaving her exposed. "Damn it," she said, pulling them up, though she took the opportunity to take a step to the side, give herself some physical distance.

Jarok let out an odd cough, and their eyes locked a moment. He opened his mouth as if to speak, but shut it with an audible snap of teeth.

"We should return to the others," Piris said into his silence, looking off in the direction of their camp for the night. She hoped to avoid whatever words he wanted to say or whatever his eyes might tell her.

"One moment," he said, his voice rougher, less controlled than usual. She didn't look to him, but heard the snap of rope against bark. When she steeled herself to turn to him again, she saw him rolling his rope tight, lashing it back to his belt. Heat rose up, delicious but unwanted, so she spun on her heels, taking the lead back to the camp. In her mind, it was best not to talk, not to look, then everything might be able to go back to normal soon enough.

No one commented on how long they were gone or what might have happened between them out in the woods, which made Piris thankful for their ragtag group. Even Gem, who was prone to jabs at her cousin for stress relief and entertainment, must have sensed making jokes right then might not be in her best interest and only stared long and hard at Piris as she prepped her bedroll. Darin ignored them, as usual. Cylian greeted them but said little else, moving to bank their tiny fire with his magic.

Piris turned her back toward everyone, damn the cold, and willed herself to sleep. It took time and a good bit of willing, but it came. When she got up the next morning, she willed herself to not reach for Jarok when she saw his sexy, sleep-addled eyes on her when she rose from her roll. They talked, planned, calculated, and all came to the same conclusion: if they picked up the pace, they'd be at Volesion Peak much sooner than expected.

This thought sobered Piris a great deal. In one or two days, she'd stroll into Volesion Peak and have to tell her parents their secret was out. Not only out but out with the royals of the Winterlands, a lord of the Autumnlands, and a famed Aurora Clan warrior. Gods willing, no other attacks would occur, else the assassin of the Springlands might also discover she was a mimic. Her mother would be devastated. Her father would be livid. Both would hurt her to see, knowing it was her choices that made them feel such pains. She wouldn't take it back, even if she could, because it had helped Strella save her prince. Still, it wasn't fun, imagining what her mother and father would say to her in a few short days.

Even with this hanging over her head, easing her lust for Jarok, it was only slightly calmed. Sometimes she'd see him looking at her from the peripheral, studying her like a puzzle he wanted to solve. Once, she'd been thinking too much on too many things and had tripped on a rock buried in the snowy forest floor. He'd somehow been right there, moving to grab her elbow and right her before she fell face-first into the ground.

"Sorry," she'd muttered, and he'd only nodded back at her, flexing his hand as he walked away.

Luckily for her, something in the air changed the closer they came to Volesion Peak, a comforting blanket of home settling around her. She'd always felt itchy, unsure, on edge everywhere else in the realm. Here, in the familiar fir forest around her estate, the sounds of the Great River rumbling closer and closer as they walked, her shoulders eased a touch and her guard dropped slightly.

"We're only a few miles from Volesion Peak," Piris called back to the four Fae following her. She'd somehow taken the lead. Darin wasn't even scouting ahead now. Murmurs of acknowledgment went up all around, and Piris smiled, thinking of home, forgetting her worries for a time. Her steps came quicker the nearer she got to the house. They were technically just inside the confines of the vast estate, which struck Piris as odd. Her father had security patrols regularly, and wards around their perimeters. She would easily slip through, of course, but the others shouldn't have been able to do so. With furrowed brows, she spun around to talk to the group about this, and as she pivoted, she felt the whiz of an arrow fly by her abdomen, narrowly missing planting itself right in her gut.

She didn't think, just reacted, shifting her weight so she dove to the ground instead of spinning fully around to face the others. Sparing a look to make sure no one else was hit, she saw everyone else crouching for cover and pulling out their weapons. Darin jumped into a thicker section of tree line, his own bow slipped from his shoulder and notched with an arrow in a blur of movement. Like a good assassin, he was off to gods knew where to hopefully pick off whoever had attacked them. The Benders were great bowmen, but she doubted they could compete with Darin man-to-man. Only problem was the fight wasn't likely man-to-man but man to several men.

Piris had no real time to strategize and instead focused on taking in as much of the scene as possible to quickly find an opening to exploit. About one hundred yards ahead, she spied three Benders atop horses, all with notched bows aimed right for them. In a blink, they let their arrows rip. She rolled several feet to her left and popped up on her feet at the last moment to make a crouched run for the tree line. The clearing offered little cover.

She noticed Jarok a second before he clamped a hand around her wrist to plant her firmly by his side and quicken her steps. Scanning the opposite side, she let out a sigh when she saw Cylian and Gem both well and mostly covered by the branches of a large fir. "Plan?" she asked.

Jarok went to open his mouth, but a steady beat of hooves filled the silence, and his focus shifted to the Benders barreling toward them. More horses sounded in the distance, and Piris prayed they weren't more Benders set to attack. Right that second, a Bender's arrow whizzed by her head—by her head instead of in her head because Jarok had pulled her a step to the side before she was skewered by the thing.

She didn't have time to thank him for the save. Two other arrows thunked into the tree trunk behind them after the prince had also pulled her to the ground. Seemed the three were set on getting them, or more likely Jarok, than going after the whole party.

A grunt, horribly close by Piris's estimation, sounded and she saw one Bender fall fast from his horse, an arrow she recognized as Darin's planted right in the man's eye socket. The assassin wasn't looking to take prisoners.

Two more arrows sailed toward them, and this time Piris dove for the save, landed hard on Jarok, and rolled him on the ground. A hiss came from the prince; an arrow had scraped across his upper arm, but she saw nothing of immediate danger.

Scrambling on the ground, she turned and saw Cylian attacking with a fireball, small but effective. His fire startled the horses, and they reared up, toppling both riders to the ground. Both rolled and popped up without hesitation. One, wielding a large hammer, plowed into Gem, who'd planted her feet in the middle of the clearing with her sword gripped tight in both hands. She was still healing from the arrow to the shoulder she'd taken in the last Bender attack, but her two-handed grip and her hard stance didn't falter. Not yet. Piris knew she wouldn't last long, and from the looks of Cylian, he couldn't help a great deal in the moment. He was clashing with the other Bender, whose massive broadsword was crashing down heavy on the rapier and dagger combination the fiery Fae favored. Even with flame dancing across his blades, the Bender looked like he might have an advantage in strength and determination on her friend.

Her friend, someone she liked. Had come to care for. Another arrow from Darin zipped through the air, thudding hard against the back of the man bringing his heavy hammer down on Gem's sword again and again as she gritted her teeth against each clang of metal. The way the arrows bounced off the men was clearly the work of some form of magic, be it wards or artifice. Not on their heads, because she'd seen the arrow in the eye earlier, but along the broader, much easier to hit parts of the Fae attacking. They had magical protection, which made the fight so much harder.

Jarok pushed into the fray, coming in beside Gem to deflect a savage downward strike of the war hammer with his slim but sturdy falchion. She took a moment to observe, watch the way the Benders moved, and could tell they were well trained, even in defense. They kept their heads down, knowing there was a skilled archer around them somewhere and that was their vulnerability. She didn't even know where Darin was, but she hoped he was ready to take advantage.

She stepped out, not with her dagger or her short sword in hand, but with her magic tingling. She needed a surprise, something to distract them. Sadly, she'd never met Engad Monti, who would be the best person to mimic for his minions. She figured they knew enough about the royals to recognize Ghel's booming voice. She opened her mouth and let it out. "Step away from my brother," she yelled, Ghel's gruff command ringing in the clearing.

The gambit paid off. The Bender fighting Gem and Jarok jerked upright at the sound. His neck exposed, Gem thrust forward and buried her blade deep into his throat. He gurgled blood as he dropped like a stone to the ground.

Cylian's attacker must have hesitated somehow too, as he allowed Cylian enough time to shove a fireball right into his chest. Whatever was protecting him from arrows seemed to keep the fire at bay, but no one was immune to the terror of thinking they'd burn to death. He flailed, screaming as he pounded his own chest in an attempt to put out the flames. An arrow flew from behind Cylian's shoulder and landed once again right in a Fae's eye. Darin was an excellent shot.

Everyone breathed hard and heavy, preparing themselves for the horses they heard coming closer and closer. In seconds they were close enough for Piris to see clearly, and she yelled to her group, "Not Benders!" She moved to stand in front of everyone else as Darin slipped in from whatever perch he'd taken to fire at their enemies.

Her father came barreling into the clearing, jumped from his trusty stallion before it had a chance to fully stop, and stalked up to grab his daughter tight in his arms. Like most healthy Fae, he looked younger than his two hundred years, only a slight smattering of gray at his mostly brown temples hinting at older age. He squeezed her hard and tight before setting her down, bronze eyes assessing her then the rest of the group. "What is happening here? Why are you traveling on foot with my daughter, and why were these men attacking you?"

He moved to stand beside Piris, taking in the members of their party. "And where is Prince Ghel?"

He'd heard her then. No more hiding it. Piris swallowed the lump of fear in her throat, gripped her father's hand, and said, "That was me, Father."

Chapter Twelve
Jarok

Jarok had met Lord Brettly Volesion only once, a few decades before, when he'd attended a week of meetings about shipping and imports held at Winterlands Palace. The summit had been overseen by his father, long before the king became too ill to do such things. Jarok remembered Volesion as a serious, quiet man who kept to himself but, when he did speak up, offered insightful comments. As he glowered beside his daughter and his massive gray stallion, steam puffing from his flared nostrils as he cut hard eyes to every person in their traveling party, Jarok saw the warrior in him, the tension marking his muscles and the whirling in his mind. The prince couldn't help himself; on instinct, he hovered a hand over his falchion where he'd sheathed the blasted thing, ready to defend if need be.

The man's large, dark-fur-clad chest heaved up hard and he hissed out a breath before looking back down at his daughter. She gripped his hand tight and held his bronze gaze with hers, her dark-auburn head only reaching his chin. Silence beat by, something without words passing between father and daughter, and he let go of her hand, closing his eyes as if resigned to whatever dark and dangerous course they'd somehow discussed without words.

"We'll talk more at the house," Volesion said, voice gruff and nearly choked. He turned on his heels to converse with his men, two of whom pulled off from the group and took off back the way they'd appeared.

Piris walked up, muscles coiled even while her voice sounded unconcerned. "Father will call for horses for us so we can reach Volesion Peak more quickly. There's a security post only a few miles from here, so it shouldn't be long."

"Thank the gods we're not walking anymore," Gem said in a rush, her eyes hesitant even if her attitude wasn't. She surveyed as she teased and stoked, like always. "Come, cousin, let's have a look at your wound."

Jarok had forgotten about the scrape of the arrow. It had sliced through his arm, cutting deep enough for blood to seep in a dark circle around his leathers. Cursing the Benders once again, he moved to where Gem sat on a rock away from the group as Piris went to her father. He wanted to go with her, shield her if he could, but thought better of it. The anger pouring out of the lord might clash against his daughter's stubborn attitude, but he didn't sense it was a danger to her. To him, very likely, but not to her, so he followed Gem's fussing command.

He watched Piris and her father from the corner of his eye as Gem grunted and poked at his sliced side, muttering about Borau princes taking arrows all willy-nilly, as she dabbed at him with a clean cloth. "Well, not much for it here. I'm sure once we reach Volesion Peak they'll have someone who can stitch this up. It's not deep, so it might not even need stitches, but it does need a good cleaning and a bandage."

Jarok, not paying the least bit of attention to Gem though his head was bent to hers, was surprised when she smacked the back of his head. "Down, boy," she huffed out with heat.

"Excuse me?" he replied in his haughtiest, most princely voice.

Gem snorted in his face. "You know exactly what I'm saying, oh mighty prince. Get your shit together, because that man there is ready for a fight, and if you keep tracking them like you are, he might find it in you."

"Lord Volesion wouldn't..." He didn't finish the thought because he himself knew the lord would do whatever he needed to do to protect his daughter. Even if he looked utterly pissed at her. Jarok could relate.

"Don't lie to yourself. In fact, stop lying to yourself in general, cousin," she hissed and Jarok finally looked at her, really looked at her, and saw the pinch at the corner of her eyes and the compressed line of her mouth.

"Turn around," he commanded, needing to see for himself how bad it was. He cursed when her shoulder flinched at his touch. "Are you bleeding?"

She wasn't injured bad enough for it to seep through her leathers, but then again it would take an awful lot of blood to seep through or out of uncut leather. She'd reopened her wound—that much was certain—and may have even done more damage.

"Cousin," he said, sorrow and pain and regret dripping in his voice.

She turned on the rock to face him again, slicing a hand in the air to dismiss whatever he would try to say. "Enough of that, Jarok. Look, we have more company."

He turned back to where Lord Volesion stood with his daughter and his guard and noted the returning men with three additional horses trailing behind them. He and Gem both rose, and Cylian and Darin converged with them, moving as a unit up to the Volesions once the men stopped and spoke with their leader.

"Three horses are all they had prepped for the journey," the lord relayed to them. "I'll take my daughter; the rest of you can double up as you see fit."

For some reason, Jarok stepped up, his hand almost reaching out to Piris, but he stopped himself from such a foolish move. Lord Brettly wouldn't appreciate him trying to keep his daughter with him. Piris wouldn't appreciate it either, so he stuffed the instinct down and turned toward Gem. "You first, cousin," he said, offering her a hand as she mounted the horse they'd handed off to him. The thing was massive, a true Winterlands horse ready to plod through anything. He adjusted the seat with Gem on it, pushing it back enough to give him room in front of it. He jumped up, ignoring the searing pain in his side, and took the reins. Slowly, to make sure his cousin wasn't pained, he followed Lord Volesion. A few strands of Piris's auburn hair fluttered behind, freed from her tight bun enough to be a beacon Jarok used to direct him on their journey, a focus for the ride.

They reached Volesion Peak after thirty minutes of hard riding. Jarok followed close behind the lord and his daughter, surveying their surroundings. The house itself was surrounded by a dense fir forest until they reached the outer limits of the yard and a lane, lined with meticulously trimmed hedges, which led to a massive black front door the height of the entire house. The building itself was two very tall dark stories, a sturdy block of stone with triangular peaks outlining each window. The footprint was large yet squat, a big square of rock with glass peppering the facade, the rush of the river becoming clearer and clearer as they moved closer to it. It sat right on the edge of a cliff, overlooking the small port where Lord Volesion commanded his fleet of merchant ships.

At the wide, squat steps up to the grand house, framed in the black of the massive open door, was who Jarok assumed to be Lady Mimi Volesion. She stood perfectly still, the air of a woman trained in the manners of the Fae nobility from birth. The lessons marked every line of her body, from the hard clasp of her hands in front of her to the perfect crossing lines of her straightened back and shoulders. There was no sign of the fighter's look or stance her daughter wore so well. Still, Jarok knew from much experience with the nobility of the Winterlands, her poise was its own form of protection, perfect for the arenas where a person like Lady Volesion would battle. Given who her daughter was, the secret the family had held for decades and the lies they'd told to cover it, he imagined she did much fighting in ballrooms and sitting rooms in her time.

Lord Volesion did not make his way to the stables, instead riding hard up to the stairs, Lady Volesion's stillness cracking when she finally caught sight of her daughter behind her husband. She lifted the soft faun-colored skirts of her refined but simple day dress to run toward Piris. The dark auburn of her hair flowed, the top part pinned back to show her broad smile and gorgeous broad face. Seeing the lady and lord together, Jarok saw the fit of the pieces that made the striking, strong beauty of Piris, the amalgamation making her who she was, physically at least. A twang in his heart, a feeling he'd known all his life as an adopted son, made his breath hitch a step, but he corrected himself quickly, long before he came to a stop at the same stairs and dismounted.

Lady Volesion hugged Piris tight, who'd herself bent down to bury her face in the hair hanging at her mother's shoulders. A different pang ripped across his chest, a wish he couldn't quite express, but he slipped his charming-prince mask on. His control was slipping more and more with each day of this journey, damn it.

He was bent to bow, an honor from a prince of the Winterlands, when Lord Brettly whispered something to his family that had Lady Mimi snapping upright with surprising speed. "Inside," he gruffly called before entering the dark hole at the front of his home, his wife and daughter following in his wake. Piris looked back, beckoning her traveling party to follow as her pale body cut through the darkness in front of them.

The entrance mimicked a dark cavern, but the inside of Volesion Peak was nothing like the outside. A softness created through luscious rugs, gorgeous wall tapestries, artwork with muted colors, and furniture with rounded lines opposite the sharp peaks of the outside made for a welcoming home. Jarok had little time to think on it as he followed along, stepping farther and farther into the house at a steady pace until they came to a small study.

When everyone from the party had entered, Lord Volesion looked up from behind a large wing-backed tufted leather reading chair, his hands gripping the edges so his knuckles became stark white against the dark, supple material. "You. Close the door."

Jarok stiffened at his tone, even though the command was for Darin, who didn't question it. He simply did as the lord asked, though the sneer that had been off his face for days came back in full force.

Lord Volesion ignored it, which made Jarok question his intelligence for the first time. No one should ignore the assassin of the Springlands. Then again, he may not know who exactly he was commanding in his home. Or he was too preoccupied to care. As soon as the door clicked shut behind Marco, he whirled on his wife and burst out with a wave of rage. "They know. The royals, and all here with her, know of Piris's magic."

Lady Volesion went deathly pale, a shaking hand reaching up to cover her gaping mouth, tears glistening in her eyes. Instantly, regret flashed across Lord Volesion as he took his wife in his arms, burying her face in his chest.

Jarok wished to do the same with Piris, who stood hugging her own chest and swaying side to side. He didn't, of course, but by gods he wanted to, so he chose to step closer to her and touch her with a quick, gentle tap of the finger on her shoulder to let her know he was there at her side. As if the warrior in her would allow him to ever sneak up on her in such a confined space.

After a few minutes of murmured grief between mother and father at what could be, Lord Volesion let go of his wife to square his chest at the others in the room. "You two in the back. Who exactly are you?"

"Gem Aurora, lord," his cousin said with a small nod of acknowledgment, which she didn't have to give him as a member of a warrior clan. No clan members were forced to adhere to the niceties of Fae nobility, so her gesture was a sign of respect Jarok took in, even if the lord did not.

"Darin Marco," the assassin said, his sneer wrapping around his name as he lifted his deep hood enough for the Fae man to see the hard set of his eyes. Jarok took in the fact he didn't add his own title, which he never did, for some reason. The more pressing matter was Lord Brettly had obviously annoyed the assassin, and as Jarok suspected, the man hadn't even known who he was, or at least the sharp breath he drew signaled as much.

With a shaking hand, he clasped one of his wife's and asked, "How many know?"

Piris, dropping her grip on herself, stepped closer to her family. "The royals of the Winterlands Palace. A very small handful of trusted guards. And the people in this room. Darin being the last."

Lord Volesion narrowed his eyes at those last words. "Did you just now, in my own earshot, reveal your power to Hooded Death?"

By the gods, he'd forgotten about Marco's whispered name—a name he doubted many used to his face outside of the Springlands, where the nobility acted with a little too much abandon at times. The assassin didn't flinch at it, didn't move, but stood, still and deadly in front of the door.

"Darin Marco," Piris spit out, stepping closer to her father, the flame of anger sparking in her eyes at her father's rudeness to one of their party, "has protected my life more than once, Father. He deserves some respect."

"I don't care about respect," the man spit, dropping his wife's hand and moving toward his daughter, his eyes mimicking hers, the heat of each feeding off one another to grow hotter, quicker.

"Obviously, as you didn't even welcome a prince into our home properly. King Frit might take offense." She added a chiding, condescending tsk sound, folding her arms and cocking her hip. It was enough to almost make Jarok laugh, as he'd seen the same from her so often, though it was usually directed his way. The tension in the air, the crackle of what could happen at any moment, and how serious it could become held the laugh back.

Lady Mimi, possibly having a similar train of thought to the prince, stepped up and laid a hand on her husband's tensed forearm. "Brettly. Please. A moment."

His eyes closed, his nostrils flared, and he took a step back, breathing in the measured, conscious way he'd sometimes noticed Piris did. A form of control she'd learned from him, it seemed.

While her husband settled, the lady stepped into the breach. "Please, Prince, Lord Cylian of the Autumnlands, Darin Marco, and Gem Aurora. Welcome to our home. We are... unsettled at the moment, so I do apologize for your first impression of our family."

Cylian, always the diplomat, spoke. "Lady Volesion, we are all truly sorry for the stress our appearance, and the news it carries, has brought into your home. However, we have spent a great deal of time with your daughter, and I must say, she is enough credit to the Volesion family to have already solidified a favorable impression."

A tear slipped from Lady Volesion, and Piris, who'd stayed at attention, deflated in front of his eyes. "Mother," she whispered, reaching for her.

"How?" the lady asked. "How could this happen? We were so careful for so long."

"I did it for Strella. To help save Prince Ghel," Piris said, an ache echoing in her words. "I wish, for you, I'd had a different choice, but I didn't. And because of that, I can't wish I hadn't done it."

Tears flowed then, tracks across the lady's sweet face from her stark brown eyes. She lifted a hand to cradle her daughter's cheek as Piris shook with a deep sigh. "You love so fiercely, Piris. I hate what happened, for you. I cannot hate how deeply you feel for those you care about." Her chest heaving, she slipped a daintily embroidered handkerchief from somewhere Jarok could not see, and she wiped the tears from her face.

"Lady Strella and Prince Ghel—" Lord Brettly bit out, venom in his words despite his attempts at calm.

Jarok had had enough. "Princess Strella and Prince Ghel. Soon to be King Ghel," he barked. The lord of the Winterlands fell into silence at the words, at the movement of the prince to his side, and Jarok's hand hovering, despite his own attempts at calm, over the blade in his belt. "You may disparage me, lord, but I shall not have you say something in anger to smear my brother and sister, my future king and queen."

Tension built again, different, more deadly, as Lord Volesion turned to face Jarok full on, his nose pinched in a look of disgust somehow familiar to Jarok.

"No," Piris said, stepping between the two men. "No. Enough of this male posturing. Father, what is done is done. We can discuss ways to soothe your concerns as rational Fae should, or we will leave, immediately."

"And you, Prince," Piris said, whirling on him but laying a gentle hand on his forearm so close to his blade. "Calm yourself. My father is understandably angry, but his anger will pass. He means no ill will, especially toward Princess Strella, who at any other time in his life, he's loved like his own daughter." She looked back at him with a glare and said, "In time, he will remember that and feel his own shame."

Lord Volesion jerked his head as if hit and rocked back a step, his wife catching his retreat with a hand at his back. She continued where her daughter had left off. "I think, Piris, it may be best you take the others to the green sitting room, yes? Order tea. Rest. We will join you soon."

Piris nodded and herded the party from the room, but not before Jarok gave the lord one last warning look.

Chapter Thirteen
Piris

Piris calmed herself, breathing deep in and out in the paced measure she'd learned from her father—her blasted, stubborn ass of a father who was the reason she needed to calm herself in the first place. Her anger bubbled to the surface again in a flash before she could tame it. This type of anger, only someone one cared for could cause, the unique mixture of rage, disappointment, hurt, and love family members could somehow so easily make rear up inside. More, however, was at stake than the building anger she might have at the average argument with her father. This was her life, and because of his flippant words about the royal family, it might mean his life if he didn't rein himself in.

Not that she thought King Frit or Prince Ghel would harm him. Prince Jarok, though angry at his words, wouldn't either. Unless pushed. Either prince, when pushed, would do much to protect their kingdom and those they loved. She'd seen it and didn't want her father to get anywhere near the line he'd have to cross to get on the bad side of one of the Boraus. She didn't want on the bad side of the Boraus either, for a more complex variety of reasons.

One reason being the prince seated a few paces across from her, his usually flippant or friendly face dark and brooding after the encounter with her parents. A small ruffle of wind occasionally whipped through the room as if his thoughts were conjuring force without him realizing it. While Piris worried her lip, concentrating on how to defuse the situation, Gem jumped into the breach as only she could.

"This big black house is drafty enough, cousin. You don't need to add to it," she grumbled with a slight lift of the corner of her mouth, her teasing clear for anyone looking. Jarok had been too busy clenching his jaw and narrowing his brown, half-moon eyes at the intricate rug under their feet.

"Not now, Gem," he grumbled, not breaking eye contact with the rug, its ivy pattern broken up only by the occasional cream flower popping up here and there.

Piris, calmed now, tried to get his attention in her own way. She didn't know what to say to him. Their usual snarky banter wouldn't work in this situation. Neither would the lust they'd cultivated over the last few days, though it continued to pulse between them like a living, breathing entity all its own.

She decided on simple. Scooting forward in her chair, she stretched her leather-booted foot forward and knocked his with a solid tapping motion. He started, blinking his eyes as he raised his head slightly to look at her. One eyebrow lifted in question, though it was a hard slash on his golden-brown skin instead of the insolent curve he'd so often directed at her in the past. Her mind blanked for a second at the thought of how he could make such an insignificant patch of hair say so much, do so much, until she shook herself from the odd thoughts.

"How about some tea?" It was all she had. Her mother, bless her, said tea cured all worries. Piris had never believed it, but damned if she wouldn't try it now.

The harsh line of Jarok's shoulder eased, as did his face, and he nodded in reply. His torso rose from his bent position where he'd dug his elbows deep into the tops of his knees, straightening him, as he cleared his face bit by bit with each inch.

Cylian said, "Allow me," and moved without much sound toward the cord pull in the corner. He didn't know her home well, but as a lord, he knew it would call a servant with tea to the room.

Piris took a moment to survey Darin, who'd refused a seat in the center of the room and stood with his back to the group, straight and tall, centered in the large picture window with its green velvet curtains. He looked to be studying the lane and bushes, but his eyes appeared distant. They weren't close and hadn't talked much during their journey, but she wanted to check on his mood nonetheless—not only because he was capable of great violence but because he didn't deserve the disrespect her father had thrown his way in his fear and anger.

She slid in close to him, though not touching, and centered her gaze out the window instead of at the man. Figured he might prefer it. "Darin, I apologize—"

He raised a hand between them, as if brushing away whatever she might say. "I have endured much worse, lady."

"I thought I stopped being lady."

"It is good to remember one's place."

She ached at the words. No one should feel that, especially not in her home, and her father would chastise himself later at the way he'd made a guest in his house feel. Swallowing hard, she pushed through. "Your place is about protection, honor, skill... from what I've seen of you. Nothing I wouldn't be proud to say about myself."

He turned to look at her, moving only his head in a rather eerie, slow creep. After giving her an up and down, he turned back to look outside once again before he asked, "Do you know what magical affinity I wield?"

She thought on it. She couldn't remember seeing him use magic or hearing any of the others comment on it, so she shook her head.

He saw her in his peripheral and answered without further urging. "I wield shadows. Handy magic for an assassin, especially one who started as a lowly, court-banned lord of his land."

Piris's breath caught. All she knew of shadow-wielders was they could blend in and out of shadows at will. Some with great power might even be able to flit between shadows for short distances. It was a handy power indeed for any fighter, let alone an assassin. Shadow-wielders weren't persecuted or hated by the average Fae. Still, like mimics, they more often than not ended up used by people in power. How he'd become Hooded Death made much more sense to her. Piris had a suspicion he'd been someone without a lot of power before his shadowy gifts had come to the attention of the king of the Springlands. Such a king as he was rumored to be would do a great deal to keep someone with that power under his thumb.

"A truly impressive magic to wield, Darin. One you use wisely." Jarok stepped to her other side, joining their conversation. She'd notice the thaw between the two men who'd at first seemed opposed to one another. The prince's words were another stone in the bridge they seemed to be building.

Darin looked at Jarok and gave a small smile, his harsh face softening a fraction. His confessions continued, bright-green eyes boring right into Piris as he spoke. "I come from a poor, lesser noble family. Barely connected to the Springlands Court after a long-ago disgrace made us fall from favor. Then, I was conscripted because I couldn't buy my way out of duty. Of course, my magic was tested first, to define my place, and I've been directly in the king's service ever since."

Piris wanted to pat him or maybe even hug him, though she wasn't much of a hugger herself, but his rigid stance and locked jaw told her it wouldn't be appreciated. It wasn't why he said all this to her and Jarok in his low, droll voice.

"I have done things... But this is not the point. I would never reveal your magic to another, Lady Piris. I'll swear any oath you require to ensure you can trust in my word."

Piris reached out then, not being able to help herself. A long history of being a tool for another, of the weight of heady power and how it was ill used by someone else, hung heavy on the Fae's head. The part of her who'd been locked away for so long, who'd been forced into lies and secrecy, knew the burden some magics could bring all too well. Darin wouldn't be a hugger either, she thought, but she did rest a hand on his shoulder as she breathed deep, looked out at her homeland, and hurt for an assassin. Something she never thought she'd experience.

"No oath required," she answered in a whisper, and she felt his shoulder ease a touch under her hand after, a silent sign he'd worried over her response.

"Darin, if ever—"

Darin took a big step backward, breaking their line and the prince's words.

"I have taken oaths, Prince Jarok. Ones I would be bound to obey despite what I might think or wish. Do not offer me anything one could in any way view as detrimental to my king." Darin raised his sleeve slightly, flashing a black mark on his forearm—the sign of a permanent loyalty oath. Piris had never thought to see one. Such a binding was often seen as unnecessary or even harmful among most Fae because it required a death price. In this case, without asking, Piris was certain it meant Darin was not free to disobey his king in any way without his life being forfeit. Before she or Jarok could respond to all he'd revealed, he pivoted on the balls of his feet and moved swiftly across the space to stand close to Cylian's chair and the two other Fae in the room talking about lighter things to pass the time.

"I-I could've—" She couldn't finish through the lump in her throat she desperately tried to shove down. She understood now, despite the hiding and secrets, what her life could have been if born elsewhere, with different parents... different royals.

"You could have, but you will never," Jarok bit out, his anger directed somewhere else, for better or worse.

After the head housekeeper, Gollan, arrived with a mass of serving trays for tea service and fussed over Piris's return, her mother glided into the room. Her father stomped behind, but in his normal heavy-footed gate and not his angry stomp, so it appeared her mother had calmed him down.

"Apologies, again, to all our guests," she said, her curtsy deep and solemn. She meant it. Piris's mother was all civility and niceties, but unlike other ladies she'd known in her life, Piris could say, without doubt, her mother did not act the part. She was the part. Sometimes she wondered if it disappointed her, having a daughter who was more fighter than lady, but she never gave such a doubt voice.

Lady Volesion gestured toward her husband, who mumbled as he bowed. His voice cleared when he turned to Jarok and Darin to offer more words. "To you, my prince, and Lord Marco, I am sorry. My words were rash, unthinking, and not reflective of my true nature. I ask your forgiveness."

Jarok, surprisingly, looked at Darin first, who with a quick nod and flick of his wrist, acted as if he hadn't cared at all about her father's words. After seeing his reply, Jarok also turned to her father and rose, offering a small bow. From a prince, especially one he'd insulted, it was more than her father deserved, given royal protocol. Jarok eyed Piris a second before offering a hand to her mother and bowing over her own, laying a soft, chaste kiss there. "Lady Volesion, Lord Volesion, no more need for apologies. What has passed is past, and we must all now deal with what is ahead of us. Thank you for your time and hospitality."

By the gods, her mother blushed when Jarok turned on that princely charm of his. Piris couldn't help herself and snorted out a laugh. Both her mother and father stared daggers at her, her mother because of its rudeness and her father for upsetting her mother more than she was already.

"You're too kind, Prince Jarok. Do sit, please." They all gave Jarok the seat at the head of the circle, if there was such a thing. Her father sat beside him, her mother beside her husband, and the rest fell in line, with Piris taking the space between her mother and Cylian. Gem lounged by Jarok, and once again Darin chose not to sit, standing along the short wall to Jarok's back so the door and the window were in view. Smart. Same could be said of Jarok, even if most would think he took his seat because it was his due. Both could be true.

Once everyone settled, her mother started right in, always ready to repair a breach or handle any issue head-on. "As you are now aware, we have held a secret in our family for many years. Our reaction may have been questionable, but I do not believe anyone can doubt our reasoning behind it. We did both because we love our daughter and wish to protect her."

Tears threatened, and Piris flexed her hands, biting her nails into her palms to counter her emotions. She'd worried over telling her parents for good reason: because of their love for one another.

"Completely understandable, Lady Volesion," Cylian said, a serious expression clouding his face. "However, I can say, without doubt, everyone here and at the Winterlands Palace is determined to keep the secret as well."

"Secrets keep you safe," her father said. His tried-and-true saying wasn't wrong. "The more people know, the harder they are to keep. We have more than ample reason to fear a slip." He'd been angry at Piris for weeks after she'd exposed her magic to Strella, but his love for the sweet, young motherless girl, so lonely yet still so kind and bright, eased his way. She had no idea what might make him feel better about this situation.

"My family has guaranteed her secret and offered their protection." Jarok paused and said, "Princess Strella is now family, and considers Piris a sister. The Boraus of the Winterlands will do much to protect both now."

"Even royals can't always keep secrets, especially when there are so many outside their purview who now know." Lord Volesion stared at Gem, Cylian, and Darin in turn. It was not completely wrong to think once more people knew her powers, it was more likely to get out, especially as the more people included an Aurora warrior, a lord of the Autumnlands, and a famed Springlands assassin.

"I'm sworn to the Boraus. No words will come from me," Gem grumbled, irked by his implication. "Besides, I like Piris, even if she's a lady. She's a strong fighter with grit."

Piris warmed at the compliment.

Cylian spoke next. "We've had dealings in the past, Lord Volesion, and I can say, without hesitation, my father, Lord-Protector Padalist, would never wish to break those financial bonds, so I will act accordingly. I, as a friend to Piris and the Borau family, also have a personal stake in keeping this secret as well. I will say nothing, to anyone in any court." Believable, and Piris suspected the lord kept much from his more-than-questionable father, as did Lord Volesion from his accepting grunt.

Darin stared, though his eyes were blocked by the shadow of his hood, only knowable because of the physical scrape across the room. He weighed his words and simply told her father what he'd revealed to her moments before. "I'm a shadow-wielder."

Shock flitted across the faces of both Piris's parents, but a hardness her father's face had carried melted slightly at the news. Someone like Marco, with his own experiences, would keep the secret as best he could.

"There are no guarantees," Piris whispered into the silence, "but these people, and the royals? I am willing to stake my life on their word in this."

"You may very well be doing just that, daughter," her father said. The words weren't harsh. They felt heavy, sounded weary. Like a man who'd fought a long, hard battle and was watching the tide turn against him.

She went to her parents. Kneeled at their feet. Took a hand of each in hers and spoke in a soft voice. "I am your daughter, always will be. I understand why you protected me as much as you could. Now, however, things are changed, and I am more capable of protecting myself. Making my own decisions." She loved her parents, always would. Understood completely why they'd taken the course they had taken in regard to her. It was time for her to carry the burden for a while—be her own keeper of secrets and not force her parents into a life they wouldn't have if she wasn't who she was.

Her mother put a delicate hand to pink lips, the tremble slight but there, before cupping her daughter's cheek with the same hand. "Oh, Piris. What have we done to you?"

"You taught me to survive, to fight, to love. I couldn't ask for more, Mother." Tears came then, and she didn't stop them. Didn't want to because they matched the ones on her mother's cheeks and shimmering in her father's eyes.

"A warrior to the core," her father said, the words strong and true, the shine of pride in his eyes all for her.

"A warrior, yes," she answered. "Like the others here. Like you."

"Still part lady, yes?" her mother asked with a little laugh.

Piris was serious, solemn, as she said, "I will always carry what you taught me, Mother. Always."

The Volesions stared at each other, devastated yet happy, freed and scared all at once.

Jarok cleared his throat, and Piris wiped her tears before standing. He stepped up and offered a hand to her father, who stood to take it.

"I will do all I can to keep your daughter—her magic—safe."

The men shook hands as her mother swiveled her head, flitting her gaze between her daughter and the young prince before a broad smile flashed on her face. Piris didn't like the smile, the idea there, but too much had happened in a short time, so she decided to ignore it. It wouldn't hurt to let her mother have wild, impossible dreams for a short time.

Chapter Fourteen
Jarok

The rest of the afternoon and evening passed uneventfully for Jarok, which he appreciated. The attack, followed by all those emotional hits, had taken a toll on his patience, which he prized. Not surprising, when he considered how often Piris and issues swirling around her put him at the end of his rope. By the gods, she was infuriating and fiery and fierce and... lovely. Worthy. Honorable. A true warrior tested and not bested, by him or anyone else, time and time again.

He was lying in his tastefully appointed guest room, with its dark-cherrywood furniture and gold accents, staring up at the large canopy structure covering the massive bed, thinking these thoughts. Jarok had never brooded before. That was his brother's domain. Now he found himself doing it more and more. Once again, because of Piris.

A small knock sounded at the door, and Jarok jumped from his bed in a flash as someone slipped right into his room. His hand was going toward his falchion on the nightstand, placed within close reach for any possibility, when the dim light revealed a nightgown-clad Piris.

His hand pulled back from his blade, hesitant and slow, not because he was wary of her but because he was mesmerized by what he saw. He'd seen her in day dresses, ballgowns, traveling dresses, and fighting leathers. She looked good in all. At the moment, she wore a nightdress of shimmering bronze, the same color of her eyes. The material was gauzy, almost translucent when she passed direct light. His fist clenched at the idea someone else may have seen her in the thing out in the hallway. He shook the thought free, literally, taking his eyes from her to get a grip on himself.

He scanned the floor, another lush rug cushioning his bare feet. Piris's feet, which he'd never seen, edged into his vision. They were perfectly formed, slim and long, her toes flexing into the rug as he stared. He'd never thought of feet before, of the delicacy and intimacy of seeing them, and now it crowded his mind. Until she broke the silence.

"I thought you might want some company." Her tone came off as coy, though an edge hovered there, a question she needed to have answered even if she didn't directly ask. Damn it, he was more than willing to give her the answers she wanted to hear. Jarok thought he could be all her answers, but pushed the idea away as soon as he had it.

He continued staring at her perfectly formed toes, knowing once he looked into her face, he'd be lost. "Your company is most welcome."

She stepped closer, her gown shimmering as it moved around her strong, shapely legs, and he took the chance. His face met hers, and he gasped at the hunger he found in her broad-cheeked, marble-pale face. Piris's eyes blazed in contrast, and Jarok was dumbstruck for a moment, his heart and head stopped for long seconds as he took her in.

Piris had no hesitation. She stepped closer, her chest brushing against his because of their similar heights. Jarok stuttered out a breath, but something drove him on, pushed him to action. His hand, almost of its own accord, came up and hooked around the small of her back to pull her even closer. The entire front of her body fell, heated and flush, against his. A smug smile stretched across his lips when her breath hitched at the sudden contact.

His other hand came up and twisted a piece of her free-flowing auburn hair around a forefinger. Staring there instead of directly at her, he muttered, "Is there something else you wanted, my lady?"

She squirmed then, her legs shifting so hard, he heard the slide of smooth, naked skin on skin and his blood pumped harder and fiercer. When she didn't answer after several stretched seconds, his deep voice broke their silence. "Tell me what you want," he demanded. He needed the words, needed to know she burned for him as he did her.

He met her eye to eye then, urging her on, and saw the moment her delicious, combative nature clicked back into place. "I want you, you arrogant—"

Jarok didn't let her finish. He gripped her hard by the waist and tossed her to the bed with force, her gasp echoing through the room as she bounced on the soft mattress. Piris caught her breath, but Jarok gave her no time to scramble about or take a dominant position. He was on top of her, crawling up her body and pulling the barely there nightdress up her form as he did. Every so often he'd pause to give her a swift, sucking kiss: on her calf, the back of her knee, high on her thigh...

Piris struggled at first, but the more kisses he placed, the more she moved in need rather than defense. Her breath quickened as her body writhed after each hard suck of his lips.

Jarok nipped at her lower abdomen, and she froze. He looked up her body, past the peaks of her breasts, and at her expression now hazy with lust. He paused, taking a moment to nuzzle, fascinated by the small swell of her belly above the triangle of auburn hair between her legs. Her abs were flexed, but a bit of softness remained, and he was drawn to the contrast. Might even love it, though he dismissed the word as soon as it flitted across his mind. To drive it further from his thoughts, he focused on moving his tongue solidly upward and over her clenching stomach, falling to her side as he slid the sheer fabric to her neck, revealing her breasts.

He'd felt them, tasted them, and seen the outline of them in the dark woods the one time they'd had together. Now, in the low light of this room, he looked his fill. Jarok moved his nose across her dark nipples, teasing her as he teased himself with deep inhales of her cold steel scent. She sucked in a breath, waiting, but he continued to explore and nudge with his nose. Not giving her exactly what she wanted. Not yet.

"Jarok," she said, a note of urgency, maybe exasperation, sounding there, and he immediately rose up and away from her body, taking her wrists in his hands and pushing himself up to loom over her.

"That's not how this goes, Piris. You want me, you take me."

She swallowed hard before her head bobbed in agreement. After, her body relaxed. She gave herself over to him. Gods, it made his cock even harder seeing her submit in this way.

"Stay right here," he growled, the lust roaring in him making his voice gruffer.

He moved from the bed to his weapon belt on the bedside, grabbing the bit of woven cord he always kept on him.

He climbed back on the bed, on his knees, and commanded her, "Up." She complied, heat in her gaze as she looked from him to the cord he clutched in his hand. When she was on her knees, her nightdress tumbled back down her body. He couldn't have that, so he ripped it off and flung it to the floor as soon as it cleared her head and arms. A soft growl left his lips as he stared at her naked form, ripe and ready for him to do what he wished.

"Arms up," he said, coming flush with her as he studied the canopy structure above them. It wasn't as secure as embedded hooks or metal rings, but it would do if he was careful in the way he tied her.

Without a word, he started working, weaving the cord so it pinned her, stretched up, and encircled her arms from wrists to elbows, pulling her arms and torso tight so she had little room to move. Delicious and safe, given where he tied her.

Still, he asked, "How do you feel?" He tugged the cord, and she shuddered at the movement.

"I'm fine."

"Fine?" he asked, an eyebrow quirked in question. He needed more from her.

"I don't hurt. I-I like it."

His heart pounded at the words, and he felt his cock weep in his sleep pants. Jarok managed to grumble out a "good" as he double-checked the binds, the wrapping, and the point where the cord was secured to the canopy.

"If you feel numbness in your hands or pain in your shoulders, tell me. Immediately."

Piris nodded, her eyes hooded, her sweet scent filling every space around him, and he knew, without checking, she dripped for him. Gods, he wanted to take her hard and fast. A part of him needed to. But she'd come to him, and he wanted her to come to him again. Needed it more than he needed to rut into her.

Instead of falling on her, he climbed off the bed, leaving her alone there in the middle, pulled tight for his gaze. He devoured her with his eyes as he slowly undressed, first removing the large nightshirt he wore, revealing the golden-brown expanse of his skin, his smooth, mostly hairless chest and abdomen glowing even richer in the low light of the room. He unlaced his sleep pants, letting them fall loose on his hips, then slowly bent down as they moved off his body, not exposing his nakedness until he stood again. By the time he finished his little show, Piris panted and strained against her bonds. Jarok didn't go to her then. He stood before her, keeping his distance. Then he took his cock in his hand and stroked it up and down at a languid pace. Waiting.

She twisted where she could, and he worried for her restraints, but she gave him what he wanted after a long minute. "Please," she whispered, the sound like sweet sugar to his ears.

He crawled on the bed, came chest to chest with her, and took her mouth in a harsh, hungry kiss. They pulsed against one another, devouring. Jarok pulled back enough to watch his hand move down her body, take her pussy in a firm grip, and test how ready she was. He brought his wet finger up between them and stared at her as he sucked her sweet juices off his finger.

"So sweet. So slick. All for me."

She didn't reply, so he dipped his hand down again and slowly circled her clit. He gave solid pressure until her body started to shake, then he backed off to a teasing, barely there touch. She whined but he didn't say anything, focused solely on her pussy at his fingertips. When her breathing evened out more, he started the cycle again. Then again. Three times bringing her to the edge of release before he pulled back.

"All for me?" he asked after her shaking stopped, a solid sheen of sweat glistening on her pale skin.

She nodded, but he again needed more. "Words," he growled, moving to cup her between her legs, holding her in a possessive grip. Even if it was only for one night. Even if he never had her like this again, he wanted to have this one shining moment in his memory.

"Yes. Gods save me. Yes, Jarok. All for you. Only for you."

Piris sagged at the confession, her eyes fluttering as if she couldn't take more. He hadn't even started, but she needed her release. He'd give it to her. Give her everything she wanted. Gods save him too. He'd give her anything she wanted.

Moving around her body, he positioned himself behind her, taking her hips in his hands to tilt her ass back. Jarok took her weight in his hands, both to ease the ache he knew she had to feel in her arms and position her to take all of him.

"Ready?" he asked, waiting for her.

She took a beat but moaned out a hoarse "yes." At the sound, he notched his cock to her entrance and pushed forward, slow and steady, despite the rigid gasp they both gave at the feel of him filling her. He moved inch by inch until they sat flush together, ass to groin. He felt somehow whole but pushed the feeling aside, lust overriding all else. Jarok pulled back, then slammed forward, hitting her limit with a hard bump. Piris cried out in pleasure, which spurred him on, so much so he was pounding into her in seconds, his original intention to be slow and teasing lost in his own frenzied need and the sound of her moans. The clench of her wet, sweet core made him mindless. Feral even. Until her body caused him to return to his mind. Focus on her.

He felt her tremble around him and he slowed, almost stopped. Gave her another command. "Not yet. Not until I say you can." He wanted her to come around his cock, but not until he was ready to come as well. Good thing he wasn't too far off.

He switched the angle of her hips and his pace so he felt the snug push and pull of her on him, driving him closer and closer. With her body sweat-slicked and shuddering in his hands, she strived to give him what he demanded, pushing herself to the brink to hold back when all signs said all she wanted was to let go.

He gritted his teeth, feeling the tingle at the base of his spine. A strangled cry ripped out of him. "Now, Piris."

She gave a hard shout as she spiraled, her pussy convulsing hard. He let go as well, driving a few final stuttering pumps into her as he came.

They both panted for several seconds, the bliss overwhelming everything else, but Jarok managed to come to his senses soon enough. He ached when he pulled out of her, but ignored the reaction and went to work untying her. When she was finally free, she sagged in his arms. Piris tried to right herself, but he held her tight to him as he stroked her arms up and down. When he finally let her move back, he did so to inspect at her arms, her wrists, make sure there was no damage or bruising.

"I'm fine," she said, easing herself from his grip.

He gave her his signature insolent look and said, "Fine tells me nothing."

"Fine. I mean, okay. My arms don't feel hurt in any way. Happy?"

"Very," he said with a sly smile as he hooked his arms around her again and brought them to lay side by side on the bed.

"I should return to my room," Piris said, attempting to move away from him, but he snagged her back.

"No. You should stay here." Jarok expected her to argue, but she moved closer, even if she did turn away from him so her back was to his chest. "Covers?" he asked and she nodded, not saying a word. He gave her that, even if he couldn't give her physical space for some reason. He'd never actually slept next to a woman, so it would be a novel experience.

As he drifted off to sleep, his naked body cupping hers from behind, he felt content. Happy, just as she'd asked.

He slept well, soundly, until icy dawn creeped into his room. When he woke, his bed was cold and empty. Jarok lay there, feeling the same.

Chapter Fifteen
Piris

The cold blue of dawn hadn't kissed the sky when Piris woke, not with a start but with a gentle ease, as if she had dived into sleep and allowed herself to float back to the top of consciousness. She took a moment to connect with her body, feel the scratch of her eyes as she blinked awake and the beautiful ache of her arms and core as she shifted, right into a hard, hot chest positioned snugly against her back. Her eyes flew open, memories of the night before crashing around her. The memories weren't horrible. Quite the opposite. A thrill raced down her back recalling what Jarok had done to her, the expert bite of the ropes, the taste of his lips, and the hard thrust of his cock into her—luscious and hard and much needed after the day she'd had.

When she'd shown up at Jarok's room, she had been unsure of her reception. Uncertain he'd wish to continue what they'd started at the inn and culminated in the forest. In the dull light of home, she did not know if he'd still want her as she wanted him, but she screwed in her courage and went to his guest room… because he'd stepped beside her during the argument with her father. He'd protected her but allowed her to battle when the Benders had attacked. Jarok had helped her at every turn but had not coddled.

And, maybe to her own surprise, she found she also needed to give up some of her control to him when they hit the bed. The twist of the rope and the gruff command in his voice made her melt as much as the touch and taste of him did. Even the memory as she lay in his bed made her insides itch and her thighs twist together.

He gave her what she needed, in and out of the bedroom—sometimes what she didn't know she needed, though if she were honest with herself, she'd Is wished for something a little harder, a little more aggressive, in her sex. She'd thought it was an odd quirk with her and never asked for more than quick release from her partners. She couldn't talk to anyone about the desires she'd buried until Jarok had unlocked them. She had two women she trusted in her life: her mother and Strella. Fae were open with their sexuality, but it didn't mean she wanted to share details with her mother, who returned the sentiment. Until recently, Strella wasn't experienced enough to give advice or guidance about desire. Piris thought now she'd count Gem among her trusted women, her friends and family, but again, there were issues. Jarok was her cousin, and Gem had come into Piris's life too recently to have such discussions before they'd begun their tryst.

Tryst it was, surely, because there could not be more. While her magical secret was open to some now, she still needed to keep it under wraps from the wider Fae world. There was still prejudice, fear. She wouldn't put the worry on her parents, who were already roiling at the handful of new people aware of her mimic powers.

Piris had willfully stepped out of her home, her hiding place, for Strella. She'd revealed who she was to save her best friend's love and help her friends in battle. It was reckless but necessary and something she'd never take back. That didn't mean she had to keep doing it, keep exposing who and what she was to more and more people. She wouldn't risk it. Couldn't. Not only for herself but for her family. It meant coming back here, to Volesion Peak, after their mission ended. She'd continue to pretend she was a null. Hide her training... spar only with her father. She'd occasionally visit Strella when she could, but she needed to stay grounded in her small, quiet life, while Jarok would go back to the palace, back to court politics and balls and battles great and small for the Winterlands. Back to his pick of ladies, none of whom he'd argue with or for constantly. None of whom would have secrets he'd have to constantly protect.

Cold had seeped out from her, pushing her away from Jarok's heavy, gilded arms. Shaking them off as gently as possible so as not to wake the prince, she'd put her fighter training to good use, moving on silent feet from the bed and out the door without disturbing him. After she'd closed the door, she took a moment to bend her head to it, feel the cool wood on her forehead, and breathe deep, in and out, to calm the absurd pounding of her heart in her chest. The beat became more aggressive the farther she moved away from the sleeping prince. As she breathed, forced air in and out to calm the rush of blood in her veins, she told herself there was no reason for it. None at all.

She was lying in her bed trying not to think too much about the night before when her father sent word for her to meet him in their training room. She'd stripped off her clothes, noting how her muscles held a slight soreness but her arms showed no redness or bruising, and pulled on a fresh set of leathers out of the back of her vast closet. She and her mother had had a grand time picking her dresses, even if she was rarely out of their house. While her mother directed her daily dress choices, she and her father designed her leathers. She thought of the care he took to protect her in all ways as she slipped on the fur-lined, dark-maroon set of leather shirt, pants, and matching boots. The fur was for warmth and comfort, as a thin bronze layer lined the inside of the entire outfit, a design from a talented artificer her father had met somewhere in the Summerlands years ago. She'd not packed the two sets he'd had made for her because she'd not imagined what would happen at the palace. Now, as she slipped them on, she knew she'd get good use of them in the coming days.

When she opened the wide double doors of the training room, familiar scents hit her nose: the odd combination of oil for cleaning weapons and wood, the icy scent of her father, and the faint tinge of sweat that she knew would become far more prominent the longer they trained.

Lord Brettly stood in the weapons corner, the black walls the same color as the outside of their home, making him almost glow in relief. He wore leathers the color of the clay and sand banks of the Great River, only yards away from where they stood. His brown head was bent over a thick staff as he said, "Let us spar."

Piris eyed him, wondering why he was being so short and quiet, but she thought he had reason. Her father was warm with her mother and her, but he was also a warrior and merchant who could be cold, even ruthless, when necessary. Here and now, it felt like armor for him.

She grabbed a similar staff from the rack at his left and followed him to the massive white ring painted on the gleaming pine floor. She could remember the first time she passed the line, an eager young girl just coming into her powers. This was where her father had taught her everything she knew. It was where they not only sparred but talked, about so much. The ring had rules she knew by heart. All matches ended when one opponent was down or stepped out of the circle. No blood was to be intentionally drawn. No permanent damage done. No anger or hurts taken outside the ring. Maybe most important-ly, anything said inside the ring remained there, between father and daughter. Each had used this rule often, for advice and confession.

Her father said nothing as he squared off with her, his knuckles white where he grasped the wrapped middle of the staff. The ring was there—was sacred—so she continued to return his silence, knowing he'd break it if and when he needed.

He stepped fast and hard, whacking out with a strike aimed at her head. Anyone watching might judge him for it because he held nothing back, but long ago he'd stopped holding back with his daughter. She appreciated the acknowledgment of her abilities. He missed anyway, her back bending sharply to pull her head out of the path of the whooshing staff.

She jabbed out, hard, fast, and low, aiming for his left knee with the tip of her own staff, but he sidestepped her, bringing his weapon diagonal to his chest. Piris righted herself, twirling her staff a few feet in front of her as she shuffled left, circling. She took the offensive, jabbing again with a swift strike to her father's gut. It didn't connect. He managed to back away in time and struck out himself, twisting Piris's staff down and away with his.

Lord Volesion brought his back up, his jab landing, though Piris stepped out of the brunt of the blow. It connected at the edge of her left shoulder, a sting of flesh and jar of bone echoing in its wake. She grunted but kept the staff tight in her grip.

"You show too much," her father said with a shake of his head.

"What?" The statement was distracting enough, her father almost got another hit in to her right hip, but she shuffled forward and blocked the blow with her staff.

"You. Show. Too. Much." He enunciated every word as if she didn't understand, and she rolled her eyes at him.

"The question was meant to get you to elaborate, Father," she said, droll and flat, as she swept her staff forward and connected with his shin. He didn't grunt, but the reverberation on her hand told her the impact must have hurt. Somewhat.

"You tell too much. When you fight and in life." Another whack from him missed because she stopped her intended progress with his words.

Shaking herself free from the impact of them, she moved forward in a flash, lashing out so they hit together, one, two, three, four times, a balance of hit and block pushing her father back from the middle and toward the edge of the ring.

"Sometimes tells are necessary."

"At times. Other times, perhaps not." Her father's breathing remained steady, even, as she blew out frustrated breaths at him.

"Say it," she gritted out as he held his ground, and they hit, over and over, her blows deflected each time by his staff. "Say it. Whatever it is, just say it."

Her father pivoted, pushing into her staff hard with his, and met her inches from her face. He deflated, lost his strong stance against her. The real pain in his bronze eyes as he looked deep into her matching pair made her stop cold, not press the advantage. "You are in danger."

Her arms slacked as his did, yet they stood with staffs still up and heads still close. "You taught me how to deal with danger. Right here in this ring. I can handle danger, Father."

He pulled away, hung his head, and whispered, "I do not know if I can. Deal with you in danger, that is."

"But you know—" She began to explain, to rationalize, but he stopped her with a quick pull forward, not in attack but to hug her close. Their staffs clattered to the ground as he held her tight, fierce, in their ring.

"You may one day know what it is to fear for a child, but not now. There is no reasoning. I know what you're capable of, Piris. Do not doubt this. Yet, I worry. Always will. I also know I will hurt you if I try to stop you from being who you should be. A hard truth I have to come to terms with on my own."

"Okay," she said, her voice soft and sweet, like she'd been with her father as a small child.

He continued to hug her and whispered, "Love does this, sometimes. You fear for no reason other than because you love."

She matched the hard hug of his arms. The love she knew he had for her, had always known he had for her, created a warm blanket that could, on occasion, feel too stifling.

They pulled back when a loud knock on the door sounded. Her father left the ring, and she felt bereft and freed at once, even wiping a stray tear from her eyes as Lord Volesion discussed some message his head secretary had received. Her spine straightened when she heard the distant voice of Prince Jarok in the hall, and she scurried to put away her staff and exit out a side door to a different hallway. She did not need to see him after the emotions she'd just expended on the conversation with her father.

After scurrying away, for reasons she did not wish to think on too long, she managed to avoid Jarok for the remainder of the day. Thankfully she could ignore the impulse to stay away from the prince for the sake of things like family and duty. Her mother wanted her own time with her daughter, so they had lunch alone in a private family sitting room. They chatted for a few hours and poured over designs for a few traveling dresses Lady Mimi wished to order soon. She tried to convince her mother she didn't need anything new, especially not traveling dresses, but her mother's soft smile and calm insistence defeated her arguments with ease.

In her room, she found a letter from Strella, so she took time reading and responding. She chatted with the butler, whom she'd not seen for months, when she sought him out to send her letter along to her friend.

She may have avoided dinner with everyone, claiming she needed rest and requesting a small plate be brought to her room. Otherwise, she thought, it was others who had kept her from the prince. Not her. Not really.

Long after full night fell, when she was preparing for sleep, she heard the quiet creak of her door opening and found Jarok slipping into her room, without a word. He closed the door and leaned back against it, watching her in silence as she sat staring back at him from her vanity, brush gripped tight in her hand.

"Piris," he said with a nod, his insolent smile in place as he crossed his arms over his broad chest. He wore simple brown leather pants with a white wool shirt tucked in the front. He had left the button at the collar open, a small glimpse of dark-gold skin peeking out. Her eyes lingered there as she remembered how his skin felt against her own.

"Prince," she finally said, though there wasn't any harsh heat to it as there might have been before. She stayed somewhat distracted by the lines of his arms, the tilt of his head, and the casual flip of his black hair. She didn't look into his eyes. She knew beyond doubt they'd somehow snare her then and there.

He lifted a hand, as if casually inspecting his nails, and said in the most off-handed manner possible, "I woke to an empty bed."

Piris didn't know how to respond. What did he expect from her? She gave a shrug and twisted back to her mirror. In a flash, Jarok was in the background, staring straight into her eyes as his warm, heavy hands landed on her shoulders. "Don't," he said.

"Don't what?" she snapped back, giving him a sneer in the mirror. "What exactly did you expect, Jarok? We had sex. That's all. I don't need to sleep in your bed to let you fuck me."

He slowly raised one of those dark eyebrows, the move questioning and flippant and infuriating all at once. "I see," he drawled, moving his hands down a fraction so he gripped the upper flesh of her arms. "This is all we are to each other," he said, sliding one hand down her chest to tweak an obviously hard nipple through her near-sheer nightgown. She gasped, closed her eyes in sweet sensation, and forced herself to nod in answer. Nod was all she could do. Her voice would betray her.

"Turn around, Piris," he said, the deep command making her twist on her small stool before she could think better of it. He gripped her chin in a firm hold, not painful but decided, to tilt her head up, make her meet his eyes. His roved over her face, looking for something, and when he didn't find it, his shoulders slumped a fraction, barely enough to notice. She noticed a great deal about the prince these days.

Her chest tightened at the sight but she squared her own shoulders and stayed firm.

"We can have this, only our bodies together, if you want," he said, inching closer to her face as he said the words, "but I need to hear you say it. Every time."

She'd agreed once, more than agreed. Possibly had agreed the first time they'd had sex, back in the forest. Piris didn't know why he needed to hear it again, much less every time, but she could give that to him to get what she wanted. Only the sex, she reassured herself, steeled herself. She said with a clear, true voice, "I want you. I want this."

His eyes closed and he breathed deep, like she did when she needed to ground her mind, before they popped back open, hard brown chips of stone trained right on her. "Up," he said, tugging on her chin to emphasize his demand.

When she rose, he pulled away, leaving her face colder. Jarok looked around the room, searching for something until he found, hanging on a hook by her closet door, a dressing robe. He strolled to it, his hips rolling with each step, mesmerizing as she stared at his firm ass in those tight leather pants. The tie of the robe made a soft slashing sound as he pulled it free, twisting it in his hands a moment before he turned back to her.

Jarok said nothing, only flicked his head to his right, toward the crackling fire in her hearth with the lush woven rug in front of it. She moved to it, her toes digging into the thick fabric as she waited for him to join her.

He did not make her wait long, and as soon as he was in front of her, he tied the robe sash loosely around her wrists, testing the twist and pull of it. "Does this feel okay?" he asked.

"Yes," she answered. A second later her arms were up and over, looped around the back of his neck. She was close to him in height, so the move brought them face-to-face, almost eye to eye, as he took her mouth in a hard, nipping kiss. She let him in, matching his fierce need with hers, stoking the fire between them as he eased them down to their knees on the carpet while maintaining their connection.

"To your back," he demanded after pulling back from her mouth. He followed her to the carpet, his weight falling onto her, pinning her down as his hips grinded into her own. Her gasp was lost down his mouth as he took hers again, thrusting his tongue in time with his hips, his hands coming up to frame and hold her face.

After several hungry minutes, one of his hands moved down between them, pulling his cock free and managing to shove up her nightgown past her hips. It took seconds to find her dripping core. He wasted no time and pulled back just enough to thrust hard and deep into her.

By the gods, he filled her so good. She cried out. He pushed up on his elbows, his hands at her head again, and ground deep inside her, moving back and forth in small motions until she sucked in a harsh breath when he hit her in some delicious spot deep inside. Grinning down at her, he pulled full back and thrust deep and hard again, right over the spot he'd found. She could have sworn the roof blew away, because she saw stars.

Her eyes rolled back as he continued his thrusts, over and over again, until she was a dripping, babbling mess of need and want, unable to do anything but hold tight to the short hair at the back of his head and moan with each hit. When her eyes refocused, she blinked and saw Jarok staring with intensity down at her, his gaze roaming her face. She felt naked, exposed, even though she was still fully dressed. She turned her head away from him, into his hand, and he let her, though the grunt he gave at the move was less pleasure and more disappointment.

Her hips met his, demanding as he gave. He pumped harder, im-possibly hard, into her, nailing her into the lush rug so it began to give a hard bite to her backside she knew she'd feel in the morning. Gods, she'd feel him in the morning, she was certain, but she couldn't think of that yet. She could only reach high for the pleasure he offered... chase it as he pounded into her.

A frustrated sound came from his throat, and he buried his face in her exposed neck. One hand snaked down to move between them, to tweak her clit hard like he'd tweaked her nipple earlier. He ground deep, hitting her spot as he did so, and she exploded. Her vision faded at the bliss of it all, at the taste and smell and feel of everything, and she was rational enough for a second to be thankful she was turned away from him, sinking her teeth into the flesh of his warm hand.

Jarok dropped his head into the crook of her neck, pumping fast and hard without the same finesse or rhythm. Then he bit down on her neck, hard enough to leave a mark, as he stuttered in his thrusts, coming to a stop deep within her.

They stayed like that, connected but not looking at one another. Piris savored the warmth of him, the touch of his leathers on her bare legs, and the weight he left on her because he knew she could take it. Too quickly, he unlooped her arms from around his neck and sat back, stuffing himself back in his pants.

She tried to straighten her nightgown too, but it was difficult with her hands still tied. Jarok stopped her progress. Gentle hands moved the fabric down her legs to cover her before he removed the knot in her sash, freeing her.

Pushing herself up, her breath still hard and heavy, she glimpsed some dark thing flash in Jarok's eyes before he shuttered them, moving to his feet in one swift, deft motion. He offered his hand to her, the prince giving a lady help up, and Piris felt a sting of longing then. But he only pulled her up, righting her with a grip on her shoulders when she stumbled on her feet.

"Well..." she said, unsure what to say or do as she wondered when she'd be alone so she could clean the wetness she felt sliding between her legs.

Jarok's jaw tightened, a muscle jumping there as it did. He gave a swift, hard nod to her, saying nothing before turning toward the door and stalking out. The prince didn't look back as he left her there alone, as she'd said she wanted, as she'd thought she wanted, so he didn't see the small step she took after him before she reined in the impulse.

Chapter Sixteen
Jarok

Jarok woke early. In truth, he'd barely slept after leaving Piris in her room. He'd gone to talk to her. Maybe bicker. To taste her again if she wanted it. To hold her. He'd woken to a cold bed and a day of her avoiding him at every turn. He'd been hurt and angry, even if he'd never actually spent the entire night with a woman in his bed.

When she'd been clear about all she wanted from him, once again, it'd been a hit to the gut, almost bowling him over. He'd breathed deep, contained his hurt, and gave her what she wanted—what he wanted too, except he needed more from her. There was something else hanging on the edge of his mind, an unspoken desire he'd not give her if all she thought him good for was a hard fuck on her floor or in his bed or against a tree in the forest.

Not that he hadn't enjoyed those encounters. He turned them over again and again in his mind, savoring the memory of the feel of her in his arms, against his mouth, warm around his cock. Yet he wanted to reach for more. He wasn't ready to articulate what the more might entail, not after Piris had put him in his place in such a firm manner. He'd stuff it down, swallow it whole, so he could at least taste her on occasion.

Such thoughts, spinning around and around his head, drove him out of his bed, and out of Volesion Peak, as morning hung fresh and new in the sky. He stalked past the manor house, back toward the line of the riverbank. It was a view he'd enjoyed the day before, the muddy waters of the Great River rolling below him, stretching across from the icy cold landscape of the Winterlands to the blooming banks of the Springlands. The other territory rested so close here, he could smell the hyacinth thick on the wind, dampened only by the bite of cold in his nose. An interesting juxtaposition, and something he figured could take his mind off one cold, infuriating woman.

His brooding prospect was thwarted before it could get started. As he got closer to the lookout point, he noticed Lady Volesion seated there, staring out across the waters. He hesitated, wondering if he could back away before she noticed, but she turned toward him, waving a hand for him to join her. He wasn't going to be rude to their host. They'd come with news of her daughter that had rocked her entire life to its foundation, news he just knew she had to still be processing after years of hiding and secrecy. The least he could do was sit by her to look out at the Great River.

He moved closer to her as Lady Mimi rose then dropped into a deep, perfectly executed curtsy. Jarok rushed forward to take her hand and help her rise, even if she looked like she did not need his help in any way. As he took her hand and looked down at the auburn shine of her hair in the morning, he thought again of Piris, the ghost he was trying to run away from, and he gritted his teeth. It was not her mother's fault, so he pulled on his charming mask for her.

"Prince Jarok," she said as she came full to standing. Several inches shorter than her daughter, she looked up into his face. "A pleasure to see you on such a fine morning."

She pulled her full fur coat tight around her shoulders, burrowing deeper in its warmth, and he waved away the most pressing winds with his magic to help make her more comfortable.

"I am well used to the winds on the river, Your Highness."

"Jarok. Please, Lady Volesion. Call me Jarok."

She nodded, a small smile on her lips. "Only if you call me Mimi."

He bowed deep and chuckled. "Not a hardship, Mimi."

She went back to the bench and sat, her back straight and her face wide open to him, and patted the seat beside her. "Share the view with me, Jarok?"

He didn't reply but he did sit, turning from her as she looked out on the waters. Following her gaze, his own got snagged by the churn of the currents, the way the muddy brown of the waters decided two distinctly different banks. The flash of meadows he could make out from there was a view he'd not seen often in his life.

"It is interesting, is it not? The first time I saw it, before I became Lady Volesion, the difference shocked me. I'd never seen the Springlands at that point. Had only experienced the Winterlands."

Jarok had visited the Springlands a few times on palace business, usually with his brother. "Have you been since?"

"Oh, yes. A lovely place, but not home. I sometimes think the cold seeps into us Winterlands Fae, makes us feel uncomfortable, too warm, anywhere else. And, maybe sometimes, a little cranky."

Jarok chuckled, thinking of all the cranky Fae he knew, including the lady's daughter. "Too true."

She turned her gaze on him then, her eyes squinting as if studying his face, looking for something there. "You know," she said, her words stretched and taut. "I've met the king and queen on occasion and always marveled at their story."

"The warrior woman tamed by the true king?" Jarok asked. It was a romantic tale, most definitely, but not an accurate one. In all honesty, his father had never tamed his mother, if such a word should even be used for a person. He loved her as she was, as she always had been. Never wished to change her, though gods knew many wished he had over the centuries, thinking a queen should be more polite and polished. In Jarok's opinion, she served her kingdom and her family well just as she was, but he was biased.

"Oh, no." She shook her head and grabbed his hand, her warm black gloves enveloping his uncovered golden skin. "Not like that, Prince. They loved despite their obstacles, which was my point."

He'd thought they were having casual conversation. "Point?"

"I see how you look at my daughter, Jarok. How she looks at you when you are not aware."

He stiffened. This was not what he wanted to discuss. It was what he'd wished to avoid by coming out here, actually. There he was regardless, having some odd intervention with Piris's mother in the gray morning light.

"Brettly and I were an arranged match, you know. Luckily we loved each other before we married. Maybe at first sight. Not many in the nobility get to experience it."

"Experience what?"

"Love." Her eyes were sharp, hard, not in anger but in insistence. She did very much wish to make some point and he'd allow her to have it, even if he wished she'd stop talking of things he wanted to ignore.

She dropped his hand and moved back to look on the river. "Your mother is who she is, and the king rightly allows her to be who she is." The change in topic made Jarok blink, but he let her go on. "We made the mistake of not doing the same for our daughter."

"Oh, no—"

"No need to console me, Prince. I realize our missteps in hindsight. I see how she's flourished with your little band of fighters, her secret being a little less secret."

She stood and looked at him as he stared up, again wondering about this point she was attempting to make. "Love sometimes makes us do things we can later regret if we forget to let those we love be who they are meant to be. Following love is never a mistake, Jarok, but it can be a stressful journey. Well worth it, but stressful and worrisome."

He couldn't look at her anymore, couldn't think about what she said, so he turned his head away from her. It was rude of him, but she didn't comment on it. "Do not fret too much, Prince. I see the two of you doing great things together." She laughed, loud and true. "And having great fights along the way—with others and each other. It will lead to an interesting and beautiful life, I think."

All he could do was nod to get her to stop and leave him be with his worries and thoughts and hidden desires somehow not hidden from this stranger. She patted his shoulder, then walked away without another word. Jarok sat, looking out at the amazing view, not seeing a single bit of it. He was lost in his head, circling again and again back to the problem of Piris. Or, more aptly, the problem of him and Piris and what they were, what they might be, if he were brave enough to reach for it. If he could somehow convince her to reach for him as well.

Jarok mulled over Lady Volesion's words for a long time, until the gray morning light brightened a touch around midday. He'd stayed outside for a time, but even a son of the Winterlands had his limits in the cold, so he'd continued his thinking in his room in front of a warm fire. Which was where Cylian found him right before he should have left for lunch in the dining room.

He called, "Enter," at a quick succession of knocks at his door, knowing from the pattern and light touch it was his friend from the Autumnlands.

"I have something for you," Cylian said, handing Jarok a scroll closed with his brother's seal. The lord took the leather chair beside his friend's as Jarok opened the letter. They'd been at Volesion Peak two days, not much time to get word back and forth between this end of the Winterlands and the palace. At least for someone whose mother wasn't able to command soaring birds of prey. She'd sent one of her small chicken hawks to the manor house ahead of their traveling party so her son could notify them as soon as they had arrived. He was certain Ghel's message had arrived tied to a similarly swift bird from their mother's aviary.

Jarok unrolled the paper, stretching it taut so he could more easily read his brother's sloppy script. It was not hard to decipher for him, but another Fae might have issues. In his direct, sparse style, Ghel greeted him and reported all was well with security at the palace and that Engad Monti and his Benders were elsewhere in the Winterlands. More of the same, except for news of their father.

"His toes have started freezing," Jarok whispered, not knowing if he was speaking to Cylian or himself.

His friend was there, kneeling by his side, before he registered the movement. "I am so sorry."

They both knew what it meant. When someone whose ice powers had turned inward and started freezing at their extremities, it was often a swift decline. Little they knew of, in any part of Fae, could help.

The scroll had dropped to his lap as he stared into the hot flames. Jarok loved his father, as a king and parent, and couldn't imagine a world without him in it. They would have to, soon, and it already broke his heart to think of what was to come.

"What do the healers say?"

Several famed Fae healers from all four lands were stationed at the palace. They'd been able to stave off progress for a good while. He hoped they could continue such progress. He gave his friend a shrug before answering, "Ghel assures me it is not immediately dire. Still…"

"You want to be there, with him. To help if you can."

"Exactly."

Cylian rose, crossed his arms over his chest, and tilted his head in thought. "You help him by being here. Give him peace of mind his kingdom is being protected. Will remain protected, after…"

"I've done nothing so far."

"Not true. You've fought the Benders on two occasions and bested them. You've come to the location where Monti was last seen."

"Not enough," Jarok growled, standing with a hard shove from his chair so the letter fluttered to the floor in front of the fire. "I need to do more. Find where Engad Monti lurks by the river and end this ridiculous rebellion."

Cylian visibly stiffened at the hard hate in his last words, and Jarok considered why. What he'd said about Monti was true, of course, but he did not want his friend to think such things applied to all rebellions, past or future. Some were necessary, as they both well knew. Some were started for personal gain, as was the case with this Monti leader. Cylian patted his friend's back and Jarok eased, understanding his silent acknowledgment.

"Do we know anything else? Anything at all about the men we track?"

"Well… You and Lord Volesion have been avoiding each other since the unfortunate events on our arrival, but I have spoken with him. He has a contingent of sailors scouring the banks for more information and expects an answer soon."

"Good. Good. Hopefully I can finally do something useful."

Cylian squinted his good golden eye at his friend, studying him in silence for a moment before he said, "Do you really think you do nothing useful?"

Jarok waved a hand. "I didn't mean it like that."

"I think you might have, and I need to assure you, you are wrong in this. You are more than useful. And good. As a family member, a prince, a friend."

Something in him cracked at the words. He knew they were true, somewhere deep down, but it felt like a dip in a hot spring to hear someone say it out loud.

He was about to thank his friend, tell him he also appreciated all he did, for his land and the Fae lands, when pounding feet sounded in the hall outside the door.

Cylian moved like a flash and swung it open in time to let a gasping guard running at full speed barrel into the space.

"The Benders. They're here," he said between hard breaths.

"Looks like we have something to do after all," Jarok growled, grabbing his sword belt from his nightstand and calling for Cylian to follow him. Hopefully they'd already alerted Darin, Gem, and Piris, and they'd have time to plan a defense.

Chapter Seventeen
Piris

Piris had been in her room, trying not to think. She'd taken the morning to indulge in some alone time, to lounge and be a tad lazy. She hadn't been lazy in a long while, not since before she had arrived at Hollythorn Manor with her trunks, ready to fight with and for her best friend. She'd been on the defensive so long, and if she were honest, she needed a break. Throw in her current madness with Jarok and the ever-looming threat of Engad Monti and his Benders, she was tense. The only time she wasn't was when she was tied up by Jarok, but the afterglow of those encounters made her tense in a different way she was unwilling to examine too closely.

It'd been ages since she took breakfast in her rooms. The soft yellow-and-cream palette was a comforting blanket wrapped around her. She remembered the days of discussion with her mother when she'd come of age and been given the opportunity to recreate her own space. The place was familiar, warm, a hug of wallpaper, paint, and carefully curated art. It represented a softer side of herself she let few see, one she wanted kept secret and safe, maybe more than her magic. Possibly because of her magic.

Needing more warm cover than her usual sleepwear gave her, she'd changed into a large wool nightshirt after Jarok had left the night before, and when she'd crawled out of bed to eat her breakfast tray by the fire, she'd slipped on an even thicker velvet robe the color of brilliantly cut emeralds with a sash of golden braids. It was a decadent piece of clothing, a luxury to wrap herself in as she nibbled on toast, drank tea, and read an old favorite book. The spine, so worn and cracked, flopped open to all her favorite parts. It was peace, calm, a moment to be alone. To be. Until it wasn't.

She heard the running steps long before they came to her door, to tell her that her home was under attack. She was gripped with equal parts fear and rage at the sheer gall of the Benders to dare attack her home. Attack her family, blood and not.

She didn't stop. Didn't hesitate. Didn't change from her lush, lazy garments. Piris grabbed a dagger belt hung by her door, the leather rubbed smooth and blades honed sharp though rarely used. They were backups maintained as diligently as the blades she favored, and she thanked herself for keeping up the habit for so many years as she sprinted down the hallway.

Gem was staying in a room a few down from Piris, and the warrior caught up with her in several hard beats, coming up on her right and yelling, "What are we running into?"

They stayed in step, Piris pushing her long legs to meet the challenge of Gem. She had no answers for the Fae, so she shook her head. Gem didn't press further as they skidded around a corner, slowing only a few steps. They'd hit the vast central hallway, its padded, intricately decorated rugs dampening the sounds of their feet as they pushed forward, forward, forward. Toward the sounds of fighting they heard clear and harsh ahead.

Piris spared a glance to her right when she heard her mother giving gentle orders before taking a small handful of guards with her as she disappeared into a darkened alcove, in the direction of the kitchens. She'd do what she could: shield and comfort the servants in the house in the lower-level kitchens, trying to keep them safe in her home. Piris cried out, wordless, fighting through the need to go to her mother, for comfort and to protect. Lady Volesion's head whipped around, worry causing lines to spider out on her forehead where there usually were none. She waved her daughter on before blowing a kiss her way, encouragement and love a gut punch she didn't need in the moment but savored nonetheless.

She and her warrior friend hit the high, black doors of Volesion Peak and followed the gravel path. Piris took a moment to thank the gods Benders were not at the doors. Not yet. She gritted her teeth and vowed they never would be, pushing herself harder, Gem having to match her speed then.

The clang of metal on metal, the neigh of frightened horses, and the men's gasps and shouts led the two down the central lane leading to the house. They found a battle in progress. Her father and his men were gathered in the center, a wall of flesh and steel ready to defend their home at all costs. Jarok and Cylian flanked them, a swirl of snow and branches around them telling her the prince was wielding magic as he wielded his sword. Burning things, cloth and steel and flesh, let her know the Autumnlands lord was also not holding back. A sonic screech, the outside edges of the sound all she heard, almost brought her to a stop.

The sound of her father's magic, his ability to direct sound as a weapon, echoed around as one of the Benders fell over, knocked unconscious by the hit from yards away. It was an imperfect weapon, she knew, because to direct sound at a single enemy and not catch others in the vortex lashing out was hard to do in the heat of battle. When Lord Volesion's screeches hit their mark, they did serious damage to his targets. She'd grown up watching it in training, when he had been trying to teach her how to hone and wield her own magic. For good and bad, this was the first she'd witnessed it used in battle.

An arrow flew by her head, nicking her ear but only skimming her because Gem had been paying attention and had pulled her friend to the side several steps. Piris whipped her head back, scanning the large hedges, a perfect place for archers to hide and hit with secret precision. Given the arrows riddling the gravel lane at the group of men ahead, she figured Jarok was using his wind as defense, which was why so many Benders were fighting with swords and daggers rather than the large bows at their back.

Moments later, a soft cry fell from the hedges, and a body followed. The Bender thumped hard to the gravel, blood pooling from the arrow piercing clean through his neck. The sold black fletches, sharp as the glinting bronze of the tip, told her it wasn't a stray arrow from a Bender. Darin was out there, in the shadows of the hedges, picking off hidden archers as he found them.

Piris had no more time to take in the scene. When she heard a cry from her father, she pushed against the wind, her eyes narrowed. Jarok must have dug through his power to reach them, because the air eased for a moment, letting her and Gem join their ranks. Piris ran right to her father and the two Benders bearing down on him as he tried to defend, only one hand to his sword while the other hung limp at his side. Every other Fae in their ranks was engaged with one or more men, so it was on her to help her father.

Without a sound save the slip of her feet on gravel, she came at the backs of the men fighting her wounded father. She leaped, her green velvet wrapping fluttering like wings around her as she used her running speed to propel her hard and high at the back of the man to her right. Her legs wrapped around his waist from behind, and she felt him stiffen for a second before she reached around him and buried one of her blades into his eye, the one place she knew for certain they were vulnerable from their previous encounters.

He made no sound as he dropped at her feet, and without stopping to consider another death at her hands, she turned so she and her father were facing off with the remaining Bender beside them. He shifted to defense, taking a blow her father landed with a hard clash at his upraised sword. With her teeth gritted so hard they felt they might crack, Piris crouched like an animal ready to pounce, ready to defend her father at any cost.

The Bender, singling her as the easier target, stepped forward with a hard swipe of his large sword. Her daggers, hilts spread wide for such defense, met his blow at an X far above her head. Piris shoved him away, to her right, so he stumbled right into the incoming sword of her father, tipped up high to bury itself in the center of his throat. He sputtered and gasped when Lord Volesion pulled out his blade and let the Fae's body fall to the ground.

They took a moment, one single moment, to send love. She blinked up at her father as he stared down at her and gave her a quick, swift kiss to her forehead before turning to his men and shouting commands. His move away, his proof of trust in her as a fighter, filled her with purpose and determination. She damned the Benders, knowing then they would forever be sorry they'd come to the doors of Volesion Peak.

Fierce energy surged through her and she spun on her heels, scanning the crowd of fighters to find a new target. She didn't need to. A Bender had pushed his way through Jarok's wind when the prince had allowed Piris and Gem entrance. She didn't hesitate, as the Bender did not, moving toward the Fae man on swift feet she then planted firm in the loose gravel.

The man swung at her with a mace of all things, a powerful swing matching the muscle and heft of the Fae in front of her. Luckily, she'd trained fighting against all weapons, her father long ago teaching her that swiftness, flexibility, and knowledge could outperform pure strength among many Fae. She bent back, her upper body going nearly parallel to the ground as the massive ball of spiked metal sailed over the space where her head had been. Twisting her waist in a move she knew would twinge in the morning, she whipped her body around toward the man's torso, shifting so her chest faced the ground and she slashed at the man's belly with both daggers. Whatever defensive spell they had was impressive, but it did little against the force of blows. Neither of her daggers sank into flesh, but the push of them made the man stumble backward, the massively heavy bit of weaponry in his right hand causing him to lose his balance.

Piris took advantage, pushing herself into his middle and tackling him to the ground so she straddled the surprised Fae warrior. Giving him no time to recover, she sliced one dagger hard across his exposed throat, spilling his blood on the ground as it splashed up over her.

She pushed off the man, who'd dropped his mace to cover the death blow at his neck, trying not to think of the multiple deaths she'd caused when only days ago she'd never killed a man. Piris did a quick survey of the fighters. Her father and his guard had formed a strong semicircle of protection across the lane, fighting man-to-man any who tried to push past them.

None did. They were not focused on the house. They congregated here, dropping into the fray as quick as they could, as if focused on a single point in the group.

Jarok, she realized when she saw Cylian singe the upraised hand of one of three men surrounding the prince and trying to wear him down. The prince. They wanted the prince.

Heat bubbled inside her. Seared across her vision. The rebels were fighting for their leader, who fought for himself. They had no care for others, not like she'd seen from the king and queen, from Prince Ghel... care she knew without doubt lay in the heart of her best friend, the new princess. Or what she now knew also rested easy in Prince Jarok—a level of care and concern for the Winterlands and all in it. The responsibility, to his people and land, hung off him like a cloak... like the bloodied robe she wore, a lush and warm thing easily made heavy with blood and fight and need.

Gem came up beside her, nodding with a quick clip of her head, before she ran full tilt toward her cousin, an Aurora battle cry ringing out loud in the air. Piris followed steps behind, pushing through the few in her way, swinging her daggers as she went. Her target, one of the men attempting to join the group surrounding Jarok, swerved before she collided with his side, somehow sensing her running attack at him.

The Bender dropped and rolled, then popped up with surprising speed to face Piris—speed he mimicked as he dodged and ducked Piris's hard blows meant for his throat. His speed did little when she tracked his direction and managed to slip a foot in a spot she knew he would hit, tripping him. He fell hard on his back. His eyes popped open on impact, in time to watch Cylian's long, thin rapier blade slam down into his throat.

The Autumn lord twirled then, sending a small blast of flame into the man who had been about to skewer his back. The attacker screamed, hitting his breast with an open hand as Gem came up from behind and dropped him, blood trailing from his throat to the singed portion on his chest.

"Jarok. Down." The words came from far away, but not. Darin was standing outside the defensive winds Jarok was maintaining around the group.

Piris took a second to look around. No more Benders pushed outside the circle. Seeing Darin outside also made her assume no more Benders skulked in the hedges of the lane. Their attackers were contained, the remainder fighting inside the vortex of air Jarok created.

Darin, his face under his hood cold and clear and stark as a bright spring dawn, stood tall, waiting with three wicked arrows notched in his bow. She felt the whoosh of wind receding, and the arrows flew, taking out three Benders at the same time. A fourth and fifth, fighting the prince, were downed by arrows a moment later, almost too fast for Piris to comprehend for a Fae without speed as his affinity. Then Darin was gone, and she saw the sliver of shadow at the hedge's edge and followed it instinctively with her eyes, seeing the assassin pop back into sight down the line so he could fire one, two, three more arrows in quick succession into the eyes of Benders still engaged with her father's guard.

They dropped, as did the swords and daggers of the rest of the group. All the Benders were now gone. Maybe some had fled when they had seen the direction of the fight, but many bodies of Benders were now piled there by the group panting from exertion around her.

"Piris," Jarok called, stalking toward her. He took her face in large, warm hands speckled with blood.

She stared deep into his eyes, still processing the heat she'd felt when she realized he was their target, the rage she tried to stuff back into a little box in the back of her mind. She couldn't say anything. Wouldn't.

Jarok opened his mouth to speak but was stopped at the loud commands of her father. "Clear the lane as quickly as possible. Prince, Piris, Lords, Gem. Come with me. We have much to discuss."

Jarok was the royal, but all followed after her father. The prince said nothing to Piris, giving her time to fit all those messy emotions back in their tight hiding spots. Still, when he let go of her face, he gripped one of her hands tight, immovably so, and she didn't fight it. She even squeezed back as they fell in line and headed toward the black doors of Volesion Peak.

Chapter Eighteen
Jarok

Jarok's hand spasmed, as if hit with a phantom ache, when he dropped Piris's, but they'd all agreed to regroup in a few minutes. Lord Volesion stalked off toward the kitchen, likely going to find his wife, and Piris trailed behind. It wouldn't be right to keep her from the assurances she might need so soon after an attack on her home.

Cylian stepped up to his side. "Prince—"

"Cylian, please, for the love of the gods. Not now." Jarok had a stray thought about what wards and spells might protect Cylian's clothes from the fire he wielded, as he'd never seen a single burn on the Fae's garments, but he shook it clear. It was an absurd thing to focus on after such devastation.

Necessary devastation, yes, but blood spilled is always a devastating act, for those who bleed and those who spill the blood.

Jarok moved to walk away from his friend, but Darin stepped into his path. The man looked like he had before the battle—clean, crisp, cold and gray. As if the prince hadn't just witnessed him take out several men in as many seconds. Made sense to him, given arrows rarely made their wielder bloody. Despite the logic of it, Jarok felt his anger rise as he remembered the smear of blood on his own hands when he cupped Piris's face. He tamped it down quickly. Unfair to the man who'd just killed for him. For Piris and her family.

"Not so quickly, Prince."

"What is it, lord?" It was petty, perhaps, to add Darin's title when he so often left it off his introductions. Or maybe he himself forgot he was a lord, given all he was forced to do by his king. The sobering realization made Jarok shut off his snark and listen.

Darin didn't show any reaction to the words and kept on with his point. "The Benders targeted you."

"Fine. They targeted me. We knew, or assumed this, already. Why is it so important right now?"

"It might be best if you—"

He cut his diplomatic friend off, this time with a slice of a hand between them. "No. Don't even suggest it. I will not leave, retreat, or hide. It is my royal duty to find Engad Monti and end this before I step foot in the palace once again."

"You're walking right into his hands, you stubborn ass." Gem seethed at his side, the blood sprayed across her giving her words even more bite.

"What if I am? I know it. We know it. We can plan accordingly."

His three companions looked at him. Gem and Cylian looked mutinous but stayed quiet. Their silence was all the confirmation either would give. Darin shrugged and relaxed his stance, all aloof then, as if he couldn't care less. "As you wish, Prince."

Jarok threw his head back and brought a hand up to pinch the bridge of his nose. "For the love of... Look, Darin. I'm Jarok. Just Jarok. Here, now, moving forward. I'm a prince, true. Because of this, the Benders target me, which is true. But in this fight, I'm just Jarok, a Fae trying to protect his family and his land. Damn the royalty of it."

Darin took half a step back, his face stone as his eyes bounced around the small circle they made. He nodded, a third silent acknowledgment that he would not be stopped in this mission. He would be the one to see it through. For his family. For his land. Now, for Piris and her family who'd just been attacked.

"Good, good. Now I'm off to wash blood from my hands and change. I suggest you each do the same."

They'd finished listening to one of Lord Brettly's guards give her report. She'd been on the border of Volesion lands when called to where the Benders breached their defenses and flooded onto the grounds. They'd had no problem with wards and magical barriers. Had surprised the few guards at their point of entry and killed them with little fanfare. She'd fought off more, captured one Bender and brought him to the single holding cell in the manor, and secured the perimeter once again.

"Thank you for the information, Betta," Lord Volesion said, clapping her on her shoulder in a warm gesture. The guard stepped back so she could see all in the room and offered a long, deep bow. Whether it was in recognition of their ranks or in sorrow over what had happened that day, Jarok didn't know, but he did walk to her when she rose and clasped her hand.

"The crown recognizes your steadfast service." He'd just argued his royalty didn't matter, but it wasn't exactly true. It shouldn't matter to the people he knew, those he fought beside. It shouldn't hinder his ability to fight his enemy. To the people of the Winterlands, the name of the Boraus, the invocation of the crown could mean something. It was little. A trinket in words. He still felt the need to say them.

She bowed again, this time with a hand across her chest, before taking hard, clipped steps out of the dark study.

The only one missing was Lady Volesion, who was off helping servants tend to the injured and organizing the funeral rites for the fallen guards. Piris stood by her father, both next to a gleaming, massive cherrywood desk littered with parchment and writing tools and a number of river maps. Jarok stood close to Piris but did not crowd her. He gave her a place beside her father as one of the authorities in the home. The home they'd just defended.

Gem positioned herself beside him, far closer than she normally did, her muscles tense and eyes alert. Cylian stood in the center of the almost semicircle, tall and straight, ever the poised diplomat, despite his rapier and blade doing a great deal earlier in the day. Darin was planted beside the other lord, arms crossed and ever-present gray hood pulled over his head, hiding most of his face save his lips and pointed chin.

Jarok asked the question on everyone's mind. "What will be done with the captured Bender?"

Volesion sighed and brought a hand up to rub his eyes before he answered. "I have a potion master on retainer and can send word to him. He'll arrive by tonight, tomorrow at the latest."

Jarok nodded in agreement with the unspoken plan. A good potion master, the type a rich and powerful lord like Volesion would have in his employ, would be able to get answers from the Bender, in ways either easy or difficult for the captive. Jarok would not ask which Volesion favored, letting the man who endured an attack on his home make his own decision on the matter.

"Do you require assistance in this, Lord Volesion?" Darin asked, low but clear.

Everyone stared at the man, ideas of how he would help, how he'd likely helped his own king in the past, running through their heads.

"No. Thank you. My men and I will handle the Bender. Until I have more information, it may be best all of you rest. I imagine much will happen after we know more."

Jarok nodded and thanked the lord but lingered, waiting for Piris.

When she looked at her father, he said, "Please. Stay a moment, Piris."

The prince's shoulders sagged a touch, but he pulled himself together and forced his heavy legs to move him toward the door, out and away from her when all he really wanted was to stay by her side.

When Jarok closed his eyes, he saw Piris, fierce and wild, flying through the air in her green velvet dressing gown, daggers drawn, and poised to jump on the back of one of the Benders who'd had her father cornered. She'd been a warrior, focused and ready for attack. Ready to defend her home and those she loved.

Still, the vision made his gut twist. He'd been worried for her before, in every attack they faced, but for some reason, seeing her so fearless and raging in the face of her father's hurt made him fear for her more. It also, oddly, made him wish for a similar expression from her, even if he was unclear about what that could be or why his chest thudded at the thought of it.

He'd sat like this, in a comfortable leather chair by the fire in his guest room replaying images from the battle, most of which featured Piris, stiff and not at all relaxed—until he heard the door open, smelled the ice and steel of her as she slipped quietly into his rooms. He didn't open his eyes at first, waiting for her to come to him.

When she stood between him and the fire, the heat of her almost as hot on his exposed skin as any flame, he turned his dark, half-moon eyes up to her. She wore what she'd had on two hours ago in her father's study: a brown set of leathers, finely made and molded to her delicious, strong body. Jarok clenched his hands to stop himself from grabbing her right then.

He quirked a dark eyebrow, a question without words. Piris breathed deep, looked off to her right for a solid minute, and whispered, "I was helping my mother."

Whatever Jarok had felt before fizzled at the pain in her voice. He'd been in enough battles, tended to enough wounds, and talked with enough grieving families to imagine how she felt then. He couldn't say anything to take the hurt away or erase the memories of what she'd had to do for those fighters, so he unclenched his hands. They reached out for her and hooked her loosely, so she had plenty of time to turn out of his grip if she chose. She did not... not as he shifted her so her back was to him, pulled her close, and brought her body down so he hugged her tall, muscular form to his in the chair. There wasn't a great deal of extra room with the two of them taking up the bulk of the seat, but the closeness was perfection to Jarok.

He breathed deep the smell of her auburn hair as he rubbed small circles on her back and both looked out at the fire in his hearth. Nothing was said until he felt her hand snake down, move between them, and rub firmly against his length in his leathers.

"That isn't necessary," he said, his voice hoarse and strained. He hardened quickly, always so quickly for her, so his body didn't echo his words.

"I think it is."

He stopped her with a hand to her moving wrist. "No 'think,' Piris. In this you need to be certain."

She maneuvered herself with a swift shift and twist, straddling his lap, until they were face-to-face. He gripped her muscled, broad hips in his hands as they stared at one another.

"I need this, Jarok. Please."

He nodded, then leaned back, putting his hand up between them as if in surrender. Piris looked at him with dubious eyes before shrugging and taking the lead.

She stood from him, taking only the time necessary to strip out of her leather pants before planting herself back on top of him, wedging her knees between his hips and the sides of the chair.

Jarok hissed out pleasure when she unbuttoned his leather pants and pulled his cock free. Piris gave him a swift, hard pump down, then up, wetting him with a droplet from his own leaking tip, before she rose up on her knees so she could perfectly position herself.

She did not hesitate. Both watched, transfixed, as she lowered herself onto him inch by inch. It was agonizing, slow, and delicious. Jarok threw his head back against the chair, gritting his teeth and flexing his fingers on her hips, doing all he could to restrain his need to take over, set the tone and pace. He knew he could give this to her, let her take what she needed. He'd prove it to them both.

When she seated herself, a breathy moan escaped her lips, and the prince leaned forward, taking her mouth and wanting to force any other moan down his own throat, swallow it whole and make it his. Then she moved in a slow, steady pace, slipping up and down in a controlled manner.

Both breathed heavy, lost in sensation and saying nothing. Only feeling. Soon, too soon, Jarok felt his orgasm rising, but he pulled away from her mouth and bit the inside of his, using a touch of pain to stop himself so she could have all she needed.

Piris didn't seem to notice, lost in her pleasure, moving in a less fluid push and pull. Gods, it was fascinating to watch her lifting herself up and down him, her head bobbing to the rhythm of her slide, her body jerking just as the maddening grip of her inner walls gripped him tighter and tighter. He licked his lips, looking his fill and committing her to memory, savoring every bit of sight, smell, taste he could.

She stuttered out a loud, low groan, then moved her hands to his chest, using them as leverage to ride him harder and faster, working herself on his cock until she slammed herself down one final time. She came hard, her pussy gripping him so hard and hot and tight, he couldn't help himself. He let go too, the look and feel of her too much to hold back any longer.

Piris collapsed on top of him, breathing heavy, each drag in and out ruffling the dark hair over his left ear as her chin rested on his shoulder.

"Thank you," she said after long minutes. Piris began to rise but he held her tight.

"You never need to thank me, you know," he replied, and he wasn't only talking about the sex.

He thought she understood as their bodies stayed connected and his dark-brown eyes met her bronze ones. Still, she said nothing as she rose from him, leaving him colder and colder with every move she made—putting her pants back on, rounding the chair, and eventually stalking from his room. All without another word.

Early the next morning, they were called to Lord Brettly's study before breakfast was even served. Without preamble or question, the lord stated, "We now know exactly where Engad Monti and his Benders are hiding."

Jarok's heart quickened. They had him. By the gods, they had him.

"I take it you wish to know, and possibly use some of my resources to confront the rebels?" Volesion asked Jarok.

The prince nodded, crossed his arms, and waited, knowing the lord asked it in that manner because there was something he wanted.

"Very well. In exchange for my information and help, I ask my daughter Piris stays behind and no longer travels with your group."

"What?" Piris whispered to her father, her words cold and seething, matching the growing fire in her eyes.

Jarok stood stunned. He couldn't say anything. He knew what he should do. Needed to do. He also knew what he wished to do. They did not correspond.

"I cannot believe you, Father. After all your talk of trusting me, knowing I could fight. Seeing me fight yesterday. You do this."

"Piris, you cannot—"

She threw up a hand. "You've said it before. I know I can't understand how a father wants to protect a daughter. But this goes too far."

"You have no need to be in this battle," he countered, his eyes becoming more and more narrowed as he spoke. "It is unnecessary."

"Unnecessary? Have you gone daft in your old age?"

A laugh from Gem was quickly covered by a fake cough, but Piris didn't seem to notice the noise.

"My best friend, my sister, will be in danger as long as Engad Monti lives. My home was just attacked. You, my father, just injured. Jarok—" She stopped herself there, saying no more of him, though the sound of his name on her tongue, in that list, gave him more hope than he'd had before. "Not to mention the previous two attacks I was in, thanks to the ex-Monti leader and his fighters. I have more than enough reason to be a part of this fight."

"Those are not sufficient. You were attacked at every turn because you traveled with the prince. Strella, the dear girl, is safe and protected in the Winterlands Palace. No harm will come to you here if you allow the group to leave without you. If the prince leaves without you."

Piris moved with dazzling speed, slamming a fist onto her father's desk so hard, she splintered the top layer of wood. "They are my friends. My—" She bit her lip, not saying the rest. Backing up, she gave her father a dismissive look head to toe, one Jarok had been on the receiving end of enough to know how cold it felt. "It would be dishonorable to leave the party. And if you make him say he will leave me behind, make it the only way he can save his family, his kingdom, then you and I are done. I will leave this house and never return."

Lord Volesion took a step back, rocking on his heel as if struck hard in the face.

"No, Brettly" sounded from the doorway. Lady Volesion, worry and stress tightening the edges of her face, said, "No more. You will not hold help and information hostage. You will not hold our daughter hostage."

"Mimi—"

"She is grown. Raised by you to be who she is. You cannot punish her for it now. You cannot stop her from what she is meant to be."

The lady moved, stopping by Jarok and giving him a hopeful look. "You will look after our girl, yes?"

"Always," he croaked, emotion making the word soft but no less true.

"Very well." With a determined nod, she slipped next to her daughter so both Volesion women squared off against the lord. "You must let go."

Lord Volesion hung his head and whispered, "Very well."

Piris watched him warily as he moved to sit in the chair behind his desk.

"Engad Monti hides a few days north of here, in a cave system. The details are here, and I have a ship prepared to take your fighting party and a score of men to confront him." He slipped a piece of paper across the desk, his head hung and his words distant.

"Thank you," Jarok said as he took the offered information in his hands. He was thankful for the information and for not having to make the decision presented to him minutes before.

"Come. Let's plan," Piris said, moving swiftly from the room, expecting him and the rest of the group to follow, so much like her father had the day before. And they did.

Jarok looked back to see the heavy lean of Lord Volesion against his lady wife, and the bittersweet smile she offered the prince as he exited.

Chapter Nineteen
Piris

The wind on the river bit through the pitch-black furs Piris wore over her matching leathers. They also matched her mood as she watched her father give instructions to his men before they boarded the vessel. He'd send along his best, she knew it for fact. He wouldn't risk his precious girl with anything less. His ship was the fastest in his fleet, prepped and ready to get their party to and from the hidden caves where the rebels hunkered down as quickly as possible, to get her back home.

A phantom bitter taste on her tongue crawled up from her gut thanks to what had passed between her and her father the day before. She'd not spoken to him since, choosing to stay in her room instead of meeting the others for dinner. She'd licked her wounds alone, once again stuffing the emotions down so it didn't show on her face when she saw him the next morning.

He'd come to see everyone off, her and her friends and his men. As had her mother, who stared at Piris from her position along the end of the wide stretch of dock. She waved her daughter over, turning away to look downriver before Piris began walking to her, assured her daughter would come when called. And she did.

She may have stomped a little hard, enough to be an outward sign of her displeasure, even if her face stayed frozen in its most imperious look—the one she'd learned from the auburn-haired mother wrapped in tawny furs in front of her. Her mother never used it with her family. No, it had always been reserved for those who whispered about her daughter behind their backs, those who thought her lesser because she was supposedly a null. A lie, of course, but a good one for a number of reasons, not least of which being it made it easy for their family to see who was friend or foe without giving up their secret.

Still, her family had given up much. She had given up a usual childhood as a young lady, though it was hard for Piris to imagine liking dancing and eloquence lessons more than her fight training, so she didn't mind. She did mind the weight of secrets at such a young age, a weight she understood but one that still chafed and choked at times. Her mother, the lovely Lady Mimi Volesion—the bright-red light of the ballroom—when Piris had been a young child, had given up her position in society. Given up her hopes for having a normal lady as a daughter. She'd never said as much, but Piris knew there was no way her mother could have wished for what had happened to them. What she had done to them. Yet her mother had borne it all with her brand of grace and love, never hesitating to protect in her way.

Piris pretended the direction of her thoughts didn't force her to swallow grateful tears as she stopped in front of her mother. Her stance eased, her feet softer as she grew closer, her eyes lighter in the morning glow and the small wet lining them. "Mother." Her word was hoarse as she tried to wrestle the inconvenient pull of emotions hovering around her for some absurd reason.

"Daughter," Lady Volesion whispered, stepping toward her only child, wrapping her tight in her small arms, and pulling her down into her smaller frame. Warmth radiated in her embrace, pulsing into Piris as if by magic, though her mother's magic was not warmth but exceptional hearing, something allowing her to pinpoint all those harsh whispers in all those ballrooms until people learned never to voice anything about Piris remotely close to her mother's presence.

Piris hugged back, breathing deep the familiar frost and winter berry scent of her, holding tight for long beats until she leaned her cheek into the thick auburn hair so like her own and whispered, "I'm so sorry," there.

Lady Volesion's eyes were sharp, assessing, when she pulled back and asked, "Sorry for what?"

"For…" Piris hesitated, not knowing where to begin. She swallowed and gave it all. "For all of this. For your life all these years. For my stubbornness even now. For the worry every bit of it must cause."

Her mother cupped her cheek, looking deep into her eyes, as she said, like a vow, "Never, never be sorry for who you are, my love. I am not." A few of the hovering tears slipped, but her mother wiped them away without a word before anyone else could see. "Your father was right about one thing, Piris. You cannot know what it is to worry for a child. Not yet. Maybe never if you choose. But, I know your heart. Know the worry and love there, so you can guess." She gave a small smile before continuing. "The real truth is no matter what, the worry would have been there, always."

Piris pushed back against the words. "Your life as a mother—"

A small, smooth hand pressed to her mouth, stopping her words. "Has been the greatest joy of my long life, and nothing you believe can change that fact. I would never change who you are. Part of who I am is your mother, happily your mother. Do not try to change that about me." She lowered her hand, looking at her husband who now stood, arms crossed, watching them both from a distance. "Your father means well, you know."

Piris gave a small sneer but also nodded. She did know.

"He was mistaken. Misguided. He will be again. Believe me. It has happened many times in our long marriage." Piris snorted, which made Lady Mimi smile a little wider. "The difference is when he makes a mistake, he learns from it. Eventually. I'll help him grasp this latest lesson a little more quickly, but he will learn."

Piris hissed out a breath, wanting to hold on to her anger, the anger that fueled her and made the worry of what might come shift to the back of her mind. "If you say so."

"I do. I also say this: it is important you learn to forgive, Piris. People will hurt you, and no one can hurt you more than those you love. If they love you as you love them, they will make amends for the hurt, and you must let them."

"Why?" Piris knew the question was petulant, childish, but she wanted to grip her anger tighter, not let it go.

"Because the love you exchange is worth more than the safety you think anger provides."

Piris didn't know what to say to that, and it appeared her mother was done with her good-bye lecture, so she took Lady Volesion's arm and led them both down the dock, sidestepping the last of the supplies waiting to be loaded onto the ship. When they reached her father, Piris paused, not knowing what to say to him either. He didn't force her to say anything. He lifted an arm to grasp her shoulder tight before bringing her into a fierce hug he released almost as quickly as he'd initiated. A silent nod, then he took his wife in his arm and moved away, to the shore, to watch the boat leave from a distance.

"Everything okay?" Jarok's voice shocked her system when his question hit her, so she spun and saw the prince looking between her and her parents, a frown on his full lips.

"Fine," she said, moving around him to walk up the landing plank and onto the ship. She knew he hated the word, but it was the only one she had at the moment, so she let it hang between them.

He muttered some curse of annoyance she couldn't quite hear, but she understood the outline, based on his tone. She didn't realize she was lost in her head until she almost ran right into Gem.

"Whoa there, Piris. Ready?" Gem hefted the pack slung across one shoulder as if in example.

Piris turned to show her own pack firmly strapped across her back, along with one of her short swords. No need to flash the daggers strapped to her sides, her chest, her legs, and ankles under the leathers.

"Good. Looks like you and I are bunkmates," Gem responded, flicking her head toward the door leading to the cabins below deck.

Piris didn't balk, knowing full well the lack of personal space on most ships. She followed her new friend down into their small quarters and flung herself on the hammock she called out as hers. She didn't sleep. She did close her eyes and think on what her mother had said for a long while before other worries and fears for what would come crowded her mind.

Restlessness urged Piris out of their cabin and up the stairs to the deck late in the night. She'd sailed the Great River many times with her father on short trips with the whole family or, on occasion, for training exercises he devised that took them farther afield than the woods surrounding Volesion Peak. She'd always been restless in the small cabins, but being stuck in a cabin with Gem made it worse. She liked her new friend. Respected her. Would fight by her any time. She didn't like being stuck in a tiny room on a ship with her as she snored in her hammock as if she had no cares in the world. Piris went above before she throttled the warrior with her tiny pillow.

There was a man at the door to the cabins who let her exit, one at the wheel, one in the crow's nest above, and another stationed along the bow. The river was smooth here, easy to navigate even in full dark, so no more were needed above. She'd heard men in the mass bunks below when she'd exited her room, chattering among themselves. They'd established sleeping shifts so fighters could be ready in case of a surprise attack, but no need for them to crowd the deck on a calm night.

All of those thoughts melted away under the vastness of the sparkling night sky above her, a river of light echoed in the actual river below, glistening with reflections as the ship cut through the glass-smooth water. It was breathtaking, enough to make her lose a sense of herself for a moment, to contemplate the beauty and depth and odd sense of mortality welling inside her. Until she heard a thump far too close behind her.

She spun on her heels, but if it'd been an assassin, she'd have been long dead. No, not exactly, because it was an assassin. If it had been an assassin out to kill her, she'd have been long dead. This assassin had no reason to harm her.

"Darin," she said, taking a step back. The slope of his shoulder stiffened a touch at her retreat.

"Lady Piris."

"Just Piris, Darin. Unless you'd like me to start calling you lord as well?" Her sarcastic tone somehow eased the stiffness of the man, and he moved to the railing, leaned down to place his forearms there, and looked out at the water and the banks of the Springlands they hugged.

"Piris it is," he said, his voice clipped but not angry.

She moved to stand beside him, not close enough to touch but close enough to talk. For long minutes, it seemed he did not wish to talk, and she was equally happy to let the silence linger as they stared out into the dark beauty of the night. Something niggled in the back of her mind, something she needed to ask, not out of simple curiosity but a need to know for her own future.

"How did you do it? Make so many forget your title?"

His head turned slowly, and he pulled his hood back so she could see all of him. He studied her, his cold green eyes looking for signs of weakness, or maybe signs of what she wanted from such a question. It was a ridiculous question to ask someone like Darin; it was prying and rude and implied so much about who he was without voicing it.

He nodded, as if finding a good answer in her face, and gave his own. "I did what my king commanded me to do."

Not exactly what Piris wanted to hear, but an honest answer to be sure. "Would you rather be Lord Marco?"

Looking out over the river, his brow furrowed and his chin jutted. With his sharp profile and shock of white-blond hair, Piris could see an icy handsomeness there. Nothing she would ever touch, but there nonetheless.

"No one has asked me what I would want in a very long time, Piris," he admitted. Cutting eyes over at her once again, he said, "If I had a choice, I wouldn't care about the title. I'd only want a quiet life deep in the fields of the Springlands, far away from people who'd never think to ask me such a question."

He'd more than earned it, Piris thought, but she was not king of the Springlands and couldn't do anything for the assassin at her side—nothing except shove her shoulder slightly into his for a second before pulling back and saying, "I hope you get your fields of peace one day."

Darin was again stoic, silent and unmoving for several beats before he cast a quick look behind them and straightened from his lean beside her. He pulled his hood back up but said, "You have the opportunity to be who you want to be, Piris. Your parents expect nothing more from you. And the royals here... They are different. I say take the title you choose and damn the rest."

He twisted around, giving her no time to reply, and gave a short hello to the Fae coming up on them from behind. She looked over her shoulder and saw it was Jarok. He gave the assassin a nod as he moved closer, to take the empty space Darin left. The prince slid in closer to Piris... touched his muscled arm down the length of hers. She had to admit she didn't mind.

Chapter Twenty
Jarok

Seeing Piris and Darin at the side of the ship, leaning together in deep conversation, punched a spike of anger through Jarok's gut. It was fleeting but there nonetheless, forcing him to steady himself as he moved toward them. Darin saw the prince first and muttered a greeting to him before turning on quick, silent feet to stalk away. As he passed, Darin nodded, his eyes hidden under his hood. Jarok thought he saw a swift smile pull up the lips Darin usually set into a hard line, but in the dark, he couldn't be certain.

Jarok did notice Piris look back at him. He moved into Darin's empty space beside her. The starlight, shining from above and reflected in the mirrored surface of the river below, bounced in her auburn hair, casting it in ruby tones. She was breathtaking, or at least for Jarok, who stared at her profile so long she turned to him with a sharp face.

"What?" she asked. For good reason. The peace between her and Jarok was still new, still fragile. Falling back into old antagonistic habits was easy, especially the way she'd been hurt by her father the day before. Somehow it felt good to give her the outlet, as the bite in her tone drummed up the familiar push and pull, the dramatic dance they'd done for months at this point.

No. Jarok wanted to fall into it in one sense, go back to something far more steady and sure for them both. Not linger in the odd space they now occupied, where he wanted things she did not. Where he thought himself a fool for feeling. Yet, he couldn't let himself do it. Maybe one day the bickering would come at a more solid and playful pace, but not now. He chose, instead, to step with honesty.

"Your hair looks like rubies in the starlight."

She blinked at him, surprised, and her face flushed before she hid it from him. Again he'd gotten nothing from her, or no words at least, so he looked away. Out on the banks of the Springlands' side of the Great River, the greenery sparkled in its own way, the light color and soft sway something rarely seen in the Winterlands. He stood looking at a secondary beauty for a time, content to be there with her, even if they didn't speak.

It almost startled him when Piris said, "The river is always so calm this time of year."

It was a small opening, but an opening, and Jarok dove into it. "Really? I always imagined the Great River stayed the same. A constant of sorts."

She propped herself up on an elbow as she angled her body to face his profile. He echoed her, so they stood face-to-face as she spoke. "No. People who don't see it year after year, through all its changes, might think it, but it's not so. After winter solstice it's often roiling, churned by snows and storms. Now, as we approach the equinox, it calms for a time. Becomes this."

She gestured out with her hands, and he followed the firm, strong line of her arm to look out at the river again. "It looks like glass."

She nodded. "Often does, at night. Deceptively calm."

He wanted more. Somehow needed more. "You spent a great deal of time on the river?"

"Yes. All Volesions have, of course, but my father expanded our shipping business in his youth, so there was more reason for him to be out on the river. He'd take us with him at times, especially if they were short trips to closer ports." She paused, thinking about something that brought a small smile to her lips. "He also brought me on the river, alone. In a smaller vessel we could navigate together. It was part of our magic training. Sound travels oddly over water, which can be a good thing when you're trying to disguise the source of sound-based magic."

She gave him a small kernel to keep, a little insight into her past, and he wanted to return the favor. "We never came to the Great River often. Only to travel to other Fae lands if need arose. I didn't spend a great deal of time on or around water. In fact, I can't swim." An odd fact to confess, maybe, but it was what came to mind.

She laughed, quiet and quick. It sounded so far from the whip-sharp laughs of derision she'd given him in the past. Her true laugh, one of amusement, was deep, rich like honey, and sent tingling tendrils of lust down his spine. "You can't swim?" She wanted to make sure, the idea so foreign to her.

"Not a stroke. I might even say I couldn't float, but I've managed to at least do that in some large bathing tubs."

She huffed out a sound of disbelief, then turned her head back out to the water. "Maybe one day I'll teach you."

The thrill of a future where Piris was by his side skittered across his senses. "I'd love to learn." He left the "from you" part of the sentence off. The way she leaned into him, he imagined she still understood.

He leaned down the inches between them. Such a small space, yet time stretched out for him. Jarok brushed his lips, soft and sweet, against hers, then swallowed her gasp before he was lost.

He came out of his lean on the railing and scooped her into his arms, pulling her firm, strong body against his. She let him, melting against him. Returned his soft kiss with more urgency and force.

Jarok didn't want that. Not then. He wanted to savor. To linger. He pulled back, peppering her lips with small bursts, setting her tone while stoking a different type of fire. Not too high. Not tonight on the open deck of all places.

She groaned, a sound of half frustration and half pleasure, so he deepened his kiss somewhat. His tongue darted into her mouth, then retreated. He felt her tense and relax as he rubbed small circles on her back, taking the pace back down. He wanted sweet and languid, and he pulled her along with him.

He also wanted it to stop there, so he stepped back after only a few minutes of kissing. Because he was a man of control, he knew exactly when his began to fray. Piris leaned in again, so he stopped her with gentle hands on her shoulders.

"No more tonight."

She cocked her head in question. She opened her mouth to ask it outright but stopped herself, pulling her shoulders back as she took two big steps away from him. A nod was all he got from her when she moved away. He couldn't have that, so he called out to her, "Piris?"

She stopped but did not turn to him, so he said to her back, "Thank you."

It was what she'd said to him the last time they'd had sex. He remembered it with perfect clarity. She'd been thankful then, for him giving her what she needed physically. He wanted her to know she'd also given him what he needed that night, with their brief chat.

Piris looked over her shoulder and one corner of her lip tipped up as she said, "You're welcome, Prince."

He watched her walk away before turning back to the water, smiling to himself as he replayed the encounter over again in his head, happy to have the little memory tucked firmly in his mind now. The memory of Piris giving him something more without a fight.

"Ahoy. Aye, matey and such. Or whatever sailors say." Gem's laughter echoed after her words before Jarok, who stood with Cylian on the deck of the ship the next morning, saw her emerge from the cabin space below. Piris followed her, laughter on her lips too.

"May be a little dismissive, Gem, don't you think?" Piris asked as the two friends stopped in the middle of the deck. The ship's crew wove around them, going about their business, though he saw a few smiling in amusement at the two women.

"I mean it with the utmost respect," his cousin called, spinning around to look at the sailors there.

"I'd be laughing a little less if I were you. Maybe be a little quieter in general." Piris, with teasing but shrewd eyes, looked his cousin up and down before she dropped the bomb. "Especially for someone who cannot swim."

Jarok swallowed a groan. By the gods, the woman was whip smart. He'd confessed to her last night, and knowing how close he was with his family, made a calculated guess. She hit her mark.

Gem gasped. "Why would you assume such a thing. Hmm?"

Piris didn't give him away by looking over at him, which he was thankful for. His cousin wouldn't hesitate to wallop him for letting such a thing slip, even if he didn't directly tell.

"I assume, Gem Aurora, because you live so far northwest, away from most standing bodies of water."

Gem squinted at the woman and hmphed loudly, as if not believing her.

"Should we test it then? The drop isn't far, and we'd be sure to fish you out." Piris stepped closer to his cousin, who crouched down in a wrestling stance.

"Come closer, lady, and you'll go overboard."

Piris shrugged, circling his cousin. "Doesn't matter. I can swim." In a flash, Piris ran at Gem, who shrieked, actually shrieked, and ran as well. Ran away. Maybe for the first time in her life.

As the women chased each other around the deck, dodging sailors, their laughter echoed in the air. A bittersweet twang thumped in his chest. The sound made Jarok happy, but he wished like hell he'd made Piris laugh like that. He was usually so good at making people laugh. Never Piris though, beyond an occasional quick chuckle.

"Truce," Gem wheezed out. "No more threats of cold water, aye?"

Piris, leaning on her knees and out of breath from running and laughter, agreed. She went up, shook his cousin's hand, then slung her arm over her shoulder. With their heads bent together, they talked as they moved up the short stairs on the deck and disappeared behind the group of men at the large wheel.

Part of Jarok wanted to follow, to linger close so he could hear more laughter. He didn't because he knew they both needed this. Piris more than Gem. She'd lived without friends for so long, it'd be a sin to come between the two now.

"A joy to see," Cylian said and Jarok started, having completely forgotten his friend was there, so engrossed in Piris and her laughter.

He nodded in reply and Cylian moved closer to say in a hushed tone, "You can—"

He stopped his friend with a hand. "You don't know what there is between us."

"I know love when I see it."

Jarok snorted. "Do you? Really?"

When Cylian said nothing, he turned to the lord and found fire and molten silver meeting his gaze. The flame and heat in his eyes masked a hurt Jarok hadn't known. Had never guessed. "Yes," he hissed when he'd held Jarok's gaze for long beats.

"Friend, I'm sorry," the prince croaked. He'd stumbled on something Cylian kept secret, buried, much like Piris and her magics. He hurt for his friend, for his own missteps working to remind Cylian of such pain. Of the love he guessed the lord had had and lost, even if Jarok wasn't told the details. Would never press for them.

Cylian shook his head, the fire banking, and gave a long, sad sigh. "I know. I know."

"If there's anyth—"

It was Cylian's turn to stop Jarok's words with an upraised hand. "Nothing to be done. Not now. Maybe never." The Autumnlands lord crossed his arms over his chest and studied the river.

Jarok gave him silence. If his friend wanted to talk, wanted anything, he'd be there for him. Cylian knew it too. Instead of prying and pushing, he leaned a shoulder into the lord before pulling away to fix his stare on a similar point in the distance.

His heart hurt for Cylian, but in his eyes he'd seen an ache he felt deep in his gut. He'd been fighting it so long, despite words from Lady Volesion and now one of his best friends. He'd denied it, but now he couldn't. From Cylian's pain, knew he shouldn't. He loved Piris. Gods be damned, he loved the strong, stubborn, beautiful woman. If only she loved him back.

Chapter Twenty-One
Piris

Two days later, Gem and Piris sat leaning against the rail of the ship, their legs bent. Piris hung her wrists on her knees, the only relaxed part of her body. Gem, quiet beside her, flipped a dagger in her hand, twirling it with such speed and precision, Piris watched with a mix of awe and jealousy.

"Want to learn the trick?" Gem asked, leaning over to knock shoulders with her friend.

Piris grinned and nodded. The warrior grinned back, training her eyes on her hands as she spoke. "First, you must be sure the blade has the right balance. Not balance overall, but the proper balance for your hand. See?"

The dagger, now stationary in her palm, sat centered, the hilt the only part touching her hand, the blade and handle perfect and even despite the small amount of air where the thing looked as if it floated above her hand. Gem gripped the weapon, flung the knife up solidly, and caught it again, with her grip switched. "You do this very well. Quickly and effectively. But you let go of the knife when you do. A risk you take to reposition. A necessary risk, sure, but a risk."

Piris nodded, watching her friend move the blade to twist in and between her fingers. "With this method, you stay in contact with the dagger at all times, never losing it." She grinned wide at Piris. "Never losing it as long as you don't drop it, that is."

She slowed her hands, allowing Piris to follow the movements. Gem nudged the hilt of the blade with her thumb, spinning it in her hand, so her forefinger hooked onto it, twisting it around in practiced control so it continued the spin. Gem's middle finger then added to the movement until she used her thumb once again to stop the blade and right it in her grip. "See?"

Nodding, Piris pulled out one of her knives, already made for her grip and balance. She echoed Gem's still-slowed movements at her side, twisting and turning her fingers independently of one another so she could flick, grip, and turn the knife with simple flicks of her fingers. Her hands were clumsy, unused to the style, but the method behind it made sense to her, enough she knew that, with much more practice, she'd be able to spin and maneuver the blade in a similar way as Gem.

"Thanks," she said, not looking at her warrior friend as she studied her hand, her knife, and the push and pull of movement in her hand with intense focus. A knock to her shoulder told her Gem's reply, and they continued their wait, side by side, spinning separate daggers.

They were waited for Darin to return from his volunteer scout mission. They'd reached the location where, according to her father's information, they'd be best able to form an attack on the hiding spot of Engad Monti and his Benders. Darin, the stealth shadow assassin he was, had volunteered to go out, check the lay of the land, and come back so they could plan accordingly. They waited, Gem and Piris seated beside each other on the deck, Jarok and Cylian leaning against the opposite railing, talking in hushed tones. The sailors and guards stayed stationed and ready for when the time came.

Piris started a bit when Darin's gray leather booths landed beside her without warning, the Fae man barely bending his knees at the impact he made when jumping back onto the boat. He looked down, a deep frown etched the lips he so often held in a firm line, and motioned for Piris and Gem to follow him. They didn't have to follow far, as Jarok and Cylian met the rest of their group in the middle of the deck, not waiting for them to reach where they'd leaned.

"What?" Cylian asked, his fiery head tipped up as if knowing some sort of blow was coming.

"It's a trap."

"You're certain?" Jarok asked.

Darin nodded once, as if he would say no more.

"How exactly is it a trap?" Cylian asked.

Darin crouched to trace a finger on the worn wood of the deck. "There is one entrance to the cave system, lined with trees in a narrow lane. The Benders have the trees and they lie in wait, in clusters, here, here, and here."

"How many?" Gem asked, staring at the places where Darin's finger had tread as if it had left some mark behind.

"At least four per position, with eight positions total. Thirty-two Benders in the tree line alone. I couldn't get close enough to the cave to see what waited beyond the entrance. I assume there are many more."

Jarok pulled his gaze from the deck to Cylian. "We need a way through without taking the lane."

Darin raised himself up as he shook his head. "The woods are dense but dead save a few evergreens, where most of the Benders hide. It is open. We'd be clear targets long before we reached the caves if we attacked in force. Without force, however, we'd be overwhelmed before we got close enough to do damage or take a defensible position."

Piris thought about what they had... how they could proceed. They needed to proceed because they had to end this. Here and now. For Jarok and his family. For Strella.

Then, with Strella flashing across her mind, a story from her friend sparked an idea. She knew what she could take and could guess how much Jarok and Gem could. Cylian and Darin remained a question. Looking from one to the other, she said, "Exactly how well can the two of you handle the cold?"

Four sets of quiet, nearly invisible feet hustled toward the left flank of their target. The fifth set had disappeared soon after they jumped ship, moving alone to take his position at the start of the lane. Darin would perch atop a cleared hill, picking off Benders where he could, as Piris, Jarok, Gem, and Cylian fought on the ground.

Piris remembered how Strella had got herself and Prince Ghel free of the Benders on the outskirts of the Aurora Outpost. She'd used ice and snow to conceal their sled. People were a little trickier, but with the help of water, ice, and a few strategically placed sets of white sheeting from the ship, the five Fae who'd traveled so far together were able to conceal themselves. Meant they couldn't attack with all their forces, but there was a plan for them as well. When the fight was in progress, Cylian would send fire into the sky, signaling the sailors and guards lying in wait.

The snow and ice packed on the strips of sheet over her leathers creaked as she moved, the only sound any in her party made as they slowly came closer and closer to their goal. The element of surprise was all they had, and they needed to use it to distract, then defeat. The plan: Darin could take out several before anyone knew, then the party, hopefully positioned by the cave entrance, would pull out the other

Benders in hiding so their forces could come through without fear of arrows from hidden archers.

Jarok had taken the command lead, and when he stopped, everyone fell in line behind him. He looked back, only a sliver of the golden-brown skin across his dark eyes showing. Not enough to fully see what he thought... why he'd stopped. He held up a hand, pointing toward the edge of the hill they were about to crest. Cylian understood his friend first, dropping to crawl up the hill for additional cover. Gem, then Piris followed, all four eventually lining the hill, using their sharp Fae eyes to track the movements below.

A few Benders wandered in, out, and around the cave entrance. Beyond the half dozen that could be seen, it looked as if no one else lingered there, unless they stayed positioned deeper in the cave. They trusted Darin's assessment and knew the rest were stationed in the trees around the lane leading to and from the massive cave mouth.

Jarok's charge would be their call to attack, the signal for Darin to begin his long-range assault. For a sliver of time, they would be exposed, open to all the Benders they could see down below as well as the thirty-two or more in hiding.

Jarok whispered, "Ready," the sound a smidge above a breath. All nodded, and Piris felt a shiver, anticipation mixed with fear, creep up her spine and warm her cooling body and limbs. She spared a full look toward Jarok, who also looked at her. Bronze met brown, and she forced herself to swallow words. The prince's eyes held sadness, but he quirked his eyebrow in the arrogant, insufferable way he had, and what had once annoyed Piris so much now bolstered her. Gave her strength.

A final, hard nod, then Jarok was up, running without stealth down the hill, flinging his wind before them all so it pushed through the Benders below before they knew anyone was there. The few who managed to remain standing found themselves hit in the chest with Cylian's fire, making them topple. They reached the bottom of the small crest and stood, shoulder to shoulder, surveying the men on the ground, either pinned by wind or flailing to put their clothes out.

It would have been an easy victory if not for the mass of arrows whizzing by their heads. Jarok threw a wall of wind up around them, deflecting the arrows in midair, while the rest crouched in defense. Unfortunately, redirecting his wind allowed the Benders he'd had pinned down to spring into action. Something crashed in the trees to the right, and Piris knew without even being able to see at least one Bender was taken down by a bronze-tipped arrow with black fletching. Darin did his job well.

Cylian, rapier poised and long dagger awash in fire, raised his weapons to clash against one of the Benders bearing down on them. Three others converged on Jarok, recognizing him because his face coverings had blown away when he'd thrown his wind. Gem intercepted, sliding on her knees in front of her cousin to take out all three men with a vicious swipe of her blade across their legs. Her sword couldn't penetrate their protective magic, but Gem was strong, and a hard hit to the knees took any Fae down. They fell back easily, but Gem didn't stop to secure them. Instead, she spun on her knees and popped up to face the Bender who was running at them from the left, having come from some other position around the opposite side of the cave.

Piris moved to the three fallen men as Jarok moved down, plowing a swift hit of the hilt of his falchion onto one's temple, who blinked out of consciousness quickly. Piris helped with the remaining two, keeping them secured with hard hits to their legs as Jarok went down the line, knocking each out. Death would come to many this day, but there was no need to deal it when unnecessary.

She moved close with Gem after, having agreed the two of them would fight with cold metal as Cylian and Jarok used magic and metal to push the Benders away from the cave. Once they cleared the mouth, and Darin picked off more Benders from the trees, Cylian would signal the soldiers and sailors with them, and the men would rally to fight in larger numbers.

The women fought back-to-back, slashing and turning like a unit. Like warriors on a mission. Metal clanged, blood sprayed, and despite a close call with a short sword to her forearm, Piris and Gem remained relatively unscathed as they made a swath of destruction across the open plain around the cave. Men lay moaning or lifeless in their wake.

For their part, Cylian and Jarok also cleared their way with ease, Jarok's wind bringing with it the smell of burning hair and skin caused by Cylian's fire. The smell was acid in her nose, but Piris knew as long as she smelled it, felt the icy winds whip her hair about, they were still fighting, so she did not divide her attention. She focused on the next man, then the next, felling Benders as she went.

A whistle sounded from somewhere deep in the trees, and a mass of feet pounded cold ground. The Benders left their posts, much to Piris's surprise. When she noticed their convergence of men moving toward Jarok, she knew why. They'd been after the prince at Volesion Peak. No doubt their orders were to capture or kill him at any cost. She pushed through, moving her and Gem closer to the duo defending their position now, coming in to help with the new onslaught.

Darin followed the Benders down, stopping every few feet to string and fire an arrow at dizzying speed, then step into shadow and melt away again before coming back up to confront a confused Bender. He picked off Bender after Bender as they moved on the prince, but there were too many.

With the Benders in the trees now on attack in the open, Cylian threw up the fiery signal, and Piris hoped the men reached them soon. They were becoming overwhelmed quickly.

Cylian cried out, the hand he had extended up to fire a flame into the sky cradled to his chest, an arrow shot right through it. Less than a second later, Darin's grunt, soft but somehow thundering in the battle, hit her ears, and she saw the man kneeling, an arrow in his chest.

Spinning to track her other companions, she watched Gem launch herself at a Bender barreling toward Cylian, who still wielded his rapier as blood dripped down a limp arm. The Aurora warrior jumped high in the air and landed on the back of a Bender only feet away from Cylian's back, burying her sword deep in his neck. She wasted no time rising and running, but she cried out midstep as a short sword found its way into her gut.

Piris felt her world tilt as Gem stared down toward the bloody wound in her center as if her taking a blow was somehow unbelievable. She screamed, bolting toward her friend as the man pulled his sword away and raised it high to land a killing blow. It never came, as a shot of wind spun him around, and it grabbed him up, twisting his body until Piris heard the crack of his bones—his neck—as she skidded to stop at Gem's side.

"Gem. Gem!" she screamed, shaking her friend's loose body in her arms.

Gem smiled up at her, blood in her teeth, and said, "Hey there, m'lady."

Piris wanted to cry and scream and rage all at once. She registered the clank of metal in the distance, a sure sign the other forces they had were coming to their aid. With the quick turn of events, she was uncertain it would help them. Arrows still flew, wind and metal howling, as she brushed a stray strand of brown hair from her friend's face. She knew she needed to get up, to fight again, but to pull away then might rip her in two.

Gem's smile faltered, her mouth in a perfect O, as she croaked out, "Pir—"

before Piris's world exploded in a bolt of pain, then went black.

She awoke, her hands bound tight in front of her as she lay on her back, staring at the roof of a cave.

"Ah. You're finally awake," a rough, deep male voice said.

Piris turned her head to the sound and saw a Fae warrior with impressive muscle but not so impressive height walk toward her. She'd never met the man, but he had to be Engad Monti. Who else would leave her tied in a cave?

He moved to stand over her. The torchlight illuminating the space flickered around him, an odd halo of orange bright in the darkness. "You shouldn't have come here, Lady Volesion."

"Because now I have to deal with your stench?"

He boomed out a laugh. "No, lady." Engad Monti shook his head, as if marveling at her gall. "You were home, safe, at Volesion Peak. I have no quarrel with you and yours. There was no need for you to come."

"You have a quarrel with my king, my royals, my friends," she spat out. "Of course I came."

"Loyalty is an admirable trait, but it did not serve you well here."

Piris snorted then. "What do you know of loyalty?"

He crouched down over her, head cocked in thought. "I know enough. More than enough. Certain loyalties only cause pain and heartache, which you'll learn shortly."

Something dark flashed in his eyes, but she didn't care about what might drive a man like him, what dark past he might have. She had no need to consider who he was. Her only care in the moment was breaking free, getting loose. Because she knew true loyalty well. Felt it deep in her bones. She understood the loyalty of a prince, who without doubt was now scheming to trade places with her right then. The stupid, insufferable man would give the rebel exactly what he wanted, all because of loyalty and honor. And Engad Monti damn well knew it.

Chapter Twenty-Two
Jarok

Jarok's rage rushed through him, cold as the wind he commanded. He'd sensed it rise in him when Cylian had taken an arrow to his hand. Then Gem took a sword to the gut and his wind snapped out like a rope, twisting around the Fae who'd done it, twirling him in the air as if he were nothing. Snapping the Bender's neck.

He'd been so focused on what he did, wanted to do, to the Fae, he'd taken his eyes off Gem. Off Piris. Only when Darin cried out a warning did he look away from the dead man and his wind lowered to the ground. Piris, knocked out. Gods, he hoped only knocked out. Flung across the shoulders of some dirty Bender, who'd bounded quick as a flash through the fighting toward the cave mouth.

His wind knew no calm at the sight. It became a tornado tearing through the clearing without course or reason. His only thought: get Piris. Save Piris. Kill whoever touched her.

The problem was he had no control in his anger. His winds flung friend and foe alike in its wake, leaving only him standing, the eye of the storm. Cylian's yells and Darin's curses did nothing to stop him as the wind whipped toward the yawning mouth of the dark cave, the same end point the Fae toting Piris had. Only when a cry of pain ripped up from Gem did he hesitate, looking back and seeing his cousin being dragged along the icy, rocky ground. A bloody line led from where she'd fallen to where his wind moved her.

Jarok blinked, the wind dying down as he calmed some. Calmed enough for Cylian to come up and grab him by the shoulders. "Think, Jarok. Think!" he growled in his face.

Shaking his head clear of the howling rage, he looked back toward his cousin, who was even then trying to get up from her bloody spot. He was running to her, to comfort her or yell at her for moving, he didn't know, when a cry from above them brought a sliver of hope.

Darin was already fighting with a Bender hand to hand, despite the arrow he'd snapped off his chest. Cylian, his dagger hand injured, was using his rapier to block the path of a Bender barreling at them. They were not safe. Piris was not safe, surely, but she'd been taken for a reason. A purpose. He had to believe she would be kept safe for the same purpose. For a time, at least. More time than the remaining party had, except their soldiers were cresting the hill, a force large enough to overwhelm the remaining Benders. If they got down here in time.

Jarok rammed into a Bender in his way, dodging the dagger the man held close. He twisted his arm, hard, and heard the snap of bone before the dagger went limp in his hand. He took his own falchion and buried it deep in the Fae's neck and let him fall to the slushy, slick ground. He didn't look back, thinking of getting to Gem only, when another Bender came upon her, sword raised high to land a killing blow. She bared her teeth up at him, wild courage and will releasing in a war cry that nearly rent his heart in two. The man's eyes widened, then a glint of silver rammed through his neck, courtesy of one of their soldiers.

The rest of their men flooded the area around the cave, cries and clanging steel ripping through the air. Jarok moved to Gem and scooped her up in his arms. "Gem," he croaked, unable to think of anything else to say.

She smiled at him, her teeth bloody and fierce. "Another scar, cousin," she said between gasps of pain. "Nothing more."

He shook his head, the rage and pain winding its way up in him once more, threatening to bellow out again, when one of their soldiers dropped to his knees beside him. No, not a soldier. A healer, from the large roll she wore on her back, which she hastily brought around and unfurled.

"Prince?" the woman asked, gesturing toward Gem.

"Give the pretty woman room, cousin," Gem called around a cough and gasp.

"You will do all in your power to save her."

The healer didn't even look up at him. Nor did she acknowledge the imperious threat in his voice. She stared at him and said, "I need more room, Prince Jarok." A dismissal if he ever heard one. He didn't mind, as Gem grabbed his hand and squeezed. Hard.

"Get her," she said, her eyes hard and angry.

Jarok nodded, patted her hand in his, and looked at the healer, who was already mixing some concoction to help his cousin. "I have her, Your Highness. She will heal. I give my word."

He didn't think twice after, already up and running full out toward the cave, flinging away arrows with his winds as he made his way to the dark hole.

He heard Cylian shout, "Jarok!"

He spared his friend a glance then, only to see if he was well. The lord of Autumnlands still fought, no sign of slowing. As did Darin, despite the hole in his chest from a Bender's arrow. The tide had turned. Their soldiers swarmed and took on Benders more than one at a time. They would have this in hand. He trusted them, his friends and the Volesion fighters, to do what needed to be done here. He, however, needed to do more inside the cave. Jarok raised a hand in acknowledgment, ignored the curses and calls to stop, and sprinted into the cave, letting the darkness swallow him.

The eighteenth time he stumbled into a wall in the dark, Jarok thought to himself maybe he should have waited. It became clear he was lost, turned around by the dark, dank endlessness of this cave. There was no light and no sound to guide him, unless he counted the battle noises he could still faintly hear from toward the entrance. He couldn't go back though. Jarok's only choice, based on the wind whipping in his gut, was to move forward. To find Piris. To make sure she was safe once again.

After long minutes, he noticed a sliver of light in front of him. He followed it, winding his way down, down, down. The cave grew colder, more still, with every step. He then heard the trickling of water, followed by a deep boom of a voice. Piris's tone, cutting and snide, sent a shiver of relief through him. He couldn't see her yet, but hearing that tone, the one she'd once used with him every time they spoke, comforted him. Jarok clung to the wall of the cave, sliding along slow and cautious as the light grew brighter.

"Prince." The boom echoed around the cave walls. "Come. No need to slink through the shadows."

Jarok pulled himself up, tossed on his other armor, and strolled into the space as if he had not a care in the world. If Engad Monti wanted a cruel and dismissive prince, he would get one.

He gave a nod with a quirked brow, insolence dripping off every gesture. "Engad," he said, not giving the man title or even the last name he'd derived from his people.

Both hits landed, the man's chest puffing and his eyes narrowing. Monti's hands went to his sword, though he kept it in its scabbard at his side. "Should I bow then?"

Jarok never expected bows, much less desired them from his people, so the intended target was off. He shrugged, moving to lean against a stone jutting up from the floor. He examined his dirty, bloody nails, flicking away what he could, letting the silence echo instead of words.

Engad Monti seethed, his anger rising with every silent second between them. Jarok knew he'd expected a direct attack, like Prince Ghel had given him on the Ice Plains. "Your brother met me in open combat on the battlefield," he called, after long moments of nothing between them.

"I am not my brother."

"Obviously," the rebel said, the word biting and harsh. A true hit, but Jarok stuffed it down.

"What is it you want from me, Engad? Am I to fight you here and now? Or do you wish to talk?"

"Are both not appropriate, given the circumstances?"

Another insolent shrug, as if he didn't care in the least. "Very well. Let Lady Volesion go, and we can talk or fight, whichever you wish."

Piris, lying on her back on the floor, let out a cry of protest. Jarok avoided her gaze, knowing looking at her could end his charade in a heartbeat. He saw her from the corner of his eye, bound so the rope cut into her flesh, no care given to her wrists or her comfort. To think of a rope used to harm, to hurt, made the wind rise in him again, but he squashed it as quickly as he could, remaining cool and aloof on the outside.

Monti, with his shrewdness, picked up on the shift in Jarok regardless. He smiled then, moving to Piris and hoisting her up by those bound hands. The jerk to her feet would have hurt her, Jarok knew, but Piris only flexed her jaw, keeping her reactions and feelings clamped down tight.

"Oh, I don't know. Maybe I keep her as a bargaining tool, for her father and the princess."

"You come at my father, he'll strike you down without hesitation. As would Prince Ghel if you dared try to manipulate the princess. I'd think you, of all people, wouldn't want to take on Prince Ghel's wrath once again." Words as sharp as knives, spit right in the face of a man who held her captive. She didn't care, could never back down in the face of a fight regardless of who she fought, and it made Jarok love her more. It also made him quake for her.

"The prince bested me, it's true, but only because of his magic."

Piris snorted and gave a long sideways look at the Fae. "Tell yourself whatever you have to in order to feel better."

Monti shook her by the bound hands, his lips curling as he said, "I'd be less mouthy if I were you."

"Please stop the endless prattle," Jarok drawled, trying his best to keep his wind and rage at bay when he saw the pain flicker across Piris's face. "We have things to do."

"Yes, Prince. That we do." The rebel threw Piris back to the floor, where she landed on her butt, the hard fall shaking up and down her body. Still, she showed no signs of pain. All she let Engad Monti see was anger and dismissal.

The Monti turned his back on her to step closer to the prince. He didn't pull his sword. He stood still, his feet planted shoulder-width apart and his arms crossed at his chest. His eyes assessed and considered.

"The adopted prince, from a great warrior clan. I expected more from you."

"What exactly did you expect?"

"More of a fight. Can't say I'm sad to see you go. I am, however, disappointed it was so easy."

A rock plowed into Jarok's stomach then, doubling him over in pain as the air gushed out of him. Monti had apparently decided to use his magic instead of having another duel with a Winterlands prince. Jarok sucked in some of his wind to gain his breath, but not before another stone pelted him, driving him a few steps back, away from the cave entrance.

Piris screamed, high and shrill and desperate, but her words were drowned out by a deep rumble. Jarok flung up his wind, slowing the fall. Yet the stones continued to fall, one by one, regardless. Giant, ancient stones loosened from their resting places in the cave.

They tumbled down, burying the prince. He looked toward Piris one last time before he was buried and said, "I love you." Then all was crushing black.

Chapter Twenty-Three
Piris

All Piris knew was rage. It dove deep, pushing everything else to the side, filling her to the brim with a surging anger she'd never known before.

"I love you."

He'd said it, soft but clear in her ears, before he was buried by a pile of boulders. Buried by the Fae standing in front of her.

She surged upward, jumping to her feet in a quick motion based in years of training. Monti turned, in no rush, to look to his captive, and his eyes flared at what he saw. On pure instinct, she called on her magic, the dark, seething well of it in the pit of her gut. The vastness she so rarely used because she feared it on some level, feared it as others did. Piris knew it lurked, waited, and that was part of what made people so afraid of mimics. The potential of what they could do if they wanted to, or if they were pushed to act.

With a blink, the ropes at her wrists went up in flame, a flash of light before they crumbled to ash at her feet. Confusion crept up Engad Monti's face as he shifted into a defensive stance. Like everyone else, he'd thought her a null. Like everyone else, outside her friends, her parents, and her Jarok, he'd thought her nothing, something to use or discard as necessary for his plans. She growled, low and deep, flashing her teeth before she took one large step back. Her foot landed in a shadow and she vanished.

She stalked the darkness, the shadows teeming as they echoed the magic and hate coursing in her veins. Monti, shocked, pulled his sword from its scabbard, turning in circles to try to track an opponent he could not see.

"What are you?" he called into the blankness of the cave.

Piris hissed, stepping out of the shadow. Stone pillars jutted out, twisting up Monti's arms in a curling gray embrace. She used his own magic to pin him, force his weapon away.

She moved in front of him, bending a moment to pull the small, wickedly sharp blade from an ankle holster. She flipped it in her hand, as Gem had taught her, and the thought of her friend and her blood still lingering on her clothes caused Piris's rage to become a consuming inferno in her gut. "I am Piris Volesion. No more, no less."

The man steeled himself, rising straight as he could in his stone chains—stone he tried to melt down with his own magic, but hers was stronger, more overpowering. Always had been and always would be, despite her need to hide it away. "You are a monster," he rasped out, the smell of sweat and fear tinging the air.

"No more than you. I suppose it takes a certain type of monster to kill one."

Monti looked frantic then, twisting with all his effort, getting nowhere. "I surrender," he gasped out, a selfish man's final act. "I surrender. I will not escape, no longer fight. Take me to the Winterlands Palace for a trial."

He'd made a crucial mistake, thinking Piris was Prince Ghel or Princess Strella. Thinking she was someone who could let the hurt and pain of her friends, her loves, stand. Still, she'd called herself a monster, but she wouldn't let herself be one. She saw him for what he was and decided to give him enough rope.

Without a word, she dropped the stone shackles. Monti went to a knee, head bowed as if in defeat, but the hard lines of his back told her to brace.

He came up clutching his sword, swinging hard and fast upward in an arc. There was enough force behind the weapon to cleave her from belly to chest, rip her open as one of his men had ripped through Gem.

Yet his sword never met flesh. It stopped, Piris's hand now cast in stone, gripping his weapon tight as it hovered around her thighs. "No honor? No surprise," she hissed, pushing back with expert strength, toppling the man to the ground.

He scrambled back and attempted to right himself, but she stomped on his chest with a foot, a foot imbibed with the mass of magical strength one of her father's guards possessed. She watched a crackle of light skitter across his chest, the flare of a symbol pulse there. A ward, then. Wards protected, but they could be busted open. Which she did, pressing harder and harder with her foot until a final white flare rose in the cave and a hard sizzle sounded. The death of a ward of protection.

Engad Monti gasped out a plea, but it was ignored. Piris instead pressed again. Without the ward, his chest caved in, cutting off the horrible scream he half released at the pain of being stomped through. She thought of Jarok's final whisper of love, how he hadn't screamed out when he had been crushed, and she raged again. Twisting her foot free of the cavity in Engad's chest, she reared it back and kicked him in the chin with all the magical might she had passing through her. With the years and years of secrets and hiding. The force of years of people not knowing her, not caring, and the love of people who now did, always would. A sharp crack rent the air, then silence. No breathing sounded except her own.

Piris stood there, over a dead Engad Monti, breathing deep, lost for a moment at what she'd done. She remembered Jarok, buried under heavy stone at her side, and she sprinted toward him. Flinging his own wind as she did, she rolled rock after rock off the pile in waves, the rocks landing on the Monti, crushing his body more. When she saw Jarok's black, floppy-haired head in the middle pile, somehow not crushed, she finally stopped using the rebel's powers. She switched to strength, shoving rocks aside, ripping her nails down to stubs as she dragged his body free.

Jarok lay unmoving, and fear clawed at her. Then there was movement. His chest rose and fell once, twice. Three times. A mangled cough came from him, and he groaned around it.

"Jarok? Jarok! Please, say something." She didn't dare touch him, too afraid that whatever god had saved him would take their blessing away.

He rolled over, looked up into her broad, so-often-stern face, and gave a watery version of his cocky smile. "Why so frantic? Do you actually care about me? I never would've guessed." Jarok's smile disappeared as soon as he started coughing again, his wind's way of helping him get the stone debris out of his lungs.

All Piris could do was scoop him in her arms, hug him to her body, and whisper over and over again, "Thank the gods."

It was nothing, with the magical strength still close at hand, to hoist him into her arms and make her way out of the cave. When she emerged, Jarok was awake but remained limp. Cylian was on her in a flash, helping her lay him on the ground. He looked her over with concern, and she read the intentions of his actions. He guided them both down partially so the prince was stabilized, and partially to not show the strength she wielded to the various Fae still lingering around the cave.

The Autumnlands lord took care with her secret, even after an intense battle—just as Piris had paused for a moment to do inside the cave, when she had known Jarok was fine and she'd made sure the tumble of rocks hid what she'd done to the Monti with her mimic powers.

"Prince, are you okay?" Worry marred Cylian's gold-and-silver eyes.

"I'm fine, Cylian. Just fine. How is Gem?" Wasn't too fine if he used the word he hated, but Piris wouldn't gripe about it.

She said nothing and let the Fae lord answer. Took in the field before her as Cylian said all was well with his cousin. The healer had already stabilized her and taken her back to the boat, saying she expected a swift, full recovery. In front of the cave, Darin squatted, letting another healer bandage his chest. Soldiers toiled around them, securing the few remaining Benders and moving the bodies of the fallen from the slush of mud, snow, and blood at their feet.

Darin was up before she breathed a word, stalking toward them, those stark green eyes nakedly roving her and the prince as he checked for any signs of damage. When he was close enough, he asked, "Monti?"

"Dead." Piris felt the word like a stone in her gut, but she wouldn't regret what she'd done. Not with Gem safe on the ship and Jarok warm and breathing in her arms, a whole land now minus one selfish, hateful man bent on power at any cost.

Darin stepped close, green meeting bronze, and after a moment, gave a deep nod. No, not a nod. A bow. A sign of respect at what she'd done and an acknowledgment of the good and bad in the action.

She almost crumpled then, would have if she hadn't felt Jarok reach up and touch her face. "Love," he said, his voice hoarse from his ordeal and the emotions whirling in his eyes.

She steeled herself with his word and called to no one in particular, "The prince needs a healer. Now."

One came running. When she growled at the man after he told her to step back, he hesitated a touch but redirected quickly, doing what he could as Jarok stayed in her arms. Eventually she would need to drop her arms, but not here, in the blood and mud of a spent battle. She'd let him go, told herself she would have to, but not quite yet.

Two days on the ship, and Piris prowled the deck with restless energy. She'd been to visit Jarok in his single quarters several times, watching him sleep as he healed. Same with Gem. The healers had put both in a magical sleep to help them recover, and neither had stirred since they'd been placed on the ship headed back to Volesion Peak.

She'd not had much sleep, spending most of her time with Cylian and Darin above deck, discussing everything and nothing to pass the time. They were one night away from her home, and additional healers if they were needed, but she wanted Jarok and Gem to awaken before then. See with her own eyes they were well and whole once again.

Darkness had crept up from the deep-orange sunset sparkling on the Great River when she heard a bellowed, "Where is she?"

Up and running before another sound was uttered, she raced through the low door leading below deck, twisting through the tight quarters until she reached Jarok's room. Piris entered without a knock and saw him sitting up in bed, his face all hard lines and angles, his brows slashing down like black blades.

The healer, the woman taking care of both the prince and Gem, spun around with quick grace to see who entered. Jarok already knew and growled at the other woman, "Out. Now," without once looking at her.

She turned from Piris to Jarok and made the best decision for her safety and sanity, slipping from between them and closing his door as she exited.

Piris stood in the middle of the small room, barely breathing. All she could do was stare at his golden face, dark eyes, and quirked slash of an eyebrow. It soaked into her, warmed her to her bones, to see him up and animated. Alive.

"Come here," he said, his voice gravelly from healing sleep. Jarok opened his right arm, flicking his head toward it, and Piris needed no more. She eased into the space he created for her. He pulled her in close, tight, as she did. Her head fit perfectly there in the crook of his shoulder.

For long minutes she sat there, still and content, feeling his pulse against her ear like a steady drumbeat. When she needed to see his face, hear his voice, she moved up slightly, though the loss of his heart at her ear pained her. "How are you? Really."

He chuckled, reaching up to tuck a stray strand of auburn hair behind her ear before he grabbed her chin, gentle yet firm in his touch. "I'm well. Truly. A little sore, a little bruised, but no more."

"Your wind buffered you. Saved you from the worst of the rockfall so you weren't crushed."

"You saved me," he insisted, shaking her chin slightly in the process. "You, Piris. My wind may have helped, but it was you who saved me."

Her heart fluttered in her chest, wishing for more, but hope was a bird she kept caged tight. Instead of voicing her hope, her need, she reached up and skimmed a hand over his face, lingering on a purple bruise blooming on his high, sharp cheekbone. He didn't wince, didn't pull away. Jarok leaned into her touch. Savored it. Then turned his head to give her a soft kiss on her open palm.

Piris shuddered at the feel of his lips on her skin. He was injured, true, but she thought there was one thing they could risk. She pulled away. His eyes flickered with sadness and loss but widened when he watched her crawl backward down his body, taking his covering with her as she did.

"Piris—" he croaked, his voice dry and yearning.

She went to untie his loose pants but stopped to ask, "Will this hurt you?"

"Not in the way you think," he muttered before he gave a chuckle. "No, Piris. If you truly wish to take me, you can have me. All of me."

She didn't reply. Couldn't say anything to what she saw in his dark eyes when he looked down at her, what he'd already confessed to her inside the cave, so she decided to occupy her mouth in other ways. Piris freed him from his pants, his hard length warm and heavy in her hands. She angled his head up, then took him slowly in her mouth, keeping her eyes on his as she did.

Her eyes closed a moment at the taste of him, salty winds and spice so strong on her tongue, and she moaned around him. When her eyes popped back open, his head was tipped back, his muscles stretched in his neck, a hard line of desire, need, and restraint coiling up his body. The most beautiful sight she'd ever seen.

Piris took him down, inch by inch, until she could take him no farther. She nearly choked on him, but the feeling of fullness—rightness—made her want to push herself.

Jarok stopped her with a hand on her head. She saw the need to do more written across his body, so she let him take over as he saw fit, adding a flick of her tongue on the underside of his cock as he pulled her head up.

Jarok paused, staring at her as they both caught their breath, then gave a gentle push to the top of her head, gripping her tight at her crown. She followed his lead, taking him back in her mouth, sucking hard as he pushed and pulled her head. In short time he held her stationary, pumping his hips up toward her. She took it all, savored his grunts of pleasure as much as the taste and feel of him in her mouth.

Too soon, he stopped his hips and pulled her head away from him. She popped free and looked up, her eyes questioning as she licked her lips.

"Gods save me." He groaned as he looked down at her. "Turn around," he growled.

She tried to ignore the request, go back to his hot, hard length inches from her face, but he held her head tight.

"Come up here," he said, the note of command dark and promising.

Her brow furrowed and she asked, "What of your bruises?"

"Damn my bruises. I need to taste you."

Her core ached and dripped. Had for some time, but the words, in his voice, his face stark with need and want, made her shift her thighs together. He huffed at her, stretching down to grab her under her arms and try to twist her around as he wished. Afraid he'd hurt himself worse, she cooperated, moving to straddle his head, her knees digging into the mattress by his ears.

He gave a hard groan, and she felt the touch of his nose trailing up her slit through her pants. "Damn, you smell so good." Without warning, he nipped her through her leathers, sending a zing of pleasure up her body.

She moaned, loud and low, and he patted her ass, hard.

"Pants off. Now."

Driven by her own desire, she no longer hesitated. She shimmied out of her pants as quick as possible, then resumed her position.

"Perfection," Jarok whispered as he gripped her hips hard. Pulling down with a firm jerk, he brought her to his mouth and gave her a long, hard lick.

Piris stuttered out a breath, the pleasure overwhelming.

When he pushed his tongue into her entrance as he flicked her clit hard with a finger, she shuddered. Before she lost all control, she moved her mouth back to him, sucking him deep as she moaned from the ministrations of his tongue.

They hovered like this, every lick and kiss and suck jolting through their bodies like a velvet blow. In a handful of moments, Piris's legs were shaking as she moaned around his cock, her focus waning. Finally, she popped him free from her mouth, ground her hips on Jarok's face, and took only pleasure. A few beats later, she exploded, her orgasm coming in hard waves washing across her body. She trembled, from sensation and emotion, and buried her face in Jarok's hard abs as she screamed through her release.

When she caught her breath, she moved back to him and took him deep, sucking hard and wanting to give him an equal measure of pleasure. A few bobs and he was straining, as if he'd only held out for her. His legs and voice were stiff.

"Piris."

She doubled her efforts, twisting one hand at his base as she focused on his head.

"Piris," he cried again and held her ass in strong hands as he pushed upward with his hips. He came in her mouth, as she just had with him, and she loved every second of it. The sound of his deep groans, the salty clove taste of his release, the sensation of him jerking in her mouth... She took every bit of what he gave her and was more than happy to do so.

When he finished, she rolled off him, spent and satisfied. Jarok moved, crunching up to grab her and pull her to lie beside him so they could be face-to-face. He kissed her deep, their tastes mingling in her mouth in a delicious echo of what they'd just done.

He pulled back, and she saw a small strain around his eyes. Piris stroked down his face. "Rest," she ordered.

"Will you stay with me?"

She nodded, deciding to stay while she could. She could give him, and herself, this.

He smiled, a bright but tired upturn of his lips, and pulled her close, burying her face in his chest. His heart once again beat against her ear, harder and faster than before but still a comfort. As she snuggled deeper in his arms, he kissed the top of her head. "I love you," he said, the words ringing clear in the quiet room.

She didn't say it back; she couldn't because of who they were, what she was. Without words, she pulled him closer, squeezed him as tight as she could, and lay with him as he drifted off to sleep, telling herself over and over again she should be happy to have had this short time with him.

Chapter Twenty-Four
Jarok

Jarok awoke to a pleasant surprise: Piris sleeping in his arms. He didn't move. Barely breathed. Savored every moment he had with her there, not running from him or pushing him away.

He could've killed the sailor who pounded on his door with five hard raps, startling Piris out of sleep.

"Good morning," he said, the smile still firm on his face.

Piris blinked a few times, tipped her neck in a quick stretch, and surprised him once again. Her arms stayed tied around him, and she brought him close, held him tight. She buried her face in his chest, and he heard her take a deep breath.

"Did you just sniff me?" He knew he stank. They'd been in battle, he was covered in the gods only knew what thanks to the healer, and he'd been unconscious for days. He did still have her scent all over his face, and his cock twitched whenever he caught the now-faint smell, the memories flooding him.

She muttered something against his chest before pulling back and, with a faint upturn of her lips he couldn't quite call a smile, said, "Yes. And?"

He boomed out a laugh, happy and free and in love, taking her in his arms as he twisted to his back and placing her firmly on top of him. She pushed up with her strong hands planted to his muscles, her tousled hair and sleepy face stopping the laughter in his throat. Jarok reached up and twisted a piece of her loosened auburn hair in his hand. He'd opened his mouth, about to let all his feelings spill, when she dropped down. Piris covered his mouth with hers, tasting him long and deep.

When she pushed back up, she flicked her head toward the door. "That was our warning. We're about to dock."

Her timing was perfect, as the ship rocked gently after a hard stop. They'd reached the landing dock at Volesion Peak.

"I need to go," she whispered but didn't leave.

"I know. You have to grab your things."

"And help Gem get off the boat."

The thought of Gem, who'd suffered so many injuries on this mission, motivated him to get out of their warm, snug bed. "I'll come with you."

Piris didn't protest, didn't say she could do it on her own. She could. He knew it. Jarok wanted to help his cousin and stay closer to Piris. Wanted to cling to what they'd had that morning so it wouldn't vanish with the currents of the river as soon as they stepped off the boat.

He wasn't exactly right. He also wasn't wrong. He'd dressed quickly, gotten his pack, and followed Piris to her shared space with Gem, who had just woken with the landing. She was grumpy, which was to be expected, so their focus went to taking care of her and smoothing her ruffled feathers as they removed her from the boat and escorted her to a richly appointed guest room in the manor house.

Cylian and Darin had joined them on the deck, fussing over Gem in their own ways: Cylian with soothing words and Darin with hard stares and barks for people to get out of the way. Gem laughed at them both, coming out of her temper because of their mother-hen behavior. The group paused in their progress when Piris saw her mother and father waiting at the end of the dock. She froze a second, taking in her family, then looked to Cylian to replace her at Gem's side. When she was secure, Piris ran. Right into her mother's arms, then after a heartbeat of hesitation, into her father's waiting bear hug. The family reunion held its own sort of magic for Jarok, who liked seeing the way Piris was loved, and loved in return.

After Gem was settled in her rooms, the battlefield healer tut-tutting at her bedside, the remaining members of the party, along with the captains on Lord Volesion's guard who'd traveled with them, met in the lord's study to detail what had happened. He cursed when Piris recounted her experiences: kidnapping, thinking Jarok dead and buried, her swift dispatch of Engad Monti, and her rescue of the prince. Pride shone in his eyes as well. After her recitation, his gruff voice said, "Well done, daughter."

Piris nodded, keeping her face trained on the carpet at their feet, maybe so the others couldn't see the emotion there. Jarok, however, caught the glimmer of unshed tears, and his chest swelled with pride and love and awe at this fierce, loyal, and loving woman.

His thoughts wandered as the others talked. A disservice to them, true, but something he couldn't help. Piris was loving. To her parents, to Strella, to Gem... even at times to Cylian and Darin. Jarok had seen it. To be honest, he'd felt it himself, in her actions toward him. But never in actual words. He'd said them. More than once now. He worried he'd never hear them returned.

Everyone else started out of the room, Piris in the lead, when Lord Volesion asked him to stay behind. Piris whirled on her father, ready to fight for him again, against her father, if need be. He waved her off.

"We have much to discuss," the prince said.

She looked from her father to Jarok, her brows furrowed and her eyes squinted, before she gave them a stiff shrug and left. She cared but wanted to act as if she didn't. He'd give her whatever she needed.

The two Fae men, lord and prince, now alone in the room, squared shoulders and stared at each other. Silence fell, and Jarok was unsure whether it was to make certain no one overheard or because Lord Volesion was hesitating. He waited until the lord finally spoke.

"I see the way you look at my daughter."

Jarok didn't respond. He didn't attempt to hide how he felt about Piris, and he was sure everyone guessed. It did not surprise him her father had caught on as well. He just didn't know how Lord Volesion might take the knowledge.

"My wife has lectured me, at length, about my missteps with you both during your arrival and subsequent stay here. For my assumptions and my treatment of you and my daughter, I apologize."

"Piris should hear that from you," Jarok said, defending his love's right to her apology on her own terms.

"She has and will again, I assure you." The lord stared out the window to their left, the first time he broke eye contact with the prince. "When she was born, she was the world held in my palms. Small and mighty. She grew to be even more mighty: in magic, strength, and spirit."

He turned back toward the prince, a father's love clear in his bronze gaze. The same look he'd always seen from his own father. "Sometimes she thinks she has to be the mighty one for everyone else, the one to take the burden. Part of that is her nature, who she is. Part is because her mother and I made mistakes when we discovered her affinity. We thought completely hiding from everyone the best course of action. It taught her to shut herself away from others. I'm coming to understand this particular trait in my daughter a good and bad thing."

Jarok waited. Lord Volesion had a point, and he'd let him make it in his own way. There was no need for interjections yet, as long as Piris was discussed with respect and love.

"I'm afraid the bad side, the sacrificing side, might be at play now. Do you understand me, Prince?"

Jarok wanted no misunderstandings between he and Piris's father. "Be clear."

"She may not admit she loves you. If she already has, and I overstep, forgive me. But I suspect this is not the case."

Jarok simply shook his head, unable to voice aloud the fear he himself held.

"She is a fighter, our Piris. To her very bones. Sometimes, she even fights herself."

Jarok appreciated what the man said, who he was in his kingdom and to his love, but he tired of the roundabout way he was speaking. "Lord Volesion—"

"Do you love my daughter?"

Direct and to the point. Finally. "Yes," he answered, clear and without hesitation.

"Have you told her?"

"Of course. I wouldn't admit it to you if I had not."

He eased his stiff posture a touch at the admission. "I believe she loves you as well but won't let herself say it or act on it in a more permanent way."

"Okay," Jarok drawled. "I understand who Piris is, and I see your point. However, why tell me all this? She's your daughter, and her needs should be your concern."

"They are. Always. Even when she doesn't want to admit what she feels or needs. And I tell you all this, Prince of the Winterlands, to ask a favor."

"A favor?"

"Fight on," he whispered, a trace of desperation in his words. "For her. Hold tight to your love and fight her for it. Maybe not too hard, because she'll resist."

Jarok laughed. "Stubborn to the core."

"Fight for you and her both. I believe she will surrender if you hold out a little longer."

Jarok understood he spoke truth, and all in service of his daughter, but their conversation made him uncomfortable, not because of the topic but because Piris wasn't there to witness it. "A favor I will happily grant," he said, then gave a quick nod. "I must leave now, Lord Volesion."

Jarok didn't let him say good-bye or add another word in, couldn't feel right if he did. All he could do was take the words already spoken with him as reassurance and a new mission. Fight. Hold on. For himself and Piris. For love.

Darin stood in the high black doorway of Volesion Peak, a slight smile touching the corner of his mouth under his gray hood. A bag was slung over his shoulder, the one that hadn't taken an arrow in battle, as he shook Lord Volesion's hand. "Thank you for your hospitality," Darin said, cool but true.

Cylian stepped up next, giving his friend a slug on his good shoulder. The assassin stumbled slightly to the side before ramming back into the lord. "I will see you soon, friend. I plan to come to the Springlands Court after a quick trip back to the Winterlands Palace."

"Safe travels, and see you soon. Friend." The word friend sounded rusty in Darin's voice, but it rang true.

"Friend," Jarok reiterated as he stepped up and offered his hand to the assassin he'd once looked down on. "I am happy to now call you that as well. Hope you do the same."

"Don't hold out hope, Prince," he replied, but the ghost of his smile was still there.

"If you need me, for anything, all you need do is send word. Do you understand?" He didn't dare say more, remembering Darin's mark, his warning. Still, it needed to be put forward, and he hoped Darin understood how much he meant it. How much he and the Winterlands were indebted to him for so much.

He nodded and hesitated, then said, "You are a true prince, one I'm honored to know."

Something swelled in Jarok's chest at the words, but before he could reply, Piris, tired of waiting, flung her arms around the man. Darin stiffened, his head slowly turning to Jarok as if in worry, and the prince smiled bright at him.

"Thank you, Lord Darin Marco. Darin. All your names. For everything."

He patted Piris on her back and stepped back. "Any time, lady. Piris. Rebel Slayer." The soldiers had started the name after she'd defeated Engad Monti. Jarok worried it would get to her, remind her of something dark and dangerous, but Piris took it on without complaint.

The assassin turned, went out the door, and disappeared within the shadows of twilight in a blink. Jarok hoped his travels went well, that his home court treated him as he deserved. Hoped one day he'd get the respect he deserved as a Fae man of true honor and valor.

It was full dark and the party had just finished dinner when a guard came rushing into the dining room. He whispered to Lord Volesion, who then directed him to the prince. The guard bowed deep as he offered a tightly wound scroll. "This just arrived, Your Highness. Tied to a red hawk."

Jarok rose without thinking, tearing into the missive as he did so. Only word from his mother would arrive so late, from such a messenger. He scanned the text, head reeling as he read. Eyes wide and words rushed, he said to the table, "My father has taken a turn for the worse. He's now confined to his rooms. My brother will take over kingly duties. I... I'm needed back. As soon as possible." His gaze landed on Piris, across the table from him, at the last sentence. Gods, he'd wanted more time. More time to fight with and for her. But it appeared there was little to no time left, not for him and his family.

"Of course, Prince Jarok. Whatever you and the Winterlands Palace needs is at your disposal," Lord Brettly said as he also stood. Lady Mimi nodded her agreement, a grave look etched on her beautiful face.

"Will you ride with me?" he asked Cylian, who stood at his right.

"Of course. Whenever and wherever," he answered, as Jarok knew he would.

Nodding to himself, he then looked back at Lord Volesion. "We will need your fastest horses. We will compensate you, of course—"

Lord Volesion waved a dismissive hand. "No. Take whatever you need without worry. For my king and prince."

"Gem, she—"

"We'll care for her like she is our own, for as long as she needs or desires," Lady Volesion said.

"I'll be with her and will make sure she is protected," Piris said as she also rose. He wanted to ask her not to, to instead ride with him. Return with him to the palace so she would be by his side as he weathered this storm. It would be selfish, possibly too soon or too much, to say such a thing, so he didn't. Only thanked her and everyone else at the table before he excused himself. They'd have to wait until dawn to leave, which felt like an eternity, so he'd much rather worry in his room.

Piris knocked on his door this time. She'd barged in so often at this point he expected it from her, but she'd given him a choice then. He appreciated the gesture, but there never was a choice. Not with her.

"Come in, Piris," he called. Seconds later, he heard the click of the door closing behind her. He'd seated himself at the fire after leaving the dining room. Stared into the flames, thinking and not thinking in turns, the room mostly dark around him.

Piris's hand landed on his head, light yet strong and sure. He looked up at her, letting the worry and pain remain settled on his face instead of putting on his old mask. Her expression mirrored his as she reflected worry back at him. "Jarok, I... I can't express how sorry I am. For everything. For everyone in your family."

He nodded and turned back toward the fire. She played gently with his hair, her fingers comforting as they pulled through his dark strands. He felt little else at the moment but her, and he thanked the gods for the relief.

She stood with him like that for long minutes before she gave his head a reassuring pat and tried to move back. Jarok caught her in a flash, gripping her retreating arm tight. I should—"

He couldn't take it. Not then. Couldn't take whatever she might say to take herself away from him.

"Stay. Please," he whispered, raw need in his words. He stood to face her, to be close to her body, and without thought, Jarok leaned over to kiss her. Like his words, the kiss was all raw need—a hungry, desperate thing, tinged with worry and love and sadness all at once.

Piris yielded to him, her back arching as he wrapped her tight in his arms and deepened their kiss. She melted, giving herself over as she so often did, and Jarok took it. Not in a greedy, demanding way. He took it for himself, for her, to feel some love in a troubling time.

He edged her back toward the large bed, step by step, until she hit the footboard. Only then did he pull back, taking in her kiss-swollen lips and heavy-lidded bronze gaze. Jarok brushed a hand down her broad cheek, feeling the flush there. "I want you, Piris. Always, but especially tonight."

She swallowed around the word but managed to say, "Same," before she reached back up, her mouth finding his. It wasn't what he most wished to hear, but he'd take it. For then. For the little time they had before he would be gone.

Gods, it still nearly wrenched his chest open, thinking of what he wanted and hoped for, and what he needed to do. Not that he didn't want to be with his family. He wanted both but couldn't have both, and his eyes pricked with unshed tears at the push and pull inside him. He'd return to the palace, do what he could for his family as long as they needed him, but he'd leave a large part of his heart here, in Volesion Peak, with the fighter in his arms.

Somehow he managed to get them around and on the bed. Get his clothes off as Piris shimmied from her demure nightdress. When she lay beneath him on the bed, naked, he took a moment to soak her in, all of her. He skimmed a hand down her side, watching her breasts rise and fall with each hard breath and the goose bumps spread across her torso. He inhaled, savoring the thick ice and steel scent of her. Her breath hitched at his touch and he shoved the sound into the depths of him, tucking it away to remember later.

"I love you," he said as he gazed into her eyes. "I have to say it while I can. I expect nothing from you in return, but I have to say it one more time. Before... before I must leave. I love you."

Her tears welled, tempering the molten bronze in her eyes. She pulled him down, melded their bodies close together, giving herself in the way she was comfortable giving. He'd take it. Take all she offered. If there was more time, he might fight as he'd promised. Now all he could do was hold onto hope, do what he could to come back to her, to fight another day. She'd have to fight with herself for a time, he thought. He hoped, with all his will, they'd win the fight. As they'd won so many.

His cock, throbbing and probing for her, slipped against her slick center, and Jarok groaned. No more thoughts. Only sensations. He slid into her pussy with ease, fitting perfect. Feeling perfect. He knew he wouldn't last long, but it didn't matter. The connection, physical and emotional, they shared was all he cared about as he sank into her warmth.

The prince adjusted one of her legs, hitching it up and around his hip, before driving deeper. So deep he felt her end. Or maybe it was his beginning, because he became new somehow as he pumped in and out of her. She moaned in pleasure, and his growl followed. No words, only sounds of pleasure and need, as they joined, again and again.

When his spine tingled, he also noticed her inner muscles tightening more firmly around him. He wove a hand between them, circling her clit with a thumb as he continued pumping. She cried out, hoarse and long, her pussy fluttering around him, pulling his own orgasm from him. He groaned to match her cry, laying himself across her as he spasmed his release. In the moment, they were one. Sadness tinged his pleasure when he remembered it would not last long.

He had to leave. She was determined to stay.

At least they'd have this, the memory of what they could be together, in good times and bad.

Chapter Twenty-Five
Piris

She stayed, once again sleeping in the prince's arms. Every second dragged and sped, equal parts happiness and agony, as she stared at his sleeping face in the pre-dawn light slipping through his guest room window. She needed to go, say good-bye and steel herself for being alone, as she always had been. Always would be.

Jarok's eyes popped open, as if he'd been awake for a long while, and he silently studied her face. A wrinkle marred his golden-brown forehead. "Piris?" His voice was deeper than normal, a rumble crashing about from sleep. It took her breath. She reached up without thought, tracing the wrinkle on his forehead, trying to soothe and memorize at the same time.

Eventually she answered with another question. "Yes?"

He let out a sigh in response, pulling her close and burying his face deep in her hair and staying there for long beats.

It felt like stabbing a dagger through her own chest, but she swallowed the pain and said, "Jarok, it is near dawn."

His head moved over hers, acknowledging her words even if he did nothing with the information at first. When he did pull back, staring into her with those shining brown eyes, he started to give her something she couldn't take. "Piris. I promise—"

Her hand at his lips stopped his words as she shook her head no. "Don't promise me anything, Jarok. Prince."

When she pulled her hand away, he said, "I love you." It sounded like a promise on his lips, but she couldn't deny him those words. She denied him the words in return, even when they burned through her body, so it felt selfish to deny him this.

She said nothing, pulling away to sit up at the edge of the bed. Piris reached for her discarded nightdress and slipped it over her head, the coldness of the fabric matching the cold creeping into her gut. She moved to rise, but a hand clasped hard around her wrist, firm as a metal band. Piris looked over her shoulder, to the tears lingering in those dark eyes she knew she'd dream of every night of her life. It was too much for her, so she shook her head to get the image out, dislodge it so it wouldn't haunt her.

Because she couldn't help herself, couldn't leave without something more, she leaned over to plant one sweet, soft kiss to the prince's lush lips. Then, prying his hand off her wrist, she exited on swift, silent feet. Piris pretended she didn't hear the cracked curses Jarok left in her wake, or sense the crack in her own heart growing wider with each step.

She'd dressed in a simple tunic and pants. No need for her to wear more. She was again in Volesion Peak, confined here for her safety and the safety of everyone she loved. The idea of love split her in two, but she shoved it down deep when one of the housemaids knocked on her door, relaying a message from Gem, who was asking to see her immediately.

Piris hurried to her friend's side, worry for her pushing out the other messy emotions whirling. At least she had a distraction, for a brief time. At least she had Gem for company in the coming days.

"Why are you here?" Gem boomed at her. The woman was sitting up in bed, her face much paler than normal and slightly gaunt, but otherwise good. Her favorite dagger was positioned at her bedside, a request she knew Gem would have made as soon as she felt ready to wield it.

Confused, Piris said, "You asked me to come, Gem."

Throwing her arms in the air, she huffed out, "I asked the maid to tell you to come see me if you were still here. Obviously you are still here, so again, I ask, why is that?"

Piris's auburn brows met in a deep V. "I don't understand."

Gem leaned into Piris's face. "Why are you here, in this room, this house, when you should be riding out with my cousin? Who just left to ready the horses, by the way."

Piris went rod straight from her crouch. "I'm needed here."

"Bullshit. There is no scenario where you would be needed here, thanks to your swift kick to Engad Monti."

Piris winced at the reminder. She did not regret what she did, but she also didn't enjoy having it shoved in her face just then. "Careful, Gem Aurora," she whispered in warning.

"Oh, careful, is it? Careful? Ha!" The woman scooted forward in bed to get in Piris's face once again. "I'm never careful, my friend. Especially when it comes to my family. Or when I'm calling out a coward."

Piris pulled back as if she'd been slapped in the face. "Coward?" she said between clenched teeth.

"Yes. Coward. A coward for breaking my cousin's heart, and your own in the process, when all you have to do is admit you love the fool."

"No. No. He's better off—"

"Oh, you're Seer Willow now, hm? You know what will happen in the future?"

Piris threw her hands in the air. "I'm no princess, Gem. I am a burden at best, a secret to constantly be hidden and guarded."

Gem shook her head. "Lies. All lies you tell yourself to hide away. True, there are parts of you you can't reveal to the entirety of the Winterlands. But, Piris, you've hidden yourself away for so long, you believe it is the only answer. It's one answer, and a shitty one. There are many other ways to be honest about who you are while keeping pieces of yourself for yourself, and those you love."

"She's right, my love."

Piris spun around at the words her mother spoke from the open doorway.

Lady Volesion moved toward her daughter to grip her hands tight. "We did you a disservice—"

"No, Mother. No! You protected me. Did the only thing you could to keep me safe and ease your minds."

Her mother's head shook, making the small tears in her eyes dislodge. "We thought so. Our intentions were true, love, but intentions have impact. What we've done to you, making you believe you need to always hide, always be secretive in all things. That was not right. It's not living. I want you to live."

Piris felt her own tears streak down her face. She wanted to argue, to comfort her mother, but she was stuck, the ideas these two women shoved at her running mad through her head, chipping away at something hard and stony inside her. Hitting the same parts Jarok's love had started to knock aside.

"I love you so much, my daughter. I want everything good and lovely in this life for you, but you have to want it for yourself too."

Piris couldn't believe when she admitted her wants out loud. "I... Gods, I want him. But—"

"No buts," Gem called from the bed. "You take what you want, like the warrior you are. Grip it tight and defend it with your life."

"The warrior you are. Always have been," her mother said, holding her hands and gaze tight.

"What about my magic?"

"You're smart. So is Jarok. Queen Alene and Prince Ghel and Princess Strella as well. Together you will figure it out," Gem said with certainty.

More and more chips in her stony wall flew away, leaving a small crack, a window into what could be if she fought for it. Like the warrior she was.

Straightening, she said, "I love you both," before she sprinted for the door, down the hall, and out the side doors closest to the stables. Hope and possibility burned bright in her, and she'd wield it like a weapon and a shield. For herself and the prince.

She arrived at the stables, winded, and found both Cylian and Jarok there, putting saddlebags on her father's two fastest horses. Well, two of his fastest horses. The second-fastest horse, a mare a reddish-chestnut color like Piris's hair, stood looking on from her stall. Piris smiled at herself then, thinking she'd also need to thank her father later for his own brand of encouragement in this fight.

Cylian turned from her to Jarok as they stared at one another, no words passing between them. After several looks, he slowly backed away, out the door Piris had entered seconds before. "I'll just... wait outside. Shall I?"

Neither answered, too lost in their stare. Jarok whispered, "Piris?" The same searching question from earlier that morning, when Piris couldn't answer. Now she thought she could. She believed she might be able to be something more with him than a secret to be kept, a burden to be hidden away.

"I love you," she blurted, without preamble. "Gods above, I love you, Jarok, even though you are infuriating at times. I love that about you too, if I'm being honest."

The prince snapped to attention at her words and prowled toward her with a predatory glint in his eyes. He took her in his arms, bending her back as he leaned into her face. "Say it again."

She didn't mind these types of demands. Liked them, in fact. She took a moment to reach up to his face, stroke the smooth expanse of his beautiful harvest-gold cheek. "I love you, Prince Jarok Borau."

"I love you, Lady Piris Volesion." He kissed her, hard and deep but quick. "Does this mean you are coming with me?"

She nodded. "Yes. Apparently there's a lot of smart people in the palace who can help us figure out how to keep my magic to ourselves while I let other parts of me roam free."

He gave a wolfish grin, looking down her body. "I do love other parts of you very much."

Piris barked out a laugh, free and clean, then kissed her prince again.

A throat cleared behind them before Cylian said, "I'm sorry to interrupt. And believe me, I'm happy for the two of you. However, we still need to make haste."

"True," Jarok said, worry warring with the love she'd seen shining in his eyes moments before.

"I'll pack quickly," she said, pushing her way free of Jarok.

Before she was fully free, another voice joined them. "No need, my lady." The pretty healer seeing to Gem stood in the doorway of the stable beside Cylian, holding up two large parcels: a saddlebag and a pack. "Gem and your mother sent a maid to your rooms as soon as you left them. All you need is here."

"Nosy," she muttered, but the action warmed her heart. Looking into the bags, she found extra supplies, three of her best daggers, and two sets of fighting leathers. It was good enough for a speedy trip back to the Winterlands Palace. She thanked the healer, who left without another word, presumably back to try to wrangle the healing Gem.

Piris changed from her day dress in an empty stall; Cylian had stepped outside when Jarok had sent him a dark look as she'd taken out the leathers. They were ready to leave in minutes. As they eased the horse out of the stables, Piris taking the swift chestnut mare, they met her mother and father in the yard. Her father gave Jarok a long handshake, their grips tight, before he nodded at the prince with sure approval. Both he and her mother moved to her, hugged her tight.

With a gruff voice laced with complex feeling, her father said, "We will see you soon, daughter. Possibly travel to the palace with the Aurora warrior when she is healed."

"I'd like that," she said, knowing it'd been years since either had attended the palace, holding their place as the lord and lady they were. Her moving on, grabbing onto a different life and wresting it in place, gave them a chance at something different as well.

After another hug between the three Volesions, Piris jumped up, threw a leg over her mare, and situated herself in her saddle.

"Ready?" Jarok asked.

"With you? For you? Yes." She held his eyes as she urged her horse into a quick jump and gallop, shooting forward like an arrow. A laugh whipped through the air, a soft but clear sound carried to her on Jarok's winds, as he caught up with her, racing with her down Volesion Peak's central lane.

"You understand what is required, brother," Ghel asked, his deep-brown eyes fixed on Jarok, who was piecing together all the military information he'd just been given.

"Yes. Of course. I've been your second for many decades. I know the outline and need to concentrate on the details now."

"Good, good." Ghel grumbled the verbal quirk of the Boraus as he rapped his knuckles on the map-strewn table in the royal meeting chamber. The two princes, one now acting as the king's proxy and one just given the position of Winterlands general, spent an hour going over logistics of the transfer. The rest of the royal family sat by, the king sickly but still present, helped by the close hand of his queen. Strella sat off to the side, beside Piris, who'd been asked to attend for some reason she didn't understand quite yet.

Prince Ghel pinned her with his eyes, then rumbled, "Lady Piris, please. Come." He gestured for her to step forward, pointing at a particular map pinned to the large winter-pine table. She moved to his side, arms crossed as she stared at what appeared to be a floor-by-floor map of the Winterlands Palace.

"I'll be busy with my general duties now," Jarok said beside her, "and when Ghel asked who would be able to take over my palace security duties, I said I'd trust only one person with the task."

Piris whipped her head to her love in disbelief, then down at the map and finally at the other prince at her side. "You agree, Ghel?"

He nodded, sure. "As does my wife, and the king and queen. You've more than proven your ability to plan, strategize, fight when necessary. Like Jarok, I'd trust no one else with the protection of my family."

She swallowed hard, worry threading its way through her joy at the honor. "What of my magic?"

Ghel shrugged. "Magic isn't required, so most will still believe you a null. But never simply a null. You are a warrior, Piris. The Rebel Slayer. One who already commands respect and rightly so, even if most of the land thinks you possess no magic."

Rebel Slayer was new. Word of what she'd done had traveled wide. Soldier and guard tongues wagged about such things apparently. She was still unsure if it fit, but it had garnered her much respect from every warrior, soldier, or guard she met in the palace.

By the gods, she could do this. Be this. She wanted to. Sliding an arm around Jarok's waist and hugging him for a moment, she looked at Prince Ghel, her future king, and said, "I am happy to serve the royal Borau line in any capacity."

"Good, good," King Frit called, his voice weaker than before but ringing in the room nonetheless, the final stamp of approval.

"Good, good," Jarok whispered in her ear, twisting his own arm around her and hugging her in return. The Rebel Slayer and the charming prince, arm in arm.

They had a private dinner that evening in the royal meeting rooms. King Frit lounged, Queen Alene hovering over him like a watchful hawk, as the servants brought in food, then promptly left them alone.

Ghel sat on a chaise with Strella, snuggled close. The large warrior prince grabbed them food on a shared plate, offering first bites to his small wife. They whispered together in hushed tones but also engaged with others, joking and laughing to keep spirits in the room high. Jarok helped with that, the other prince at her side, an arm slung around her shoulders, holding her close with a firm grip.

Piris loved to see her bonded sister in a family, happy and loved. She'd needed it, with the lonely existence she'd lived with her traitorous father before she came to the Winterlands Palace. It hit her then, like an arrow straight to the chest. She'd needed it too. Maybe in a different way than Strella. She'd never had family issues. But she'd also never extended her family beyond three people: her mother, father, and Strella. She hid. For good reason, she'd hidden herself away, living a half-life of sorts.

Now, however. Now, life was full. Filled with more people she cared for and who cared for her. More people who knew exactly who she was and still cared. Like the people in the royal meeting rooms, who looked at her with laughter in their eyes as they all talked. Like Gem, who was likely with her parents, giving them and the healer sass. Like Lord Cylian and Darin. Cylian had left for business in the Springlands and Marco was already there, but she knew they carried not only her secret but friendship and respect for her with them, close and tight.

Like the man beside her, who'd stopped his jokes to peer into her eyes. It was only then she realized she'd shed a tear or two. "Piris?" he asked. The simple question held so much: memory, meaning, and future.

"I love you," she said.

Piris looked around the room, which had also grown quiet, more tears threatening to spill. Everyone gave her space, as a good family should. As her family always had. And now she had so much love, so much family, she nearly burst with it.

She felt Strella at her knee before she noticed her friend move toward her. The princess knelt there, concern etched in her stiff posture and small frown. She echoed Jarok's question. "Piris?"

"Thank you. For all this." She knew Strella never wanted to be a princess. Never wanted to marry until she had been forced into it, then came to love Prince Ghel. Her journey to the palace started all of this for Piris, all the love and freedom and purpose she now felt roiling inside.

Piris knew Strella understood, because she'd likely experienced the same epiphany at some point. Who wouldn't, surrounded by the love and honor of the Boraus at their side. The two had always been sisters by bond, but now they shared another bond. Strella nodded, her bright-white smile lighting up the room as she rose.

"All is well," she said to the others, taking the attention away from her friend and starting a conversation about the plumage of the kestrel perched on the queen's shoulder.

Jarok's hand gripped her chin, and he pulled her face to look into his. He studied her a moment, those dark eyes darting over her to make sure all was well. Whatever he saw made his face soften and his eyes burn with some dark inner light. "All is well," he repeated with a nod.

"Yes. All is now well."

He hugged her to his side a moment, then thought better of it. Rising quickly, he dragged her with him, gripping her upper arm tight. "We have somewhere to be," he announced with imperious certainty, daring anyone to challenge his words.

Ghel snorted at him. The king gave a soft, indulgent smile. Queen Alene looked them up and down, as hard-eyed and assessing as the kestrel by her side, before she nodded in turn. Strella heard Piris giggle to herself but had no time to respond to any of it before she was pulled out of the room.

"But dinner, your family," she managed to sputter out once they were in the hallway.

Jarok spun her to his front, loosening his grip on her arm to band both strong arms around her middle. She landed at his chest, nearly eye to eye, where his light still burned. "I love you, you love me, and we are now free to do as we please. And right now, I'm going to wipe away your tears and make you produce a different, far more pleasurable, type of cry."

Piris couldn't argue with any of it. She didn't want to. She'd argue with Jarok again. Their back-and-forth made her blood boil in a delicious way, and she would never be a pushover for her prince. Right then, however, the idea of being with him, bound to and by him, felt right. As she now felt right.

"Oh, so cocky, Prince." Tilting her face up, she took his lips. It started soft, sweet, and full of the love she'd come to find surrounding her. Then, of course, it turned far more heated.

Jarok pulled back first. "I'll show you cocky." He laughed, the sound deep and full of joy. They walked hand in hand, side by side, and Piris would not wish it any other way.

Thanks so much for reading! Please take a moment to rate/review *Land of Ice and Intrigue* on Goodreads or an online retail site.

Epilogue
Darin Marco

People often forgot his title, which he never bothered with, but for some odd reason, it'd been a topic of conversation recently, when he had been serving his king's interests in the Winterlands. Those Winterlands royals and nobility behaved in odd ways he had found refreshing, even if he disliked the questions about himself. Or maybe he hadn't disliked it so much. Learning more of others, finding others who wanted to know more about him, was at the very least novel. Definitely a different situation than the one he was currently in, where every person in the ballroom scuttled back a step at his approach.

He was Lord Marco by birth, but by use he'd long ago become Darin Marco, assassin, Hooded Death in his homeland. The last of his line, his parents and any wealth or holdings from his family lost long ago, he himself felt he had no need for the title. It didn't fit him, oddly, but it was now of the utmost importance to his new mission.

His hand clenched at his side, a flex to anyone looking but a silent scream to anyone who knew him. But no one in the Springlands knew him, not really. He was his job, his duty, the swift hand of his king. Nothing more than something to be feared. Now, after decades upon decades of cultivating this fear, honing him as a weapon to use in and out of his own lands, the king needed him to do something that flew in the face of all his history. He had been tasked with infiltrating the courtiers who feared him as the king's assassin, somehow gain their trust. Find the ridiculous weapon the king of the Springlands should have destroyed centuries ago but for some reason hadn't. It was a job for a courtier, not an assassin.

Still, he had to do what he was tasked with doing. The king helped him somewhat in his endeavor, using the success of the Winterlands mission as a ruse to bestow his ancestral lands, rotted and overgrown as they were, back to him in an official proclamation as a prize for helping squash a too-close rebellion of warriors. The uprising had spooked the king, to be sure. Now, assured in his absolute reign, he made Marco officially a lord again, even if he'd technically never lost the title, just the lands. All to remind his court his assassin was a member of the nobility and would be allowed to walk among them as one now.

Darin hated it, as he hated everything about the Springlands Court. The simpering, the lies... the backbiting and cuts with words. He preferred a more direct approach in all things, but understood sometimes finesse was needed. Didn't mean he had to like it.

There'd been a few moments he could classify as not completely horrible. He'd discussed some treaty with the Winterlands with one of the king's newest, and less sycophantic, advisers—Lord Elligin Gralax. The Fae had hailed him, in fact, rushing over to talk about his recent trip to the other land. This lord was no warrior, but he reminded him of the Winterlands party: thoughtful, engaged, and bent on doing well. He hated to think it, but with an attitude like that, he'd be out of the king's favor in no time.

He'd spent a few moments discussing military issues with a contingent of lordly soldiers in attendance. They hadn't stopped him as Lord Gralax had, but they had not moved away after he'd entered their circle either. Good soldiers stood their ground.

Mostly, he had an early taste of what this latest mission would entail. A great deal of trying to pry his way into the inner circle of the courtiers with them fighting him at every turn. Gods, he wished he could carry his bow into these glittering halls, wear his hooded leathers instead of the stifling gray silk tunic and breeches, and demand answers with a glare of his icy-green eyes.

But no. Such tactics wouldn't work, although he remained unsure what tactic might actually work for him. He was Hooded Death to these people, not someone they might let their guard down around. He had no in, nothing to humanize him after years spent seen as a deadly weapon. He could find any angle on a battlefield. Hit any target required when he had it in sight down the length of an arrow. None of that mattered in a ballroom, where he would need to engage in a fighting style he didn't know.

His shadows might help. He could slip in and out, eavesdrop. However, the king was convinced Darin needed to employ a different approach. The king always got what he wanted, so Darin's shadow magic became a tool he might occasionally use rather than his main form of attack.

Needing a break from the cutting looks and whispers behind hands and fans, Darin stopped his turn around the ballroom midway to exit onto a terrace. He breathed deep the lush smell of freshly cut grass and perfectly tended hyacinth in the meticulously planted gardens outside the ballroom. More than that, he basked in the silence, happy to be outside the range of the prattle and hyena laughs of the glittering court of the Springlands.

Silence, that was, until he heard a whispered "damn" from behind him. He'd been so focused on the quiet, on the feel of his hands on the cold stone railing and the scents of the night garden, he hadn't heard anyone behind him. A surprise indeed, to have someone sneak up on the assassin. He spun around on swift feet, taking two large, menacing steps toward the sound before his eyes fully registered the source.

There, in the pale light filtering through the glass doors of the ballroom, stood a small woman. Petite would be the proper term, Darin knew, but he was not one to always be polite. She stood no more than neck height to him, though her body was rounded, flaring in the right places. Small but lush for certain, like a blooming flower. Her eyes, a melted caramel color, were wide in a rounded face. Those eyes didn't leak fear of him. No, he knew the fear of him well. It was more as if she were caught. A child about to be gently reprimanded for having a hand in the dessert before their dinner.

He stepped closer, eyeing her perfectly tailored, floating lavender dress at odds with her haphazard brown bun of curly hair. It was a nod to fashion, but only a nod. Her hands moved, wringed in fact, in front of her, before she pulled herself together. She gathered her breath and her body, rising to a firm posture and tilting her head up to look right into his eyes. As no one had done before tonight, except Lord Gralax. Who, he remembered, had strikingly similar caramel-colored eyes and brown hair. Though, admittedly, much more height and fewer curves.

"Lady," he said, moving closer into her space, fully expecting her to back away as he did. She did not. The woman held her ground, and his gaze.

"Lord." The sound was strong, belying her stature, her voice firm, deep, and assertive. It was the voice of someone used to arguing and not losing.

Darin threw a slight smirk her way and a nod, but he did not give up his cold stare at the mystery woman.

She broke first, casting a furtive look at the glass doors behind her, a frown marring her smooth face. It'd disappeared in the time she looked back, having found what she needed to find. Or not. She was, obviously, a lady. As he'd said. Maybe an unmarried lady. If so, with this crowd, being caught out in the dark with a strange man could be disastrous for her ambitions, whatever they may be. For most ladies of the Springlands Court, that would be marriage, but he wouldn't assume such with her for some reason.

"Feel free to return," he said, flipping one of his hands toward the ballroom before he clasped them behind his back.

She cocked her head and really looked him over for the first time. "Do I know you, sir?"

He shook his head in reply. No need for more.

"Very well," she said, jutting a hand out in greeting. To him. "I am Lady Harwel Gralax."

Her hand hung there, long enough for her to look down at it and back up at him with a frown as he debated whether he should actually take it. Mostly for her sake. He did not think she would wish to have her hand in his once he said his name. Still, he took it, and marveled at how warm, firm, and strong it was in his. For such a small hand, it packed a great deal of power. Also told him a great deal about the woman who wielded it.

"Darin Marco, my lady." He didn't bow, but he did nod his head deeply, breaking eye contact for the first time. When he looked back at her, her eyes had flared slightly but she didn't shake. Didn't step back. The woman didn't even take her hand from his.

"A pleasure to meet you, Lord Marco," she said, pumping his hand once before taking hers back, not because she feared him but because it was appropriate to do so.

"And you, Lady Gralax."

She gave a small curtsy, the first he'd ever received in his life as far as he could remember, and moved to the side, toward the ballroom door. "Could you?" she asked, gesturing toward the door. Not for him to open it but to ensure he did not follow. No one needed to see them emerging from the dark garden terrace together.

He bowed then, deep at the waist, and gave her a smirk in reply. A promise without words. As he watched her leave, her dress swaying, lovely in the soft lights inside, he thought to himself the promise extended further than Lady Gralax could understand. She was not the lord's wife; that much he knew. The lord was unmarried. He had, however, heard talk of a sister who was his ward. Much younger and his sole responsibility.

Part of him balked at the idea forming in his mind, but he'd seen a few women stop to speak with the lady in lavender before she had been swallowed up by the crowd. She was part of the crowd, accepted where he was not. Also, for whatever odd reason, she appeared unafraid of him. Another tool he might be able to use.

He needed more information first. Needed to be sure she would serve his purpose. Possibly even find something she might require in return for the vague plan churning in his mind to come to fruition. A full smile hit his lips then, where no one could see it. It felt rusty on his face, but he didn't mind. He might now have a way into the courtier crowd, and it happened to be a lush, petite woman with a strong voice and firm handshake.

Want More?

Get all the latest info, updates, and even some book deals over on Sonya Lawson's Substack.

Follow Sonya Lawson on social media. She's @sonyalawsonwrites on TikTok, Instagram, Facebook, and Threads. Get new book notifications by following her author profiles on Goodreads and BookBub, too.

You can find all things Sonya Lawson on her website and her Books page lists all her current publications.

And, once again, please consider rating/reviewing *Land of Ice and Intrigue* on Goodreads and/or wherever you purchased this book. All honest reviews are greatly appreciated!

About the author

Sonya Lawson is a recovering academic who now writes fantasy (in a wide variety of sub-genres). Her work offers a glimpse into different yet familiar worlds that are sometimes dark, sometimes dramatic, sometimes a bit funny, and always steamy.

While she remains a rural Kentuckian at heart, she currently lives in the Pacific Northwest. Her days are often filled with writing, editing, reading, and walking old forests.

Acknowledgements

My editors at Novel Nurse Editing, Janna and Angie, are the absolute best. They have eagle eyes like a Fae, I swear. Without them, none of my books would be what they are, so they deserve all my praise and thanks.

100 Covers made the cover and did a fantastic job matching the vibe of the book and extending the look of the overall series.

My ARC readers, those on my email list and those who find me in other ways, do a valuable service every single time. I thank you all for your time and honest feedback.

Kenzie Kelley once again lent her awesome beta reading skills and made this book better in the process. Thanks so much for all the input and encouragement.

Nicole Wells gave me amazing feedback on my blurb. So good, in fact, I want to thank her here for it. Her constructive criticism was top notch and her help made the end product so much better.

As always, my family, friends, and husband do a lot of heavy lifting in my life. I can't thank them enough for all the love and support they offer. I love you right back.

Last but never least, thanks to all my readers. You allow me to tell you stories and I'm so thankful for that opportunity.